Double Takedown

A Mike Stoneman Mystery

Double Takedown

A Mike Stoneman Mystery

Kevin G. Chapman

Other novels and stories by Kevin G. Chapman

The Mike Stoneman Thriller Series

Righteous Assassin (Mike Stoneman #1)
Deadly Enterprise (Mike Stoneman #2)
Lethal Voyage (Mike Stoneman #3)
Fatal Infraction (Mike Stoneman #4)
Perilous Gambit (Mike Stoneman #5)
Fool Me Twice (A Mike Stoneman Short Story)

Stand-alone Novels

The Other Murder
Dead Winner
A Legacy of One
Identity Crisis: A Rick LaBlonde Mystery

Short Stories & Novellas

The Car, the Dog & the Girl
Ghost Creek (a romantic mystery novella)

Visit me at www.KevinGChapman.com

For Sharon, who knows my characters better than I do and who cares about them more than anyone. All my love

Chapter 1
A Night at the Ballet

May 23, 2022

NEW YORK HOMICIDE DETECTIVE MIKE STONEMAN was decidedly out of his element. The David H. Koch Theater's palatial lobby resembled the red carpet outside the Academy Awards. Bejeweled women sipped champagne under crystal chandeliers while celebrities mingled and posed for pictures. *What's a cop doing in this crowd?* he thought, not for the first time.

Mike's black tuxedo pants were annoyingly snug. Standing in a crowd of people, only a few of whom were wearing face masks, exacerbated his discomfort. Every one of the glamourous members of the Broadway community swirling through the room was either taller, thinner, or younger than him. Most were all three.

Jason Dickson, Mike's partner, on the other hand, was happy to show off his tall, fit physique in a perfectly tailored tux. His dark skin contrasted with the snowy white collar of his dress shirt. Mike was used to being the older, shorter, and paunchier member of his team. His only solace was that all the other homicide detectives in their Manhattan precinct looked more like Mike. He had overcome the jealousy years ago, but at a formal occasion like this, he felt a tiny pang.

Mike was also not a fan of ballet, which would follow the cocktail reception. He appreciated the dancers' physical prowess and the fluid beauty of their performances. But the story that others claimed they saw within the dance eluded his perception. This was supposed to be the first big post-pandemic event for Mike and Michelle. Time to get back to something approaching normal after more than two years of social distancing. Mike felt like an old war horse at the Kentucky Derby.

Michelle, by contrast, was smiling, laughing, and having the time of her life alongside Jason's wife, Rachel. For Rachel, one of the most outgoing and people-loving individuals Mike knew, the pandemic had been torture. Tonight, Rachel was resplendent in her sparkling purple gown. Jason had quietly revealed to Mike that she had not fit into it since the baby. A solid month of near-starvation and workouts yielded the eye-catching results before them.

These musings were interrupted by the clinking of silverware on crystal. The crowd hushed and all eyes turned to a white-haired man standing on the red-carpeted stairway leading to the theater. Once he had everyone's attention, Albert Edward Gooday the Third thanked everyone for coming and for donating to the Broadway Cares / Equity Fights Aids foundation. In a three-minute speech, Mr. Gooday gave his personal thanks to a list of people who made the event possible. Mike paid little attention until their host encouraged everyone to drink the wine and enjoy the hors d'oeuvres before the performance began in thirty minutes.

Michelle's soft voice penetrated the growing murmur of the crowd. "Thank you, Mike."

Turning to his left and looking down at Michelle's beaming face, most of Mike's discomfort melted away. Four inches shorter than Mike, Michelle's smooth skin and dark eyes produced the illusion of being much younger. Passing men admired her soft curves and slim legs and neck, wrapped in a black, sequined cocktail dress. He often marveled that Michelle was his wife. When he started dating the Manhattan county medical examiner during the Righteous Assassin investigation, Mike never imagined that, five years later, they would be together at a Lincoln Center charity ballet.

"I didn't do anything."

"You agreed to come, and you dressed up for me. I appreciate it. I'm having a wonderful time. I hope you don't hate this too much."

"I'm fine. Looks like Jason and Rachel are loving it." He tilted his head toward their companions, who were deep in conversation with three women in progressively more revealing gowns and one tall man with perfectly groomed hair. An actor, of course, but Mike did not recognize him.

"I'm sure they are. Thank you for agreeing to spend the money."

"Yeah, well, it's a good cause, right?"

A booming voice caused Mike to swing his attention to his left. "Detectives Stoneman and Dickson!"

"Well, I'll be damned," Mike lowered his voice, hoping only Michelle would hear.

"Shhh! Be nice," Michelle whispered back.

A rotund man accompanied by a glamourous blonde advanced toward Mike, extended his meaty hand, and gave Mike's an enthusiastic shake. "Victoria, allow me to present two of New York's finest homicide detectives, Mike Stoneman and Jason Dickson. I can truthfully say I owe these men my life."

"Well, I guess we shouldn't be surprised to see the great Max Bloom at an event like this," Mike said.

"Allow me to present one of my protégés, Miss Victoria Franklin, an up-and-coming actress," Bloom gushed.

"Actor, Max. Please." Victoria extended her manicured hand toward Mike. Her ears dripped with a three-tiered cascade of diamonds, matching a necklace dangling between her exposed cleavage.

Michelle said, "Are you one of Max's clients?"

"One of my cast members," Max crooned, placing an arm around Victoria's slim waist. "Since the tragic death of my wife, Sheila, I'm happy to say that I'm now a producer of one of this year's biggest shows, *Godfather: The Musical*. It's up for eight Tony Awards. Sheila always loved the theater. It's what she would have wanted." Max patted his companion's hand, as if grieving deeply over his loss.

"You're producing *that* show?" Rachel blurted. "I should introduce you to my brother, Jackie. He's a brilliant performer. You should give him an audition."

"Oh, I'd be happy to, Miss Robinson. Anything for my favorite detectives." Max held out his business card, which Rachel placed into her purple clutch.

"And it's now *Mrs. Dickson*." Rachel flashed a satisfied smile at Jason and extended her left hand, displaying her own diamond ring.

"Wonderful!" Max bellowed. "Congratulations. I owe your husband everything I have. You can have your brother call me anytime." Max then squeezed his date's shoulder, pulling her gently. "Come, my dear. There are many other people who need to meet you." Without a glance back, Max and Victoria disappeared into the crowd like Shoeless Joe Jackson melting into an Iowa cornfield.

Michelle clutched Mike's forearm, pulling him forward. "We don't have much time before the performance. I want to meet Alex Bishop. I saw him over this way. He's the lead in Max's show, so now we can tell him we know his producer."

"I'm not sure I want to be associated with Max Bloom," Mike grimaced. "He's probably here playing some angle."

Jason, who had been listening, said, "I'll bet you ten bucks Max got somebody else to buy his ticket for this shindig." Mike laughed, but did not take the bet.

When the lights dimmed and the guests made their way toward the stairs, Mike and Michelle walked past a large placard listing the names of major donors. She pointed out that Maximillian Bloom was listed as a $50,000 benefactor.

Mike looked over his shoulder at Jason. "Well, I guess you were wrong."

* * *

FORTY-FIVE MINUTES INTO THE FIRST ACT of the ballet, Rachel pulled down her sparkling purple facemask and whispered into Jason's ear, "What's going on down there?"

They were seated in the next-to-last row of the orchestra level. At the front of the house, partially illuminated by the stage lights, someone was standing. Rachel could not see who it was, but could hear the buzz of people talking. Then, a woman's scream attracted everyone's attention. Necks strained to see. More people stood.

The music stopped in the middle of the piece. The performers continued dancing for several seconds on a silent stage. The conductor, standing on a raised podium so she could see the stage and the orchestra pit, turned toward the audience. She was talking into her headset microphone. There was another scream. Then the conductor's voice boomed over the sound system.

"Ladies and gentlemen, please remain in your seats. We have a medical emergency in the front row. If there are any doctors in the house, we need assistance right away."

Rachel's EMT training kicked in before the conductor finished saying "emergency." She leapt over Jason's lap, then kicked off her heels as she sprinted barefoot down the long, sloping path toward the stage. Dozens of people began filming on their phones. Despite the conductor's instruction, half the house seemed to be standing.

Mike jumped up as soon as he saw Rachel leave her seat. He grabbed Jason's sleeve. "Let's go, we need to work crowd control down there. Michelle, call 9-1-1."

Jason and Mike were forty feet behind Rachel. When they reached the front of the theater, a small group of gawkers had already gathered in the aisle.

"NYPD! Please take your seats and keep this aisle clear for emergency services!" Jason shouted, his baritone carrying throughout the auditorium.

Mike gently eased several men in formalwear away from the space between the front row and the orchestra pit. Jason did the same. The two detectives took up positions on either side of the aisle, casting authoritative glares at anyone who seemed interested in venturing toward the commotion in front of the stage.

Jason glanced down the front row and saw Rachel's bare back hunched over someone lying on the floor. The straps of her purple dress flashed in the house lights, which had come on. Rachel and two men worked together to drag a figure on the floor toward more open space. Jason saw black shoes and pants, but could not see the man's face. An usher ran down the aisle, holding a small red case that Mike assumed was an automated external defibrillator. He dashed past the two cops and handed the device to Rachel, who had taken charge of the emergency situation.

Rachel barked instructions while prepping the AED, then administered an electric charge to the victim's now-bare chest. On the elevated stage, twenty dancers leaned over the edge to watch.

One minute later, an actual EMT team barreled down the aisle with a gurney on wheels carrying their own equipment. Rachel remained on her knees, working on the supine man, while the two tuxedoed doctors stepped back. The public address system announced that there would be an intermission in the performance due to the medical emergency and asked everyone to calmly return to the lobby. As the crowd slowly rose and meandered to the exit, those still filming remained standing until Mike, Jason, and several ushers shouted them into submission and herded them toward the doors.

On the floor, the EMT crew loaded the unconscious man onto their gurney, then hustled out an emergency exit door at the left corner of the stage. As soon as the crew passed them, Jason and Mike rushed toward Rachel. Jason gently pulled her to a standing position. She hugged Jason in her bare feet as Mike stood back. Before Jason and Rachel disengaged, a tap on Mike's back caused him to spin around. Michelle held out Rachel's sparkling heels with a concerned expression.

"Don't like following instructions, huh?" Mike said.

Michelle flashed a tiny smile. "I told the usher I'm a doctor and he let me stay."

"Thanks," Rachel said, slumping into a front-row seat and working to slide back into her shoes.

"Do you know who that was on the floor?" Michelle asked.

Rachel stood. "Oh my God. You couldn't see, could you? It was Alex Bishop."

"The lead in *Godfather?* He was just nominated for a Tony!" Michelle grabbed Mike's sleeve.

"He was," Rachel said, "but unless the EMT crew works a miracle, he won't be there to win it."

Chapter 2
Happy Birthday, JJ

August 19, 2023

IN THE SWELTERING AUGUST HEAT, more than a year after what became known as The Ballet Murder, Mike and Michelle pushed through the unlocked door of the Robinson family home. The humidity diminished only slightly inside, where a pair of window-mounted air conditioner units chugged away in their endless battle against the Brooklyn summer.

"Hey, it's Uncle Mike!" Jason's deep voice filled the living room. The assembled Robinson clan watched in amusement as a flash of blue and orange sped across the worn rug atop the aged hardwood floor. The flash shrieked in excitement before colliding with Mike's left leg. After peeling the tiny arms off his gray slacks, Mike hoisted Jason Dickson, Jr., his three-year-old godson, into his arms.

"Happy birthday, JJ." Mike gave the boy a kiss on the cheek, before the tiny whirling dervish squirmed his way out of Mike's grasp and slid downward. Michelle met him at

Mike's feet and engulfed the bundle of energy in a hug. When released, JJ dashed back across the open floor.

"He never stops, does he?" Michelle directed the question toward Rachel, who appeared next to her friend.

Rachel kissed Michelle's cheeks. "Only when he passes out from exhaustion."

Michelle handed over a gold gift bag while Mike shook Jason's hand. Rachel then paraded the newcomers around, introducing them to all the Robinson relatives. When they had circumnavigated the room, Michelle bent down to give a long hug to Rachel's mother, Olivia. She was a lean and spry sixty-five, still managing the house and taking care of little JJ when both Rachel and Jason were working.

"How was New Orleans?" Michelle asked Rachel when they had finally taken seats on a sofa while their husbands went to the kitchen seeking cold drinks.

"It was great. Relaxing." Rachel then lowered her voice and leaned in toward Michelle. "It was great getting away. It was the first time since JJ. But I'll tell you that things have sure changed in three years. When we went to Vegas for the wedding, we got to the hotel and had crazy sex. When we got to the hotel in New Orleans, we got into bed and took a two-hour nap."

The women exchanged hushed giggles. "Did you eventually leave the hotel and get some of that great NOLA food?"

"Oh yes," Rachel patted her tummy. "It's a good thing we didn't stay any longer or I'd be as big as a house."

Michelle assured her friend that she looked great and did not mention that the belt around her waist was looking a little tight over her orange dress. Blue and orange were the theme colors for JJ's party. The birthday boy was wearing a t-shirt replica of a New York Mets jersey with a big number twelve on the back. Francisco Lindor was his favorite player, according to Jason.

"Well, it's great that your mom can watch JJ. He's quite a handful."

"I know. I keep hoping all his energy will start to slow down. I worry that he's got ADHD or something."

"Oh, honey, he's an active little boy. I wouldn't worry too much."

"I know. I just worry about everything." Rachel sank her head against Michelle's shoulder.

Michelle glanced at the high-backed chair against the far wall. Propped up on the seat, a photo of Ernie Robinson surveyed the room, as he would have if he were there in the flesh. A long-time New York City Sanitation department worker, Rachel always thought her father was the strongest man in the world. He had a dominant personality, which made it that much harder to accept his illness, quick decline, and eventual death at the hands of the unsympathetic virus. After Ernie's funeral, Olivia fell into an understandable depression. Being JJ's grandma helped get her through. After Rachel and Jason moved into the house, she also had them to mother. Together, the family put the tragedy behind them. But Ernie's absence still lingered.

"I can't imagine raising a little boy like JJ in the city." Rachel's cousin, Mary, seemed immensely impressed. Mary was fifteen and had lived her life in northern Westchester county.

Rachel lowered her chin. "I love it. Lord knows I owe my life to JJ."

"Your baby saved your life?"

"You bet, Mary. I had some early-term complications and had to take disability leave. That was in March of 2020 — right when COVID hit. My EMT friends were out trying to save lives. A bunch ended up catching the virus. A few of them didn't make it." She paused, her lips quivering. "By the time I was feeling well enough to go back to work, I was too far along for the city to let me back in an ambulance. I worked dispatch duty until I gave birth. Working in the office kept me away from COVID, and kept me and JJ safe. So, that's why I say JJ saved my life. By the time I was ready to go back after JJ was born, I'd gotten the television job."

"It's too bad Ernie wasn't as lucky," Mary said. Her face then froze in embarrassment as everyone suddenly stopped talking. All eyes turned to Olivia.

"It's OK, dear," Olivia soothed, allowing her guests to exhale. "It's been three years. It's alright to talk about it."

Rachel took her mother's hand. "I'm glad Jason and I were here for you."

"They must have been such a comfort," Mary said.

"Oh, hell no," Olivia laughed and sat back in one of the folding chairs they had brought up from the basement to accommodate all the guests. "Jason drove me crazy. JJ got me through. Taking care of that little baby was just the tonic I needed to pull me past the loss."

"Big ol' Jason take up too much space in the house?" Mary enjoyed needling Jason.

"It's been fine," Jason said.

"Except for the bedroom," Mike muttered. The comment drew a round of muffled laughter.

"What bedroom?" Mary looked around for someone who would let her in on the joke.

Mike said, "You see how Jason is such a big man, and Rachel's a tall one herself. So they got a big king-sized bed and put it in Rachel's room. It takes up pretty much the whole space."

"We have plenty of room," Rachel protested. "We're very happy to be here. You should have seen Jason's tiny little apartment in the city. We could have never had a child there. We love being with mama." She looked at Jason, who nodded his affirmation. "Mama even offered to give us the big master bedroom, but Jason and I said 'no way.' We're not forcing mama out of her own bedroom. Right, Sweetheart?"

"Absolutely." Jason's voice instantly held everyone's attention. "We're fine where we are. Comfortable. We're lucky to be together."

"I know how it feels." Michelle was perched on the arm of the sofa, her slender legs dangling. "After Mike and I got married, we had a bit of a battle. Now we're both comfortable in the new apartment. We're settled in, plus, now we have Topsy."

"Topsy! Topsy!" JJ's high voice penetrated the general murmur. The birthday toddler barreled around the edge of the sofa, looking expectantly at Michelle.

"Not today, Dear," Michelle soothed. "Topsy is at our house, sleeping. You'll see her next time." After a few seconds, JJ turned and sprinted away.

"Who's Topsy?" Mary asked.

"She's Michelle and Mike's cat." Rachel stooped to clean a spill from the floor. "JJ adores her."

Olivia turned to Jason, who was holding a long-necked Budweiser bottle. "I saw on the news that they're gonna start the trial soon for the man who poisoned the actor at the ballet. That's one of yours, right?"

Jason and Mike tried to avoid talking about police business in social situations. They certainly did not want to say anything about a high-profile case that would be in the center of a media storm when the trial of Nathan Matthews began in September. Mike and Jason had weathered the press attention during the short investigation and then ducked under the continuous barrage of coverage concerning the details of the indictment. They both dreaded how the upcoming trial would put them back inside the 24-hour news maelstrom.

"You're right. It's one of our cases. Which is why we can't talk about it," Jason said politely but firmly.

Mike attempted to deflect the conversation. "The investigation was pretty quick. We found evidence implicating the director. It was open and shut. Our testimony won't be very exciting. I hope."

"It's not open and shut at all!" a female voice broke in. All the men turned toward the strikingly beautiful face of Cyndi Linderman. She was tall and slender. Even wearing jeans and a simple, bare-shouldered white top, it was obvious she was accustomed to glamourous situations. Rachel had introduced her to Mike as an actress friend.

"Do you know something about the case?" Mary asked, eager to have someone willing to share information.

"I know Nathan Matthews." Cyndi's voice carried over the general party din. "He's a wonderful person and he's devoted to the theater." Her voice got louder and more emotional as she spoke. "There is no possible way he would have poisoned one of his actors. He treats us all like his children. He's nurturing and compassionate. He could not have done this, which is why he has been saying from the start that he's innocent. It's awful that more people in the theater community haven't come out to support him."

When Cyndi took a breath, Mike noticed that all the conversation in the room had stopped. Everyone's eyes were fixed on Mike and Jason. The last thing he wanted was to create a scene at JJ's party, or embarrass Rachel. "I appreciate your support for someone you obviously know well. At this point, it's out of our hands. It's up to the DA to bring an indictment, evaluate the evidence, and take the case to trial. If the state can prove its case to the jury and the guy is convicted, then fine. If the state can't prove the case and he is acquitted, then that's fine also. I have no reason to think he's a violent criminal or a menace to society. If he's innocent, I won't lose any sleep over it. Good luck to him."

By the time Mike finished, Rachel was easing Cyndi away from the two detectives. Jason led Mike to the front door and suggested they get some fresh air.

Once outside, engulfed in air that was anything but fresh, Mike apologized. "It's JJ's day, and yours and Rachel's. I don't want to take anybody's attention away from you."

"No worries, Mike. I like what you said. Deciding guilt or innocence isn't our job." Then he lowered his voice, despite nobody being within listening distance. "Except for Ronald Randall."

Mike dropped his head. "That was different."

"I know. Nathan Matthews is no serial killer. But if he poisoned Alex Bishop, he's going down, even if he's otherwise an angel."

"Right." Mike turned to reenter the house, with Jason in the lead. As he closed the door behind him, he noticed a Black man wearing a blue sport jacket, standing next to a maroon sedan parked across the street. The man seemed to be watching the house. Mike closed the door, ignoring the tiny flicker of suspicion in his brain.

A few minutes later, Rachel brought out the birthday cake and everyone made a fuss over what a big boy JJ was. He blew out the three candles, then dipped his fingers into the icing. Everyone laughed as he licked orange buttercream off his hand. Rachel, holding a slim point-and-shoot Nikon, waved her hand and called JJ's name, trying to get him to look up. The boy ignored his mother, focusing on the slice of cake Jason had placed on his high chair. Rachel continued to call out and snap photos.

When the camera had been packed away, Michelle put her arm around Rachel's shoulders and gave a squeeze. "He's a beautiful boy. You and Jason are doing a great job with him."

"He is wonderful," Rachel sighed. "I just wish he would look at the camera. I can never get a decent picture of his eyes."

"Don't worry, honey. You have a lot of years in front of you. Maybe he doesn't like paparazzi. He's sweet and everyone loves him."

Rachel turned toward Michelle and enveloped her in a hug. Michelle's diminutive body nearly disappeared inside Rachel's long arms. "Thank you. And Mike. You're the best friends."

* * *

AN HOUR LATER, the bulk of the party guests had left. Mike and Michelle stood on the porch, saying their good-byes. Rachel held JJ in her arms. The boy's droopy eyes and diminished squirming signaled that he was overdue for a nap.

"Thanks for being here," Jason said to them both.

"We wouldn't miss a big event like this for the world," Mike replied. "I'm just glad we can have a party without masks on. Things are starting to feel like they're back to normal."

"Amen to that," Rachel agreed. "We'll see you Labor Day, right?"

"A day at Coney Island with my favorite little boy?" Michelle reached out and pinched JJ's plump cheek between her thumb and index finger. "Wild horses couldn't keep me away."

Rachel and Jason watched from the porch as Mike and Michelle walked down the sidewalk toward the subway. As he looked back to give a last wave, Mike noticed the dark sedan he had seen earlier, still parked across the street. He wasn't sure, but he thought he saw the back of a man's head sitting in the driver's seat.

Chapter 3
A Shadow of Doubt

JASON WAS CARRYING a mostly eaten platter of cut vegetables and dip toward the kitchen when the doorbell rang. All the party guests had departed, leaving Jason, Rachel, and Olivia to clean up.

"Can you get that, Jason?" Rachel called out, her arms elbow-deep in the kitchen sink.

The tall detective set the platter on a still cluttered table, wiped his hands, and approached the front door, wondering which family member had forgotten their purse. He was surprised to see a stranger standing four feet back from the threshold. The man wore pressed gray slacks, a dark blue button-down shirt, and a light blue jacket — no tie, but much more formal than a sweltering Saturday afternoon normally required. He had skin nearly as dark as Jason's and was easily six feet, with broad shoulders.

The man flashed a disarming smile, not approaching without an invitation. Jason combed his memory, thinking he looked vaguely familiar. "Sorry to bother you, Detective Dickson. I'm Sterling Wright. We met at Jim McMillian's funeral. I was Jim's partner in property crimes. I'm a private investigator now. I hate to impose, but it looks like the party is over. Can I talk to you for a few minutes? It's important for my client."

Jason processed the information. *What does this guy want on a weekend?* "How do you know about the party? Are you surveilling me?" Jason put a hand on the door, ready to slam it shut on the PI, ex-cop or not.

"I'm not watching you or anything, Detective. I asked around and people knew you were having a birthday party for your kid today. It wasn't a secret. I'd wait until you were on duty, but this conversation needs to be off the record. Tell me to leave and I'll go, but I know you don't want to put an innocent man in prison and let a killer go free. I want to make sure that doesn't happen." Wright rushed through the explanation, as if wanting to finish before getting cut off. He adopted a serious expression, the friendly smile now gone.

Jason appreciated the technique. The man had not identified what case he was working on or what Jason's involvement was. His pitch was calculated to pique Jason's interest and play on his sense of justice. It was working. He stepped onto the faded wooden planks of the front porch and half-closed the door behind him. Wright held his ground.

"Off the record, I don't know what you're talking about. Who are you working for?"

Wright didn't hedge or hesitate. "Nathan Matthews. I have new information, but most importantly, I want to talk to you about the planted evidence."

"I can't talk about it. The trial is coming up. Good-bye." Jason stepped back inside, his right hand back on the door's edge.

"You don't have to say anything." Wright stepped forward, holding up a hand. "I don't want you to violate any confidentiality or tell me anything about the DA's case or your testimony. We know what it's going to be. I just want you to listen. I need five minutes. That's all. Then you go back to your family and I go home. Please."

It was the "please" that made Jason pause mid-slam. Also the anguished look on the man's face. They had shared a partner in Jim McMillian, even if it was a short stint for them both. Jason now recalled having a moment with Wright at McMillian's funeral. They were both Black detectives in a department with pitifully few. They had a connection. Jason didn't know the circumstances under which Wright left the force, but he could take a few guesses.

"Not here." Jason leaned into the house and called, "Rachel, I'm stepping out for a quick walk. I'll be back in five minutes." Without waiting for a response, he stepped onto the porch and closed the door. He took the four wooden steps two at a time onto the concrete walkway leading toward the street. He did not look back as Wright scrambled to catch up.

The PI pulled abreast after Jason turned left onto the sidewalk. "Didn't you wonder why the investigation was so easy?"

Jason turned his head toward his impromptu companion. "Fall back. Stay behind me. We're not having a meeting or a conversation. You have something to say? Say it to the back of my head. I'm taking a walk around the block. When I make it back home, you're going to keep walking. You have until then to say your piece."

Wright fell into step one stride behind Jason before they reached the corner. While they took a tour around the Brooklyn neighborhood, he made his pitch.

"Detective, you've probably never had a case fall into place quicker and more easily, have you? Don't you wonder about that? You interview two or three obvious witnesses who tell you that Nathan Matthews and Alex Bishop had a running conflict since the start of *Godfather: The Musical.* Then you grab his laptop and there just happens to be specific evidence about his internet searches on it. Like he's a killer who wants to be caught. But think about it. If you were planning to murder someone, would you research the killer drug interaction on your own laptop? Isn't it possible that somebody else who had access to Nathan's laptop planted those searches, knowing you would find them and arrest Nathan? That takes the real killer off the hook. Nobody is looking at other suspects, because the most obvious one has evidence pointing right at him. When was the last time it worked out that way for you, huh?"

Jason turned left again. He could see the top of the Robinson home in the crack between two row houses. His pace remained steady as the private investigator continued.

"There were other people who had motive and opportunity. But you and Detective Stoneman never finished the investigation. The planted evidence pointed you in one direction and that was the end of the road. Arrest, indictment, case closed. Tunnel vision. Nathan has maintained his innocence for the last fifteen months. He's been offered a plea deal, but he insists on a trial. Does that make sense if he's guilty? Why wouldn't he take a plea if the evidence is so damning? Sure, he had a team of lawyers, but they bailed on him five months ago. He ran out of money to pay them. Now he has a solo attorney — and me — and we're at a serious disadvantage, but Nathan still won't take a deal. It should make you think.

"I've been working this case for a year, and I truly believe it's a set-up. Nathan didn't do it. He's being framed, and the DA has taken the bait hook, line, and sinker. There's another guy who could have done it, who had motive and opportunity. He was the understudy to Alex Bishop. He thought he should have been the lead. Greed and jealousy; we both know they are common motives. But I don't have the resources to dig up the kind of evidence you could get. All we want is a deeper investigation. We need you to re-open the case."

Jason figured the speech had been rehearsed to fit into five minutes, since Wright had suggested that amount of time. He made the final left turn, back toward Rachel's mom's house, a few seconds after Wright finished talking.

"Are you going to say anything?" Wright asked from the sidewalk, arms at his sides with palms out. "We still have time to find the real killer before the trial."

Jason stopped and turned. "That's not happening."

"Can you at least think about it? We can talk again."

"I don't think that's a good idea."

The PI held out a silver business card toward Jason. "If you change your mind, give me a call."

Jason took the card and stuffed it into his front left pants pocket. He walked to the porch and went in without looking back.

When he opened the door, Rachel was nearby. "Where'd you go, honey?" She held five half-full plastic cups in her hands.

"Just for a walk. I needed some air."

"Who was at the door?"

"Some guy who wanted to sell me on something. It's not important." He took two cups and headed for the kitchen.

Chapter 4
Faded Memory

THE MONDAY AFTER JJ'S BIRTHDAY PARTY, Mike and Jason worked on the final paperwork on a case they had been calling "Two Hands." The moniker was ironic, since the corpse they found had zero hands, hence, two *missing* hands. The stiff also had no teeth, which was an elementary tip-off that the killer wanted to make it difficult to ID the victim.

Unfortunately for the lowlife named Oscar Infante, he neglected to excise two tattoos on the victim's chest, which matched a missing person's report. The stiff had some obvious gambling debts. Oscar was a known enforcer for a bookie named "Big Al" Henderson. So, the pieces fell together fairly quickly. Mike lamented not being able to arrest Big Al, but at least his muscle would be put on ice for a while.

They had adjourned to the fifth-floor conference room, next to the communications department. It was larger than the tiny space next to the bullpen, two floors below in the old brownstone the city had converted into a police station house. The whiteboard on the wall opposite the door still bore the shadow of a square box in the upper right corner. Mike, Jason, and a task force assigned to hunt down the serial killer known as the Righteous Assassin had toiled for months in that room. The marker stains would never come out.

Jason snapped a folder closed and stuffed it into a cardboard box, already over-filled with case files. "I had an interesting conversation after JJ's party with a private investigator about the Ballet Murder."

Mike looked up from his own stack of documents. "What were you doing talking to a PI about a case we're prepping for trial next week?"

"He showed up at the door after the party broke up. He's an ex-detective named Sterling Wright. In fact, I remember him. He was Jim McMillian's partner for a while, before me. I didn't exactly talk to him. He talked. I listened, then told him to shove off. But what he said made me think."

"About the Ballet Murder?" Mike put down his pen and rolled his neck clockwise, listening to the cracks. He had been sitting at the conference room table for two hours.

Both detectives expected Oscar to take a plea, serve his time, then return to Big Al's operation. There was no percentage in contesting the charges. Big Al would not want a trial and Oscar knew better than to rat out his boss. They were buttoning down the file just in case, but the chance of these documents ever seeing the light of day again was miniscule.

Mike's stainless steel, vacuum-insulated coffee cup was mostly empty, so he took the opportunity to get a refill from the cistern perched on a plastic-covered counter in the back of the space. The smell of burnt toast escaped from the container when he pushed the spigot. "You know better than to listen to somebody working for a defendant. I hope you didn't say anything that will compromise this case. The DA is counting on a conviction."

"I know." Jason sat back in his chair. "The problem is that the guy had a point. The investigation was too easy. The evidence pointed to the director so clearly. Did we develop tunnel vision and not look at anyone but Matthews?"

"It was clean," Mike confidently replied. "Matthews was already a suspect. He had motive and opportunity. The internet searches nailed him. If you remember, he claimed he wasn't in his office at the time they were made. But his alibi didn't check out. He had time to run those searches and still make it to his Directors Guild dinner. He was busted and he knew it."

"I know." Jason leaned against the conference table, looking at Mike. "That's why we didn't follow any other leads. We focused on Matthews and only Matthews. Is it possible it really was too easy? The guy has been protesting his innocence and claiming he was framed for over a year."

"What do you expect him to say if he's not taking a plea?"

"Of course," Jason said, shaking his head. "I know. I can't figure out why it bothers me so much."

Mike, who had put his feet on the table, took a sip of the stale coffee before responding. "Jason, it's like I said to that actress at JJ's party. The quality of the evidence and the arguments the defense might make at trial are not our concern. That's up to the DA. He made the call to indict. Our job was to collect the evidence. We did. The DA thinks the evidence is enough to convict. We don't need to tell the prosecutor how to do his job. And we sure as shit don't need to be helping a PI working for the defense. Anything we say can only hurt the case. I don't care if he's an ex-cop. He probably quit so he could make more money working private. We should *not* be talking to him. I shouldn't have to tell you."

"I know." Jason stood and paced across the ten feet of available space. "I didn't say anything to him. And he didn't quit. He got pushed out. I asked around. Nobody seems to know the details, but he didn't leave voluntarily. And it's not about helping or hurting. Isn't it about the truth? Isn't the point of an investigation to find the killer, no matter what?"

"You know the answer," Mike scolded. "That's what the trial is for."

"Sure, but if we arrested the wrong guy, then there's a killer on the loose who got away with it. What if we missed something and let that happen? Isn't that something we should care about?"

"Of course we care." Mike tapped his pen on the table. "We don't arrest people unless we think they're guilty. The evidence said he's guilty. It's solid. Remember, we work for the city and the DA. We're on their side. We don't do anything that could jeopardize the case. You have any doubt about that?"

"No," Jason conceded, staring at the blank whiteboard. "But let me spin it out for a minute. Let's assume Matthews wanted to kill his actor. He searches the internet for a drug interaction with the medication Bishop was taking. He somehow gets the killer drug into the victim's system during the gala. Then, we start an investigation. It has been a few weeks since the internet searches. Matthews has to know that we're going to look at his laptop. Why does he leave it sitting there for us to find?"

"He deleted his browser history. Maybe he figured that was all he needed to do. He's an older guy. Not so tech savvy. He screwed up. He thought he covered his tracks, but our forensics techs restored the search information. That's not out of the question." Mike looked to his partner for confirmation.

"Yeah. It's possible. Like you always say, Mike, never underestimate how stupid a criminal can be."

Mike stared at the faded square on the blank whiteboard, instead of his partner. "I'll admit it potentially raises some doubt. But it's doubt that the DA needs to worry about, not us. They convened a grand jury. They got an indictment. We checked the box, Jason. The case was successfully closed. We moved on to the next stiff. Like always. We couldn't re-open the case even if we wanted to. We need to forget about these questions."

"I know," Jason said. "I'm just not comfortable about it."

Mike tossed his last folder into the evidence box. "We'll be meeting with the DA before Labor Day. You can tell him about your concerns if you want to during the trial prep. Just don't say anything about talking to a PI."

Chapter 5
Trial Prep

ON THE TUESDAY BEFORE LABOR DAY, Mike and Jason met at the Manhattan District Attorney's office in Foley Square. Mike entered the dreary interior conference room on the 17th floor and held out a hand to Assistant District Attorney Keith Harris. Mike and Keith had worked together for more than ten years, which was considerably longer than the average ADA's tenure. Most lawyers as talented as Keith moved into more lucrative private firm jobs after accumulating the connections and experience that were the primary currency of an ADA. But Keith valued justice over Hawaiian vacations. He and Mike had bonded years before. Mike relished testifying in a trial when Keith orchestrated the action.

"We really doing this?" Mike asked playfully. "I thought you were better at getting guilty pleas. We figured this one had 'deal' written all over it."

"You and me both." Keith released Mike's handshake and gestured toward the ancient chairs surrounding a Formica-covered table that smelled of industrial cleaning solution. The light fixtures, which had once been white, were now colored like the teeth of a medieval serf. "Not that I mind having a simple case. I wish the evidence was this clean for all my trials." Keith's waistline was wider than Mike's, but his suit was well tailored. With short brown hair and a square chin, he could have passed for a cop in different clothes.

Jason helped himself to a cup of tepid coffee from a plastic carafe while his companions claimed their seats. "Aren't you a little worried about the publicity and the public sympathy for Nathan Matthews? The tabloids are already ramping up their coverage. By the time you start the trial, every prospective juror will be saturated with sympathetic stories."

Keith inclined a confirming nod. "I'd be more worried except the Broadway community isn't rallying around the guy. If there were a batch of A-listers making noise and crowing about his innocence, we'd have a problem. But they're pretty quiet. He killed one of their own. He's so obviously guilty that even the usual activists won't touch him."

Jason sat, a blank pad of paper on the table at his elbow. "Is the evidence really so clear-cut?"

"Let's find out," Keith said, opening a large three-ring binder dotted with labeled tabs and sticky notes. "That's what we're here for, right? Let's see how compelling your testimony is going to be."

For the next two hours, Keith carefully walked the two detectives through their upcoming testimony, making notes about which witness would best deliver the key facts for the jury. It was typically slow going, but necessary for Mike and Jason to be fully familiar with all the documents and to have their stories engrained for the witness stand.

On the night Alex Bishop died, nobody knew he had been poisoned. It was a medical emergency, rather than a suspected crime. Only after Michelle finished the autopsy and got back the toxicology results did anyone even think about murder.

Keith put down his pen and stretched his neck forward and backward. "I heard a rumor the other day that Dr. McNeill was so upset about the guy's death she conducted the autopsy the night of the Broadway Cares gala, still wearing her heels and evening gown. You believe that shit?"

"I believe somebody would start such a rumor," Mike responded. "You know her, Keith. It's not entirely impossible." The three men shared a laugh and a consensus that Michelle would have done it if she thought there could have been foul play involved.

Keith then spent fifteen minutes with Jason, covering the information in the toxicology report. This was the first weight-bearing leg of the prosecution's case. The tox report showed the presence of digoxin in the actor's blood. That drug was widely used for heart rate control for patients with atrial fibrillation. It was not anything lethal on its own. However, because Bishop was already on a high dose of a beta blocker called metoprolol for a different heart condition, the digoxin sent him into complete heart block. The ADA would get this information into the record through a forensic toxicologist, who would testify in great detail about the drug interaction. It was important to establish that Jason and Mike knew about this when they began their investigation into a possible homicide. Jason needed to handle this testimony, since Mike being married to the medical examiner placed him in a conflicted position when it came to evaluating her report.

Keith turned back to Mike, who had been checking messages on his phone. "Had you been assigned to the case before the tox report came back?"

"Yes. It's routine for a detective team to be on the case of any death where there is no clear cause. Since it was a celebrity case and the media was all over it, Sully gave it to us, but we didn't have any focus until we got the report. We spoke to his personal assistant and took a look around his apartment and his dressing room in the theater. His heart condition was a closely guarded secret. Casting agents and directors wouldn't want to take a risk on a lead who might drop dead mid-production. She couldn't tell us who in Hollywood knew he was taking the meds, but there were only a few people in New York. One, of course, was Matthews. As the show's director, he had to know in case there was a medical emergency during a rehearsal or a performance."

"When did you come to the conclusion that the other drug in his system was, essentially, a murder weapon?"

"As soon as we got the tox report back. We guessed that an amateur killer could figure out digoxin would be lethal for Bishop, but might not realize how obvious it would be on the tox screen."

"Great. So, I'm guessing the next thing you needed was a list of people who had a motive to poison Bishop and who also knew he was taking metoprolol, right?"

"Not immediately. The ME's report included a notation that the drug interaction would have happened pretty quickly — probably within an hour or so. As soon as he began digesting it, he would feel symptoms and eventually his heart would stop. That meant somebody slipped him the poison during the party before the ballet. If he had been poisoned before he arrived at the theater, he would have started to feel sick during the cocktail hour. We wanted to determine who had an opportunity to slip him the Mickey during the party."

"So . . . ?" Keith prompted.

"So, we wanted to see if there was surveillance video from the gala that might show us something. We also wanted to see if there was any possibility of identifying a glass he drank from with traces of the drug, and maybe fingerprints."

"I don't recall seeing anything in the case notes about you finding a drinking glass." Keith leafed through his binder.

"That's because we came up empty," Mike said. "All the glassware had been washed. Nobody impounded it since we didn't know it was a crime scene that night. We had Bishop on camera taking food or drinks from seven waiters and accepting glasses from two other people. Any of them could have given him the drug. Plus he was off camera several times. Nathan Matthews was one of the people who handed him a glass. That turned out to be significant later. At the time, we didn't think much of it. Any one of those servers could have done it."

"So, why are we talking about it?"

"You asked." Mike kept his poker face on, not showing any sign of emotion.

"Did you question the people who brought drinks to Bishop?"

"No," Mike answered. "We were still waiting to track them down when other events made that line of investigation moot."

Keith flipped to a new section of his binder and carefully pulled out a stapled bundle of papers. He left the pile on the table, leaving Mike and Jason to wonder when the prosecutor would let them see the evidence. "OK. What was the next stage of the investigation?"

Mike and Jason looked at each other, then Jason responded. "We went to the theater to interview members of the cast and crew. We wanted to know if anyone had a grudge against Bishop. We asked a standard series of questions about whether the guy had any altercations or disputes with anyone, or if he was sleeping with somebody's wife. We had multiple witnesses tell us that Bishop and Matthews had a rough relationship."

Keith ticked off information from his notes. "The witnesses were the stage manager, Rich Cohen, one of the actresses, Virginia Healey, and Bishop's understudy, Brock Taylor." Keith flipped over his pile of papers. He pushed half of it across the table to Jason, then handed the other half to Mike. "Are these your notes from the witness interviews?"

Jason, a veteran of enough testimony to know the drill, carefully flipped through all the typed pages of the package. "They are. I made notes during our interviews on the dates indicated on these pages, then typed my notes when I got back to my desk. I then destroyed the original handwritten notes, which is my normal practice."

Keith gave Jason a silent thumb's up. "You have been trained well, Detective. How many witnesses did you speak with?"

"We spoke to a dozen or so people, but the three you mentioned each told us that Matthews and Bishop had some problems."

"Without worrying about the exact words, tell me the highlights of what you were told by the three different witnesses."

"Won't that be hearsay?" Jason asked.

"Who's the lawyer here?" Keith leaned back in his chair, smiling. "Don't worry. We're not relying on the truth of the statements, so they're not technically hearsay. Just answer the question."

"They said the director was unhappy that Bishop was cast as the lead in *Godfather*. Matthews criticized Bishop regularly, complained to anyone who would listen that Bishop was a washed-up film star who had no business on a Broadway stage. He yelled at Bishop during rehearsals and eviscerated him whenever he made a mistake. At a rehearsal a week or so before they opened, the two got into a heated shouting match on the stage. Matthews made a statement to the effect that he wished Bishop would drop dead so he could bring in somebody who could act. This was verified by multiple other witnesses later."

"Were there any other incidents described to you that you considered relevant?"

"There was a situation a month or so into the show's run where Bishop was sick and called to say he couldn't perform. Matthews shuffled around the cast and had the understudy ready to play the lead. Then, a few minutes before showtime, Bishop showed up and said he was feeling better. He demanded that they hold the start of the show so he could get into wardrobe. Matthews told him it was too late and that he should go home and rest up. He allegedly made a remark about them being a better cast without their star. Bishop apparently made a big stink backstage and threatened to walk out into the theater and tell the audience that he was ready to go on, but the director was forcing them to see the understudy instead. Matthews relented and delayed the show. Several people reported overhearing Matthews say that Bishop was ruining his show and that his behavior was unprofessional. Matthews called him a Hollywood hack."

Keith smiled. "Based on the information you heard from these witnesses, what did you do next?"

Jason handed back the witness statement sheets. "We interviewed Matthews, who admitted having disagreements with Bishop, that he yelled at the guy during rehearsals, and that he was unhappy about the late-arrival incident. He even admitted saying Bishop was ruining the show and that he was a hack actor. We asked him why he would bring Bishop a drink at the benefit gala if he disliked him so much. He said he wanted to bury the hatchet and didn't want to hurt his own chances for a Tony Award by being an asshole in public."

"Did you believe him?" Keith asked.

"Are you going to ask me that question on the witness stand?"

"God, no. I'm asking you now, here in this room. Did you believe him?"

Jason looked at Mike, who answered for both of them. "We talked about that. Matthews seemed to be forthcoming and honest during his interview. He admitted to things we thought were pretty damning. He's smart, so it was possible he was playing the good guy. He's around actors all the time. Who knows how good an actor he might be. It made sense, but it also sounded like a good line that somebody who was a murderer would have thought up. We didn't exactly believe him, but we weren't sure. Once we found out about the evidence on his laptop, we stopped thinking about it."

"OK, let's not get ahead of ourselves. After interviewing Nathan Matthews, what did you do next?"

Jason picked up the story. "At that point, we considered Matthews to be a potential suspect. He had a motive and he had handed the victim a cocktail, which could have been an opportunity to poison him. We searched his office in the theater, with the permission of the stage manager, and discovered a laptop computer on his desk. We secured the computer and held it until the district attorney obtained a subpoena authorizing a forensic search of the machine. Then, we turned it over to the tech team."

Mike leaned over the edge of the table toward Keith. "We're not going to be able to testify about the data they found on the computer, right?"

"I won't need you to, Mike. We'll have the forensic tech take the jury through what they found."

"We got the report of what the techs found on the laptop." Mike pointed to Keith's binder. "The summary said he had deleted his internet search history, but they were able to recover the data. Two weeks before the benefit at the ballet, he searched for the heart drug Bishop was taking. He also searched for drug interactions and accessed some medical websites that talk about how digoxin should never be used in combination with metoprolol. He even searched for information about where he could obtain digoxin, which is a prescription drug. That was enough for us to arrest him and turn the case over to the DA."

Jason stood behind his chair, leaning into it. "What are we going to say on cross-examination about whether it's possible that somebody could have planted the evidence by running those searches on the laptop to frame Matthews?"

Keith dropped his pen on the huge binder. "What do you think, Detective? How would you answer that without me prompting you?"

"I'd say I'm not a computer expert. I don't have an opinion about whether that scenario is consistent with the attributes of the data on the machine. I just don't know."

"Perfect answer. We'll make a lawyer out of you yet." Keith flashed another satisfied smile.

"You think it will matter to the jury that Bishop won the Tony for best actor, posthumously?" Jason asked.

"The critics didn't think he deserved it, but when you die at a Broadway Cares benefit, there's a lot of sympathy." Keith carefully clipped his papers back into the big binder. "I doubt people even remember now. That was more than a year ago and the show closed a few weeks later."

Mike leaned in toward the prosecutor. "Keith, what would you say if I told you that Jason and I both have some concerns about whether we completed a thorough investigation here? That we never considered the possibility there might be another killer?"

"I'd tell you to put such thoughts out of your head. I need you two on the DA team here. What's bothering you?"

Mike explained their doubts about the lack of physical evidence, the possibility that the evidence on the laptop had been planted, and the fact that the director had not ditched the laptop once the investigation started. He didn't mention that these doubts had been brought to Jason by the defense team's investigator. "It's possible we relaxed once we got the laptop information. What if there was somebody else and we never looked for them?"

Keith reassured his witnesses. "I get it. I know you guys always look for doubt. But this was a clean bust. The evidence was there. The search history on his laptop is not circumstantial. It's real evidence. The stage manager said that Matthews kept the door locked and never let anyone in there when he was away. There's not much chance that somebody broke in, leaving no trace, planted the evidence, then deleted the browser history. If somebody was trying to frame him, why delete the evidence?"

Jason had a quick answer, "Because anybody knows that if the police confiscate the laptop, anything in the deleted browser history will be discovered. It would look more suspicious if the history was *not* deleted. Deleting it makes it more plausible."

"You're assuming this hypothetical other killer is thinking two moves ahead and is a genius-level criminal. It doesn't generally work that way." Keith grabbed his briefcase and started packing up. "It's a clean case, guys. It should be a piece of cake. I'm frankly surprised Matthews hasn't cut a deal."

"Doesn't that worry you?" Mike asked. "Doesn't the fact that he has maintained his innocence all this time make you wonder?"

"Not really. He's not a normal defendant. He isn't rotting on Rikers Island while he awaits trial. He has been under house arrest with an ankle bracelet, and he has a nice apartment. He has had a comfortable year, so there hasn't been much incentive for him to take a plea."

"Must be nice to be rich and famous," Jason observed.

"Yeah. I wouldn't know anything about that." Keith stepped toward the conference room door. "I'll get the preliminaries out of the way in the first few trial days. Once we have all the foundations set, I'll bring in Doctor McNeill, and then you two. Be ready starting on the third day after jury selection."

"We'll be ready." Mike led Jason toward the exit. While they waited for the elevator, he said, "We need to put our doubts away for the trial. Keith thinks it's a good case. His opinion is the only one that counts. We're on the prosecution's team."

"Is that supposed to make me feel better?" Jason stepped into the car.

Mike faced the door, not looking at his partner. "It doesn't matter."

Chapter 6
On the Boardwalk

ON LABOR DAY, Mike, Michelle, and Michelle's niece, Star, accompanied Jason, Rachel, and JJ on an outing to Coney Island.

The day was humid and in the mid-90s. The whole summer had been hot, leaving everyone testy. A miniscule sea breeze on the boardwalk provided slim relief, particularly for JJ, riding in a folding stroller and straining at his bindings. Rachel had outfitted her son in a floppy sunhat and yellow-rimmed sunglasses, complementing the coating of SPF 30 sunscreen. The three-year-old squirmed and struggled, fussing and squealing as the group paraded down the beachfront. The child banged a yellow plastic mallet against the stroller's side over and over, drawing attention from passing sun worshipers.

Mike stopped at a cart selling sno-cones and bought a round of icy treats for the group. JJ's immediately found its way onto the toddler's New York Mets number 5 t-shirt. Mike had strategically suggested a blue flavor option, so the stain complemented the color scheme. The group rested on a wooden bench, facing the conglomeration of multi-colored beach umbrellas and shelters that nearly obscured the sand. Seagulls squawked nearby, fighting over a stray French fry.

"What do you think of Coney Island?" Michelle asked Star, who was gazing longingly at the beach. Her dark skin was dappled with beads of sweat.

"I'd like it better if I was wearing a swimsuit."

Eunice Albertson received the nickname Star in junior high school in the Atlanta suburb where Michelle's sister Rosie lived with her husband, Clarence. The oldest of Rosie's three kids, Eunice loved music, dancing, and acting. She was on the drill team and played the lead in the eighth-grade production of *Once on This Island*. Her friends began calling her Star.

When she was fourteen, Star made a trip to New York to visit her Aunt Michelle. The two attended several Broadway shows as well as off-Broadway theater. Star fell in love with the Big Apple and set her sights on the performing arts school at NYU. Throughout high school, Aunt Michelle watched from afar, thanks to the internet, Zoom, and YouTube. After Star received her NYU acceptance, Michelle looked forward to spending much more time with her favorite niece.

Rachel gathered the now-blue napkins, along with the soggy sno-cone wrapper, and deposited them in a garbage can next to their bench. Looking at Michelle, she said, "When do you testify in the Ballet Murder case?"

"Keith said it will probably be on the second day after opening statements. They picked the jury on Friday, so the case should open tomorrow." Michelle reached down to tickle JJ's tummy, which prompted a squeal of laughter. "I'll go before Jason and Mike."

"Hey!" Mike scolded, "No shop talk today. We're here to have some fun."

"I'm sorry, Mike," Rachel said. "I'm trying to pitch to my bosses that they should let me cover the trial. Not that I'm complaining about my job. I love covering the medical and emergency stories, but I'd like to branch out a bit."

"Oh, honey," Michelle stroked Rachel's upper arm. "We know how talented you are. You should be anchoring the evening news. It'll happen. Remember, luck favors the prepared mind. It's kinda funny, since it was the Ballet Murder that got you the TV job, huh?"

"How did that happen?" Star asked.

"We were there," Jason answered. "Rachel was still an EMT then. She jumped in and tried to save Alex Bishop's life in the theater. Afterward, she got interviewed by ACN — American Cable News. They thought Rachel was so good on camera that they brought her into the studio for a follow-up. Then they offered her a job."

"It wasn't quite that quick." Rachel playfully slapped Jason's shoulder. "It was several months later. But I was ready to get out of the EMT stress, so I'm pretty happy about it."

"And you'll be moving up very soon," Michelle said. "You keep pushing them until they can't ignore you."

"I know." Rachel munched her melting strawberry ice. "There's so much more I can do. Who would be better to cover this trial than me, huh? I have inside information from the ME and the detectives who worked the case. Plus, I was there when it happened! And I would be so good as the Broadway reporter."

Jason put his arm around his wife's shoulders. "There's nobody better than you, honey."

Mike slurped the last remnants of his cherry ice from its paper cone. "You're young. Plenty of time to climb the ladder. We're looking forward to watching you. It's nice that you're not out on the streets with the EMT crew getting assaulted." Michelle slid her arm under Mike's and squeezed, nodding her agreement. Mike gazed at the sweltering bodies splayed across the beach. In the distant surf, hundreds of revelers bobbed in the refreshing Atlantic. "How's the bedroom situation?" Mike asked casually.

Jason stiffened. "It's fine. We're happy to let Olivia stay in the main bedroom suite. It's her house. We're fine in Rachel's room. JJ has plenty of space, so everything is fine."

"I thought you would have changed that arrangement by now," Mike said to Rachel.

"It's none of our business," Michelle said, grabbing Mike's arm and pulling him off the bench. As they moved away from the others, she said, in a hissing whisper, "Let it be, Mike." Then Michelle turned back to Rachel. "When are you bringing JJ over to play with Topsy?"

"We'll be over next weekend. He loves that cat."

"Topsy!" JJ squealed. The toddler had a limited vocabulary, but Topsy was a word he spoke clearly.

"So do I!" Star gushed. "She's so loving and cuddly. Maybe you should get one of your own."

Rachel gripped Jason's arm. "My mom is not a cat person. And, frankly, Jason isn't, either. We'll have to settle for visiting Topsy."

"Star, did Mike and Michelle tell you how they got their cat?" Jason asked.

"Aunt Michelle said she was a stray they adopted."

Jason let out a deep belly laugh. "Oh, sure. I guess that's true. But not the whole story."

"Do we really need to?" Mike asked.

"Absolutely," Jason pulled Star gently toward him. "Your Aunt Michelle's chief assistant, Natalie, found the little kitten huddled in a corner outside their office. The thing was malnourished and had a chunk bitten from her ear, and another from her tail. Natalie scooped her up and brought her inside the lab, where she and Michelle, along with the whole ME staff, nursed her back to health. They couldn't keep her forever in the lab, and Natalie couldn't take her home because she lived in a no-pet building. So, Michelle took her home, without telling Mike."

"That's not true," Michelle protested, although a smile played at the edges of her mouth. "I told him I was bringing home a present. It was during COVID. We were trapped in our apartment, except for going to work wearing masks all day. Lots of people got pets. And I always wanted a cat. And Topsy is so happy with us."

"She's happy with you," Mike mumbled.

"You're growing on her." Michelle squeezed Mike's hand.

"Two years later and she only occasionally lets me touch her. But that's fine with me. I'm more of a dog person, anyway."

"And, Star, did Michelle tell you how Topsy got her name?" Rachel asked.

"Sure. She said it was after the cartoon cat from *Tom & Jerry*."

"Well . . ." Rachel got a mischievous grin, "Michelle does love those old cartoons. But it was really Natalie who named the stray cat. Her full name is Autopsy. So, Topsy for short."

"That's so funny!" Star's voice raised an octave as she laughed. "Well, I love her."

"She loves women and children," Mike said. "I must admit it's fun watching Topsy play with JJ."

They spent the rest of the afternoon meandering along past the ice cream, t-shirt, and candy stores along the boardwalk, listening to happy screams from the beach and the constant screeches of seagulls. When JJ finally became so fussy that not even a warm churro would console him, Jason and Rachel announced they were heading home. Mike, Michelle, and Star stayed for another half-hour, unwilling to retreat to the subway and the long trek back to Manhattan until absolutely necessary.

"I guess it's just as well that you never got married and had kids while you were coming up as a detective, huh, Mike?" Michelle asked as they watched a family with three children scampering across the sand, chasing a beach ball. Star had insisted on dipping her toes in the surf, leaving Michelle holding her shoes. "Must be hard to juggle a family while being a cop."

Mike didn't turn his eyes away from the happy family. "I watched Darren and Marie do it for two years, before he got himself shot. He handled it pretty well, but I know Marie always worried about him. I guess Rachel must feel the same way about Jason, sometimes."

"I feel that way about you." Michelle stared at the side of Mike's face, wondering if he would turn to look at her. "I try not to, but it's impossible not to think about it. If we had kids, I'm sure it would be far worse."

Mike finally turned his head. "I don't ever want you to regret marrying me. But I'm a cop, and that's what I'll always be. Maybe I'll hang up my gun someday, but until then, I can't change who I am or how I do my job. I'm glad you can handle it. I'm not sure whether Rachel can, and how Jason will handle that."

Michelle leaned her head onto Mike's shoulder. "I know what you mean. I'm not sure, either."

"It will probably get worse after baby number two arrives."

Michelle straightened, surprised. "Did Jason tell you?"

Mike shook his head softly. "No. I figured it out. I'm sure you already knew."

Michelle pursed her lips. "I was sworn to secrecy, but since you know, I guess I can confirm your suspicion. Rachel doesn't want to tell anybody officially until after the first trimester. Have you told Jason that you know?"

"Hell, no. And I won't. He'll tell me when he's ready, or when Rachel tells him to. And I'll be suitably surprised. It's the least I can do for my partner."

"I'll never understand you men," Michelle said, returning her head to its resting place.

When Star returned, her feet and ankles covered with sand, they strolled along the smooth boards in the general direction of the subway. They were in no hurry for the summer to end.

Chapter 7
Party Girl

THAT NIGHT, ON MANHATTAN'S UPPER WEST SIDE, Kayleigh Bronson held a champagne glass over her head as she danced to Taylor Swift's "Shake It Off." Her sheer blue lace top rode up nearly to the base of her breasts, exposing her toned abs above designer low-rise jeans. Long, golden hair flowed back and forth across her oval face in time to the music, exposing and obscuring her blue eyes. Her friends cheered as a few drops of golden liquid spilled from the glass, splashing on the edge of a Persian rug. Five other young women, all wearing skinny jeans or tight-fitting dresses, bounced to the music in Kayleigh's living room. A dozen other party guests stood around the perimeter or sat on the plush sofas and high bar stools. The mood was carefree and festive.

Summer had been a sweltering slog for most New Yorkers. For Kayleigh and her party guests, the unofficial end of summer was an excuse for revelry and the sad conclusion of the vacationing months. Those with traditional jobs lamented the return to office life, at least three days per week in the post-COVID hybrid work environment. For Kayleigh, it was merely time to start planning a Halloween party.

The party mix emanating from hidden speakers transitioned to Cyndi Lauper's "Girls Just Wanna Have Fun."

Kayleigh drained her glass and skipped in time with the music toward the bar. It was tucked into the corner farthest from the windows, which displayed the lights of Weehawken, New Jersey shimmering on the surface of the Hudson River. Her wide smile exposed bright white teeth, surrounded by deep red lipstick.

"Lori!" Kayleigh cried out happily, holding her arms wide and enveloping her friend in a bouncing hug.

"Happy anniversary, girl," Lori said, clinking her half-full glass against Kayleigh's empty one. "I can't believe it's already been a year. I guess time really does fly by when you're having fun. And you have more fun than anyone I know." Lori burst into an uncontrollable giggle as both women began swaying their hips to the music.

"Best year of my life," Kayleigh called out above the noise. She refilled her glass with Dom Perignon, draining the last drops before tipping the bottle onto its side, where it rolled against a silver ice bucket. "And I'm getting a surprise later."

"Oooh!" Lori raised her manicured eyebrows. The hair piled on her head gave her the illusion of being much taller. She wore an orange tube top, leaving her smooth shoulders and long neck bare. "Is this surprise coming from your actor or your landlord?"

"I can't say." Kayleigh flashed a mischievous smile. "It's called a Montezuma's Delight."

Lori's face turned serious. "You be careful with that crazy shit. Don't be taking anything unless you know what's in it, no matter what that psycho dude says."

"He's not a psycho. He's a doctor, and he gives great advice. Brock loves him, and I don't know anybody who ever had a problem with his stuff. He always tells you when to avoid something because you're taking something else. Don't worry."

"I worry. You're too trusting, Kayleigh."

"Oh, Sweetie. I'm always careful." Kayleigh put a soft hand on Lori's arm. "Just have fun. It's a holiday, right?"

Before Lori could respond, three other guests crowded around the bar, laughing and jostling for space. They all greeted Kayleigh, who smiled and chatted with each of them.

Nobody in the room was over thirty, and nobody was sober. Kayleigh circulated through the crowd expertly, making sure no one felt neglected and offering drinks and recreational drugs. Outside the south-facing windows, the adjoining apartment tower glimmered. The new World Trade Tower's pinnacle rose in the distance, bathed in yellow light. It was a view everyone in the room envied.

At a quarter to midnight, Lori grabbed her host by the hand near the entrance foyer. "Kayleigh, this has been amazing tonight, but I have an early appointment."

"Oh, Lori. We need to have a night for just the two of us. Text me tomorrow. We can get some lunch."

"Don't go too crazy tonight, Hon. Are you still planning to do the Montezuma thing?"

"Oh, you bet! I'll post it later, so look for it in the morning!"

"OK. But be careful. I love having you in the building." Lori gave Kayleigh a kiss on the cheek, then left the apartment.

The music shifted to Katy Perry as Kayleigh mingled with her guests. As she passed by a leather sofa, a strong hand clasped her arm above the wrist and pulled her down onto the beige cushion. "Hey, Babe. I've hardly seen you. Trying to make me jealous?"

Kayleigh leaned in to dispense a lingering kiss on Brock Taylor's willing lips. Brock was the most handsome man she had ever met. He was actually beautiful, with smooth cheekbones, flawless skin, and soft brown eyes. She had been amazed when the Broadway actor paid attention to her at a nightclub six months earlier. He was so talented and confident. And his hands were so soft . . . and slow. She fantasized about making love while he was in his drag costume, which Brock had hinted about. It hadn't happened yet. Brock was amazing. He also loved sharing her drugs.

One kiss morphed into another. Brock's hand found Kayleigh's denim-covered thigh. Kayleigh's eyes opened and darted across the room to the bedroom door. She detached from Brock's lips. "You are incorrigible! I can't make out here. It's my party. I have obligations." She stood abruptly, but smiled seductively down at her lover. "There will be other nights. You relax and have fun." Brock flashed a mock pout, then reached for a joint smoldering in a crystal ashtray on a nearby side table.

Kayleigh continued her interactions with the party guests, dancing, laughing, and sipping champagne. Three guests were first timers. She spent time with each, exchanging stories and hugs. One woman wearing a Halston dress said she wanted to pitch her an idea, which Kayleigh casually brushed off. "It's a party, silly. Save business for daylight hours. Text me tomorrow."

Shortly before midnight, Kayleigh slipped away to the bathroom in the primary suite. Examining her face in the lighted mirror, she took a moment to appreciate her good fortune. She was twenty-three, fully self-sufficient, and debt-free. It had been an amazing run. The apartment was spectacular. Her TikToks were trending multiple times per week. Her Instagram followers had recently topped two million and her social life was flourishing. Estee Lauder wanted her to plug their new facial cleanser. She had all the fine food, booze, and drugs she could enjoy. Life was good, and only figured to get better. She had multiple men courting her, although she was having enough trouble juggling the two she was regularly fucking. She didn't think more would be a good idea, although it was an exciting prospect.

"Ready?" came a deep voice from the bedroom.

"You bet!" she replied, bouncing on her toes. She expected the next hour to be memorable.

Chapter 8
Back to Work

TUESDAY MORNING, Mike staked out space in the fifth-floor conference room while Jason walked to the basement records room to visit Sophie LaFontaine. Sophie's ever-present smile and island accent made her counter a popular destination for cops looking for a few minutes of diversion during a busy day. Thirty-three years on the force had not slowed her mind. She showed no signs of retiring from her perch as the queen of the records room. Even with digital records taking over the day-to-day paperwork of policing, the maintenance of physical evidence and original papers created during investigations was a critical function. Sophie guarded her realm with the tenacity of a mother bear. Nobody knew the contents and organization of the records better than Sophie.

Today, Sophie's blue uniform was accented by bright red nail polish and matching lipstick. A mound of thick, black hair was carefully arranged atop her slender neck. With expertly applied makeup on her cheekbones and eyelids, Sophie could pass for a Queen Latifa impersonator, although the popular actress was two decades younger.

"Well, look who's come down to see ol' Sophie today. It's the father of the year and the husband of my favorite local TV star. What can I do for ya, Detective?"

"You can start by giving me some of the Jamaica sunshine you keep inside that smile of yours." Jason reached across the waist-high counter separating Sophie's domain from the Linoleum-covered hallway and engulfed Sophie's hands. "C'mon, beautiful. Gimme some of that Sophie sugar."

Sophie turned her head demurely to the side, fighting to keep a straight face. After three seconds, she burst into full toothy bloom. "Oh, you Cassanova. You know I love you. You can come brighten my day anytime. Now, what can I get you?"

"I need our evidence box from the Nathan Matthews file."

"Oh, the Ballet Murder. That trial's comin' up. Let me see if there's anything still here. Most of it went downtown to the DA." Sophie dragged a huge bound ledger book from under the counter. Its scratched black leather cover spoke volumes about its history. Jason had seen the same book in Sophie's manicured hands since his first day working homicide. Inside, purple script writing recorded all the materials coming and going from the massive storage room. The same data was in the department computer, accessible from the keyboard inches away, which she ignored. Sophie ran her index finger down a page of dated entries. "Here we are. We sent six boxes down in June, but I still have one. It has the physical investigation notes and photo prints. Mostly things duplicated in the electronic files. You can see all that on your computer screen upstairs. You still want the box?"

Jason said he did and Sophie scribbled a note, handing it off to a young female clerk, who hustled off into the rows of metal shelving. The detective leaned onto the counter and placed a hand on the edge of Sophie's ledger book. "Why do you still use this old thing, Sophie? It's a lot of work to duplicate the same information that's already in the computer."

"It's worth it to make sure." Sophie gently removed Jason's hand from her precious book and closed the tome with a thud. "You should know, Detective, anything in that computer can be messed with. Somebody knows how, they can change it or make it go away. They can even put somethin' in. You can never trust 'em. But if it's in my book, ain't nobody going to change it or put somethin' in that don't belong. You can take that to court."

"I can't argue," Jason agreed. "But there's information in a computer you can't find anywhere else, including things people think they deleted. You can't burn it or throw it in the trash, so it can come back to bite you, unless you throw the whole machine in the river."

"Maybe. But when you look in that file box, you'll see things that are actually there. Plus, you sometimes see the things that aren't there, but should be. You know what I mean, Detective. It's the things that are missing that may point you in the right direction."

"I wish I had you upstairs sifting through all the files with us, Sophie."

"You and Stoneman prepping for the trial?"

"Yes. We heard the defense is going to argue that the evidence on Matthews' laptop was planted by the real killer."

"Oh, my. That would be an effective argument, seein' as how it's about the entire case for the prosecution. Things would be a whole lot different if you had proof the director had some of the drug that killed Alex Bishop. I love his movies. He could've played on my stage any time."

"How can you remember every detail about every case, Sophie?"

"I don't. I only remember what concerns my evidence."

"But there was no evidence of the drug. We figured he ditched it after he spiked the guy's drink. We didn't expect to find a bottle in his dressing room. The absence of that evidence isn't surprising." Jason realized he was arguing the case with Sophie and wondered if she was just busting his balls.

The clerk returned, carrying a medium-sized cardboard box bearing a round yellow sticker with Sophie's handwriting. After checking the box number and making a notation in her immense record book, she slid a slip of paper across the counter for Jason to sign, acknowledging that he took possession of the box and its contents. As he turned to leave, the evidence box held in both hands, he said, "You think it's a big hole, not being able to put a bottle of that drug in the director's hand?"

"Honey, what do I know? I'm no detective. To me, it's a little bitty hole, but if you had filled it in, it would make the rest of the pail hold water a whole lot better."

Jason lifted the box up six inches in a kind of wave to Sophie, then trudged back up the stairs to the fifth floor. There was an elevator, but since Rachel chided him about developing a little "spare tire" around his waist, he had pledged to only take the stairs.

Two hours later, the conference table was littered with photo prints, pages of typed notes, and a few assorted sheets bearing several styles of handwriting. Mike and Jason had barely unpacked the box and organized its contents when a knock on the door jamb caused them to look up. Their captain stood with both hands on his hips. Like every other cop in history named Sullivan, all his officers and detectives called him "Sully." He was a bulldog in supporting his detectives, but he would also call them out if they made him or his homicide unit look bad. In his police uniform, the detectives in the bullpen liked to joke that he looked like the Skipper from Gilligan's Island, with plump cheeks and a ruddy complexion.

"Are those files from the Ballet Murder? I thought you already prepped with the DA?"

"We're reviewing some loose ends that surfaced during the trial prep," Mike responded. "We don't want to leave any holes in the case."

"That's admirable, Stoneman. Shows dedication to the prosecution. If you didn't have more important things to do, it would be a fine use of time by two experienced homicide detectives."

"We don't have a current investigation requiring any immediate attention, Cap," Jason said.

"That was five minutes ago," Sully barked. "We got a dead girl in a high-end apartment over on Riverside. The communications department called after the uniforms got there. Seems that she had a million social media followers, so it's a high-profile stiff. You two are on it as of right now." Sully held out a thin folder. "Get over to the site. I'll have somebody clean up this mess while you're out."

Mike gathered a small stack of manilla folders and deposited them back into the evidence box. "See, we're a credit to the department for being so dedicated to supporting the prosecution."

Jason opened the new case folder. "We'll make sure Keith knows," he said absently, staring at the case intake form. Looking up, he said, "You'll love this, Mike. We're headed back to a familiar crime scene."

Chapter 9
The Influencer

WHEN MIKE AND JASON STEPPED off the elevator into a vestibule adorned with an ornate golden-framed mirror, plush maroon carpeting, and crystal wall lamps, they each felt a sense of déjà vu. The Park Towers, overlooking the Hudson River at the south end of Riverside Park on Manhattan's Upper West Side, was a jewel of the neighborhood's redevelopment. No buildings to the south were more than ten years old. None to the north were less than a hundred. From 72nd Street to 126th, Riverside Park was lined with stately pre-war buildings, most of which had been renovated and all of which retained their old-world charm. The new constructions, starting with the Park Towers, were shiny steel and glass, with modern conveniences and a decidedly younger clientele.

Four years earlier, in the summer of 2019, Mike and Jason spent some intense hours in the building after one of its most famous residents, NFL quarterback Jimmy Rydel, disappeared from his swanky penthouse apartment. Rydell turned up a few days later, his body naked and partially frozen on the Central Park carousel. The subsequent investigation revealed corruption with more layers than a tailgate party fiesta dip.

"The last time we were here," Jason said, "there was no body in the apartment. At least this time we don't have to search for our corpse."

"Sure, but we're right back in the celebrity murder craziness. We're now the cops in *Only Murders in the Building*. Let's hope building security can keep the press away from our crime scene." Mike turned right down a short hallway. There were only eight apartment doors on the section of the 37th floor served by their elevator.

"If it's a crime." Jason reminded his senior partner that the intake report said the probable cause of death was a drug overdose.

"Yeah. They wouldn't bother sending us, except the victim is somehow famous." Mike stopped at their target door, where a uniformed officer stood sentry. "I honestly don't get it. It seems like there are hundreds of these young people now who have millions of internet followers, but they haven't done anything. They're not actors or singers or artists. They post home-made videos and cell phone pictures. They're somehow rich celebrities for nothing. It's like they didn't earn it. Now we have to treat them like Sophia Loren."

"Who?"

"Screw you, Jason," Mike snapped. "I know damned well you know who Sophia Loren is. You're not that much younger."

"A lot happens in two decades, Mike." Jason kept his poker face in place, but winked at the officer guarding the door. Beyond the threshold, two EMTs leaned against the wall. A wheeled gurney stood idle in the corridor, awaiting a passenger.

Mike pushed past his partner and entered the apartment. Once inside, Jason was all business as they cycled through their familiar crime scene routine. The apartment was as opulent and impressive as they expected. A short entrance hallway adorned with a huge pink vase, used as an umbrella holder, spilled into a sunken living room. Across the room, three panels of floor-to-ceiling windows displayed a downtown view featuring the pinnacle of One World Trade Center. Polished hardwood flooring peeked out between Persian rugs and plush leather sofas and chairs. On the wall opposite the windows, a sixty-inch flat screen's black surface reflected the view.

"Some party," Jason mumbled, scanning the debris around the room. Glasses dotted the end tables, an oval glass-topped coffee table, the marble countertops of a bar, and the pass-through to the kitchen. Some were half-filled with left-over booze and melted ice. The bar area was strewn with bottles. All were opened; a few were empty. Jason noted the brand names: Grey Goose, Bombay Sapphire, Macallan, Don Julio, Dom Pérignon. Spent cigarettes, tobacco and marijuana, lay like perimeter spikes on a large crystal ashtray. A long table against one wall held platters of mostly eaten food, plates of which were abandoned around the room. A stain of white powder residue on the coffee table's surface and the amoeba-shaped remnants of spilled liquid marring the hardwood completed the picture.

"Ya think?" Mike deadpanned. He turned to the officer who had joined the detectives when they entered. "This your scene, Hernandez?"

"Yes, Sir," came the crisp reply. Emmanuel Hernandez had secured hundreds of crime scenes in his career. He was a solid six feet, with a square chin and alert eyes. Hernandez and Mike knew each other well.

"Give us the quick version. I'm sure you've done some of our legwork for us." Mike made eye contact with Jason, who pulled a spiral notebook from his jacket pocket and prepared to record the relevant information.

"We got the call at ten o'clock this morning from a building security officer named Jimenez. One of the residents called down, concerned about the tenant. Kayleigh Bronson was not responding to knocks on the door or to text messages. The building security team agreed to conduct a wellness check and entered the apartment using the security override code on the door lock."

"Electronic passcode locks, right?" Jason interjected. "I remember from the last time."

"Affirmative," Hernandez said. "Jimenez found Ms. Bronson unresponsive on the bed. He called 9-1-1. He reported no obvious injuries or signs of violence on her body, which I can confirm based on my observations. The assistant ME left a few minutes ago." "Jimenez told me this apartment frequently hosts parties and that there was one last night with more than twenty external guests."

"External means other than other building residents?" Mike interrupted.

"Correct. Miss Byrd said there were several other residents at the party."

"Byrd is the one who called security?" Jason asked.

"Correct." Hernandez remained at attention, reciting the case facts without referring to any notes. "Miss Bronson is a known drug user and there is drug paraphernalia and what looks like residue of drug use in the apartment. It looked like a possible overdose situation. No indication of unlawful entry or violence, which is why we didn't immediately flag it as a possible homicide."

"What changed?" Mike asked, although he suspected the answer.

"Nothing, except that Ms. Byrd snapped a photo of the dead girl and posted it on Instagram. Then the internet had an aneurism. We were ready to release the body but we got a call from Captain Sullivan to secure the scene and wait for you detectives. The forensics unit is on its way. We left the body in the bedroom for you." Hernandez gestured toward the apartment's interior.

"Do we have a guest list of party-goers?" Jason asked.

"One of my officers is downstairs with the building security guys putting it together, but they're not sure if everyone who attended was identified and recorded. As long as they were confirmed by the resident when they arrived, they got admitted."

"We'll need to review the security camera video," Mike said as a mental note for himself and Jason. "Anything else?"

"We secured an iPhone, which was on the floor next to the body. It's locked and now on the kitchen counter. We also secured a laptop computer, which is on the desk in the master bedroom. It's also locked with a passcode, but the tech guys will probably be able to crack it."

"I guess we'll get a report on that along with the forensics." Jason made a note on his pad.

"One other thing that might be important." Hernandez, for the first time, consulted his pocket notebook. "Ms. Bronson is not the owner of the unit, according to Jimenez. She's a subtenant. The apartment is owned by somebody named Logan Summers."

Mike looked at Jason. "Ring a bell for you?" Jason shook his head. "Me, neither. Good work, Hernandez, as always. We appreciate you saving us time, even if it turns out to be a routine overdose. Thanks. We'll take a look around."

Mike and Jason pulled on their blue latex gloves and crime scene booties and walked carefully into the living room. After slowly surveying the scene, they ventured into the primary bedroom and met the corpse. She lay on the soft mattress, clothed in satin sheets the color of ocean foam. One slender arm hung down as if reaching for her dropped phone.

The young woman's chalky face still sported carefully applied makeup. Her blonde hair flowed around her shoulders onto the bedspread. She was wearing jeans and a light blue top with spaghetti straps and a lace bottom, which left her midriff bare. A gemstone in her belly ring sparkled. She was dressed for a party. No red stains on the clothing suggested any wounds beneath. Her face was unscathed.

Jason held the iPhone he had plucked from the kitchen counter. When he pressed the dead girl's index finger against the sensor, the unit sprang to life. "Bingo," he declared when the screen lit up. Its app icons completely covered the underlying photo of its owner wearing a black strapless dress with the logo of the People's Choice Awards in the background.

"You want to spend some time with that before we bag it?" Mike asked.

"Sure." Jason sat on a day bed, the color of which matched the sheets and bedspread. He punched the text message icon and scrolled through the most recent communications.

Mike circled the bed, viewing the corpse from all angles and scanning for anything out of place on the floor or furniture. He wandered into the walk-in closet, surveying the young woman's magnificent clothing and shoes. Nothing seemed disturbed or missing.

When he returned to the main bedroom, Jason held out the phone so Mike could see. The Instagram photo showed Bronson in the same jeans and lacy blue top, her hair flowing down over her shoulders. She was holding a champagne glass, surrounded by five women in similarly festive attire.

"Rachel's been teaching you well," Mike said. "You sure it's from last night?"

"Yes. There's a time-stamp and a caption. It was some kind of anniversary, maybe for her vlog."

"You gonna make me ask?"

Jason took back the phone. "Video blog. She's got a YouTube channel. She's also big on TikTok."

"Great. I can't wait. We'll get a young uniform to view all her online videos and photos and report back to us if there's anything important. You find anything obvious yet?"

Jason replied without looking up from the phone, "Not yet. The texts from last night are all about the party. Who was running late, who wanted to bring a friend, stuff like that. One big group thread for her regular guests. We'll be able to track them down later. I don't see anything like a threat or a cry for help."

The two detectives examined the bathroom. Amid scattered cosmetics and toiletries, a roughly square space had been cleared on the marble countertop. A line of fine white powder residue crossed its center. The medicine cabinet's contents included a dozen pill bottles, along with unmarked phials of powder in several colors.

"I'll have Rodriguez bag those up," Jason said. "We can send them out to the lab for analysis if we need to later."

The woman's drawers were filled with colorful and mostly skimpy clothing and lingerie, coordinated exercise clothes, and all the other accoutrements of an affluent twenty-something. One jewelry case held expensive-looking baubles, while another held only a cannister of loose weed and neatly packed bags of rolled joints. The fridge was filled with yogurt, fruit, water bottles, and wine. The stove showed no signs of use. A guest bed was rumpled, as if somebody had spent some time on top of the bedspread. Otherwise, the apartment showed no signs of being lived in. It was the abode of a typical rich, party-happy young woman who had plenty of friends ready to eat her food, drink her booze, and smoke her weed. Nothing at the scene suggested anything other than an overdose or some other natural explanation for the girl's death.

"Why are we here, again?" Mike headed toward the exit.

"Because the victim has two million Instagram followers."

"Sully said it was a million."

Jason shrugged. "I guess he figured after the first million it doesn't matter. Or maybe he was not fully informed. Either way, she's an influencer. So, people care."

"And that means she was murdered?"

"It means that if there's any chance she was murdered, we need to be on top of it because the department will look bad if we miss it. We're the commissioner's insurance policy. Sully can't give it to Cook and Vega. They'll start to think they get all the celebrity stiffs."

"They can have 'em all as far as I'm concerned." Mike stepped into the wood-paneled elevator car. "I've still got the Ballet Murder on my mind. You think there's any chance one of the drinks at that party upstairs was spiked?"

"Huh?" Jason grunted, while staring at his phone's screen.

"Never mind. We'll need to see if anyone who was at her party last night had a motive to kill her."

Jason looked up. "I haven't read all her messages, but it looks like there are a few hundred possible suspects, according to her online followers."

"What does that mean?"

"Remember the riot at Washington Square Park a few weeks ago? A few thousand people arrived expecting to get free PlayStation 5s and computers and then were all pissed off when they didn't get any free stuff? They tore up the park and turned over cars and we had to call in the riot squad?"

"That was her?"

"No. It was a friend of hers, but she's big in the gaming community. She re-Tweeted her friend's post about the game system giveaway. So she had to apologize afterward. Some of her Twitch followers now think the other guy is out to kill her for not supporting him. Other people think Sony wants her dead because of all the bad publicity. Some others say the police want to kill her because of some comments she made after the riot, about how badly we treated the kids. You get the idea."

"What the hell is Twitch? Is that a dance they do on TikTok?"

Jason turned away to avoid Mike seeing him laughing. "Oh, Mike, you are so old."

"I know. You don't have to remind me. So, the point is that the internet crazies are out on this one. Great."

"Let's go talk to Stafford and see if he can give us any insight into Miss Influencer."

* * *

MIKE AND JASON APPROACHED the building's front desk. It was the size of a Texas saloon's bar, but without the stools. Two desk attendants in dark blue uniforms with gold trim handled the intake of guests, package deliveries, and miscellaneous tenant needs. Two other doormen staffed the doors, fetched taxies, greeted those entering and exiting, and shooed away any vagrants. At the moment, the doormen were fully engaged keeping a group of people all holding cameras away from the doors. Without specifically recognizing any of the photographers, the detectives immediately knew a media horde when they saw one.

"Great," Mike lamented. "Just what we need, a gang of freelance photographers trying to get a scoop at our crime scene."

"Maybe that's why Sully wanted us on this one," Jason said. "He knows how good you are with the media." Mike scowled and marched toward the desk.

Jason asked for Charles Stafford, the building manager. Stafford was visibly unhappy upon seeing Mike and Jason. He had spent hours with the detectives after the Jimmy Rydell murder. Management hated the negative publicity created by a police investigation.

"Detectives Stoneman and Dickson. I can't say I'm happy to see you, but I assume this is about Kayleigh. It's a tragedy, of course, but a drug overdose shouldn't create much of an investigation, I trust?"

"We hope not," Mike said, shaking the man's hand. "We'd be happy if there's nothing here but an unfortunate accident. You were on a first-name basis with her?"

Stafford shrugged. "Everybody was. That was her online persona. Most of the staff didn't even know her last name. She was just Kayleigh."

"We heard she was a subtenant; the lease holder is Logan Summers. It's probably not significant, but can you confirm the information?"

"That's private," Stafford said. "I really can't say."

Mike put a hand on Stafford's arm. "OK. You said it and I believe you meant it. But let's get real. I don't want to come in with a subpoena for all your tenant records and I don't want to give this guy, Summers, a hard time. Level with us and we can get out of your hair as quickly as possible. Whaddaya say?"

"Fine. Don't tell anyone I did this without a subpoena. Mr. Summers is a close friend of Woody O'Meara, who owns the building, as you know. I'm not entirely sure of the circumstances, but Mr. O'Meara agreed to allow him to purchase the apartment as an investment. He had another subtenant who moved out last September. Since then, Kayleigh has been his subtenant. We've been fairly happy having her here, except for the parties."

"Does she pay her own rent?" Jason asked.

"I don't know. Mr. Summers takes care of payments. He owns the place and pays the monthly maintenance bills. He also pays for the housekeeping. I have no knowledge of the arrangement between him and Kayleigh."

"Tell us about the parties," Mike said.

"They have been an issue. There are people coming and going at all hours of the night and day. Some of her guests are celebrities, whom the other residents like to see around the building. People they recognize. Others have been disruptive and we have had to ask her not to invite them back."

"OK." Mike turned toward the front door, confirming that no press photographers were inside the lobby. "Do you have a list of who was present last night at her party?"

"We have some names on the desk register, but I can't say for sure if those were everyone who attended."

"Right," Jason said. "We understand. There may have been building residents there, who would not have had to sign in."

"That's right, but . . ." Stafford lowered his chin and massaged his forehead with one hand. "It's possible there were others there, also."

"Like who?" Mike asked.

"I can't say for sure. But, for example, Mr. Summers often visits her parties. And he sometimes visits at other times. He would not need to sign in."

"We can verify him from the lobby security video, though, right?"

Stafford fidgeted with a plastic card in his hand, the size and shape of a standard hotel key. "Detective, you may recall from your last investigation that we have a street-level breezeway under the building where delivery vehicles enter and exit. It can also be used as an entry for tenants and guests who have permission."

"There's a security camera down there, though," Jason cut in. "We would be able to see guests entering and leaving."

"Not necessarily," Stafford replied. "The camera is focused on vehicles, and pedestrians are often accompanied by building security so that their identities are not obvious on the video."

Mike held eye contact with the building manager, whose expression was sending a clear message. "I get it. The celebrities, mistresses, and tenants tip the security guys to help them get in and out without having their faces on camera. Am I right?"

"I can't say I'm specifically aware of such a practice, Detective. But you may be right."

"Fine. We'll need to talk to the guards who were working last night and see if they remember any names or faces. The rest of the guests should be on the front door video. We'll get an officer to come look at the video in your security room."

"Like old times," Stafford said ironically.

Looking at Jason, Mike said, "I'm guessing we'll also need somebody to sift through the girl's social media accounts looking for photos or videos, right?"

"We'll need somebody young," Jason suggested. "You never know. There might be something there. That's what she did, took photos and posted them online. And videos. So much TikTok video."

"Joy," Mike muttered. "Do we know who the last people were to leave the party? The ones who would have been the last to see her alive — assuming she was still alive?"

The building manager shrugged. "We have no way of knowing. We don't sign people out with specific times, and any building residents would not have been recorded as leaving. We have cameras in the elevators and lobby, but not in the residential hallways, so we can't specifically track everyone's possible movements."

"Great," Mike sighed. "OK. We'll start reviewing the video as soon as we can get somebody on that. We need to know who was there last night, and who was the last to leave. Maybe the friend who lives in the building will be helpful. I'm not making any assumptions about whether this was an accident or a homicide, but until proven otherwise, we'll treat it as a possible crime and cover all the bases. We appreciate your cooperation, Mr. Stafford."

When Mike turned toward the exit door, he saw the forensics unit arriving. He had the building manager clear them inside, then spent a minute talking with the unit chief about the iPhone waiting for her upstairs. Then he said to Stafford, "With all the press out front, maybe it's best if we exit through the breezeway and avoid causing more of a stir than necessary."

Chapter 10
Too Much Information

BACK AT THE PRECINCT, the evidence box from the Ballet Murder had been moved to Mike's desk. He considered those files to be infinitely more interesting than tracking down leads on the likely drug overdose case that he and Jason instantly dubbed "The Influencer." They made a report to Sully and requested that he assign three uniformed officers. One would review security video at the Park Towers and work with the building staff to identify the people who attended Kayleigh's party. One would track down all the publicly available social media records of the dead girl's activities leading up to her death. The last would get the iPhone from the forensics unit and sift through all the content there for anything that might suggest foul play.

"You think homicide?" Sully seemed disappointed. "I was hoping not to waste a bunch of resources on this. Can't we call it a likely drug overdose and leave it until the tox report comes back?"

"Sure, Cap," Mike quickly replied. "I'll be happy to make a note that, at your instruction, we're standing down until we have some indication from the ME that it should be treated as a homicide. I'm sure any witnesses who would be available in the next few days will still remember everything later. Jason and I can get back to prepping for the Ballet Murder trial. Is that what you want us to do?"

"On my instruction? You're a prick, Stoneman. I've already had two calls today from the mayor's communications office, asking for updates. The internet is apparently losing its mind over this girl, like she's the queen of England or something."

"The death of the queen would certainly merit the expenditure of some resources," Jason mused in an exaggerated deadpan.

Mike nodded seriously at his partner, then made eye contact with Sully. "Jason and I certainly can't handle all the leg work on our own. We'd be slowed way down. But if the case isn't a priority, I guess that would be fine."

"Oh, for the love of Aunt Millie," Sully spat out. "Fine. I'll assign you the resources. But don't squander them. Keep 'em busy. And keep a lid on it. I'm sure the vulture reporters will be snooping around soon enough."

"We'll need young officers for this, Sully," Mike said. "It's a lot of social media stuff, TikTok and Switch and such."

"Twitch," Jason quietly corrected.

"Like Sully knows the difference," Mike hissed back.

"Fine!" Sully barked. "I don't give a shit. The younger officers are better for me anyway. I'll give you three, but the moment you don't need them, you give 'em back. You get me?"

"Got it, Cap," Mike said.

He and Jason left the captain's office and moved the evidence box to the bullpen conference room. They attempted to get back to reviewing the Ballet Murder files, but before they could finish extracting the papers from the box, a young female officer knocked on the door jamb. Mike thought the Black officer with the tight braids didn't look old enough to qualify for police duty. She had pointy shoulders and thin legs. The brass name plate on her uniform shirt pocket read "S. Martin."

"Um, Detective Stoneman?" she hesitantly inquired. "Captain Sullivan said I should report here for an assignment."

Mike was used to the phenomenon. He made young officers nervous. Male or female, they all knew that Stoneman was the senior homicide detective. Most new officers had taken his classes on crime scene protocol and evidence handling while in the academy. They knew his reputation, even if they had not followed the news reports of his investigations over twenty-one years as a detective. If they were even born twenty-one years ago. The academy cadets called him *Culo de Piedra*, which translates to *Ass of Stone* or simply *Stone Ass.* He liked being thought of as intimidating. It got the officers to move a little quicker for him.

"Come in, Officer Martin," Mike said, gesturing toward a chair. "What's your first name?"

"Um, it's Sue, Sir." The young woman took two steps into the room, but remained standing.

Mike turned to Jason and made eye contact. Jason said, "How are your social media skills?"

"Y-you mean doing research on social media?" she stammered.

"Exactly. Ever heard of Kayleigh Bronson?"

"Kayleigh? Oh, sure. She's huge. I mean, most of my friends aren't that into her, but of course I know who she is. Doesn't everyone?"

"Not everyone," Mike said sternly.

"N-no. Of course not," Martin snapped to attention, as if she had offended Mike.

Jason told her to relax, then explained the assignment to research the dead girl's social media accounts and report back on anything that might be connected to the party the prior night and her death. Martin gasped upon hearing that Kayleigh was dead, but then absorbed the information and scampered away, seemingly relieved to be beyond the scrutinizing eyes of *Culo de Piedra*.

In the next thirty minutes, Mike and Jason gave assignments to two more young officers, who bounded away to their tasks. They were then free to ponder their next activity. They re-organized the evidence documents from the Ballet Murder and reviewed the case.

"The PI said he wanted us to look at the understudy. That would be Brock Taylor."

"What? He killed the lead actor so he could get the part? Seems like a pretty thin motive," Mike said.

"It's at least plausible."

"Yeah, sure," Mike said, "but here's our problem." He held up a stapled group of pages. "We interviewed Taylor. On the night of the ballet gala, he said he was performing in New Brunswick, New Jersey. We never verified the alibi, but it seems pretty solid. If it checks out that he was on stage fifty miles away when somebody dropped a Mickey in the actor's drink, then he's pretty clean."

"True." Jason looked at the ceiling. "I guess he could have hired somebody else to do it, but that's pretty speculative. An amateur like him, or Matthews, doesn't have access to hired assassins. The understudy was one of the witnesses who pointed a finger at the director. If he was the real killer, it would make sense that he would immediately try to focus the investigation on the guy he framed."

"Sure, but he wasn't the only one. Seems like everybody in the show knew about the conflict between Matthews and Bishop."

Before they could get further into the discussion, Officer Martin interrupted them. She stood at the door, carrying a thick folder of documents. "Excuse me, Detectives," she said haltingly. "I have a preliminary report for you on Kayleigh's social media information."

"That was fast," Mike said. "Let's see what you have."

Martin inched forward and, at Jason's invitation, took a seat at the head of the table, with the two detectives on either side. She put the folder on the table. "There's still a ton of information I haven't looked at. I've downloaded all her TikTok videos for the past month, but haven't watched them all yet. I'll come back with more as soon as I can."

"Alright," Mike soothed, trying to get the officer to focus and calm down. "You obviously didn't come back to us with nothing. Tell us what you found."

Martin sat on the edge of her chair, breathed in deeply, then closed her eyes and blew out the air through her mouth, as if in a trance. When she opened her eyes, she looked at Jason. "At twelve twenty-four last night, Kayleigh posted a one-minute video to TikTok and Instagram. She said she had just done a hit of a Montezuma's Delight cocktail, which was recommended by The Pharmacist. She said she was feeling wonderful and was dancing on her sofa. Then she signed off with a peace sign. Here, I'll show you."

Martin pulled out her phone and played the video for Mike and Jason. Kayleigh was smiling with her arms extended over her head, gyrating to a Dua Lipa song. Several party-goers behind her held drinks aloft and hooted their approval.

When the video stopped, Mike said, "Great. That's a place to start. Do you have any ID on the people in the background?"

"No," Martin said meekly, as if she had failed the assignment. "None of them are tagged anywhere and I don't recognize them."

"That's OK," Mike replied. "Do you know who her pharmacist is?"

"Oh, it's not *her* pharmacist, it's *The* Pharmacist," she said. "He has a pretty big YouTube channel. He talks about drugs and combinations of drugs that will produce specific effects. He's like a guru for drug-users. I need to find the show where he recommends this Montezuma cocktail, but it has to be some combination of drugs. You think that's what killed her?"

Mike looked puzzled. "There are people on the internet recommending drug cocktails for other people to take? How is that not criminal?"

Jason ignored Mike's question and took the folder of documents from the table. "Thank you, Officer. Good work. Keep digging. Are there URLs here for us to examine?"

Officer Martin brightened. "Yes. I sent you both an email with the hyperlinks to make it easier for you to look at them."

"Well done. We'll take a look at what you have. You get back to it and I'll text you if we have any follow-up questions."

She quickly pushed back her chair and exited the conference room. Jason flipped open the folder and read the top page. "OK. This is a place to start. Do you want to pivot to The Influencer, or stick with the Ballet Murder?"

"We're not going to get anywhere with the Ballet Murder. Let's see what Officer Martin has here for us."

Mike and Jason dove into the images and comments and were immediately down a rabbit hole of posts from Kayleigh's followers. They included insane speculation, conspiracy theories, wild claims, threats, impassioned pledges to kill themselves, memes, jokes, and an avalanche of sympathy. It was impossible to decipher whether any of the posts and comments on various social media platforms were potentially helpful to the investigation.

"It's like a tip line on steroids," Mike observed.

"And unsolicited," Jason said. "People are spontaneously writing comments on her accounts. It's possible that some of them might contain actual information. But, Jeez."

The most obviously helpful items were the videos and photos from the party and from prior parties. The posts traced the dead woman's life and movements in more detail than Mike could fathom. Her Instagram account showed everywhere she had gone and seemingly every meal she had eaten in her life. There were a dozen images of her wearing the same outfit in which she died, all taken the night before. They showed happy, smiling faces and posed groups of people in her apartment. Mike and Jason instantly recognized the surroundings. They didn't recognize any of the faces, but many were tagged with their names. Jason suggested sending the others out for facial recognition matching. Those people were the last ones to see her alive, so they might have information. But Kayleigh's own TikTok showed the most likely cause of her death. If the toxicology report came back matching whatever this Pharmacist recommended in his Montezuma's Delight, then it would be a pretty clear case of voluntary overdose.

"We need to get these photos over to the officer at the Park Towers. We'll see if the doormen or desk attendants can match the faces to the names they have on the guest list," Mike said.

Jason copied the hyperlinks and sent them to their officer on the scene. "There's too much information here, and too many people who might have more. They're all possible witnesses, but I don't see how this is a murder."

"You're probably right. The most obvious explanation is usually true. But let's see what the tox report tells us. I'm betting that eager-beaver Sue Martin will find the recipe for the Montezuma's Delight on the internet and we'll be able to rule out homicide."

Jason dropped a bunch of print-outs to the table. "We can only hope. We'd better get some lunch. Looks like we'll be here for a while."

* * *

AN HOUR LATER, OFFICER ROBYN KONOPKA, who had been assigned to Kayleigh's phone, arrived with a pile of text messages. Each print-out noted the sender's name, based on Kayleigh's address book or reverse-look-ups of the numbers. There were additional notes describing the known senders and what their connection was to Kayleigh. The detectives were less than a half-day into the investigation and were already referring to their stiff by her first name.

There were two sets of text messages from burner phones. One string was intimate. It included messages arranging for meeting times and locations and asking if Kayleigh was alone. They went back 30 days, which seemed to be the auto-delete setting for the texts.

"It's not unusual for somebody to have a burner phone," Jason observed.

"Yeah, but it raises a question. Somebody who didn't want his name to show up."

"You assume a man?"

Mike smiled. "Sure, based on the language. Women are more polite."

"I agree," Jason said while studying the thread. "All the meet-ups were at the apartment. It's like this guy didn't want to be seen with her out in public. That's a little odd, since she's such an influencer. Being seen with her would be a good thing for most people."

"Not if you're a cheating husband," Mike said. "Or maybe somebody high-profile who doesn't want to be associated with a drug-culture maven."

"You could be right," Jason conceded. "Sex, jealousy, infidelity, and secrecy are all possible ingredients in a murder. But it's a burner phone, so we can't get an ID on this sender."

Jason passed Mike several print-outs of Instagram posts. Most mourned Kayleigh's death without much substance. Those who commented in detail all said they blamed The Pharmacist for recommending a dangerous drug cocktail. They said Kayleigh would never overdose on purpose. It could not have been a suicide.

"That's what they all say," Jason commented.

"Based on her video dancing on the couch, I'd say it's a pretty good bet the girl was not in the process of killing herself," Mike said.

"Probably not, but it still could have been accidental."

"I'm definitely on team accidental overdose." Mike tossed his pen onto the table with a clatter. "We'll all be happier if we can put this one to bed quickly. Let the internet crazies blame this Pharmacist guy. Better that he take the heat than us."

At a quarter to four, Officer Martin returned to the conference room with a fresh stack of print-outs. She had sent a supplemental email filled with more hyperlinks.

Overwhelmed, Jason and Mike tapped two junior detectives from the property crimes division, who were working a swing shift. Both were young and eager to please Stoneman and Dickson. They didn't tell Sully about their appropriation of additional resources.

Between the four detectives and the three officers working the leads, they created a massive list of possible witnesses to interview if the case turned into a homicide investigation. Kayleigh's friend Lori Byrd, who alerted Park Towers security, was at the top of the list.

When six o'clock rolled around, they left the conference room strewn with papers and placed a sign on the door reading, "Investigation in progress."

Chapter 11
Faces in the Crowd

WEDNESDAY MORNING, Mike and Jason arrived at Park Towers, where Charles Stafford led them to the building security room. The officer who had spent most of the prior day reviewing video from the security cameras, Janice Harris, was already there. She gave Mike and Jason a rundown on the prior night's party-goers. She flagged the last four people who appeared on the lobby cameras and who were known to be Kayleigh's guests, between twelve-thirty and one-fifteen a.m. She could not be sure there were no other guests who left later, including building residents, but it made sense to speak to these four. Mike asked Harris to work on identifying and contacting the potential witnesses for interviews.

Stafford then led the detectives to apartment 7-D, the home of Lori Byrd. She had been alerted to the imminent arrival of the police and met them at her open door. Byrd wore a pink track suit with a half-sleeved top, leaving her midriff bare, exposing a belly ring that glinted under the hallway lights. Her blonde hair had dark roots, held back by a thick terrycloth headband matching her exercise gear. Despite appearing to have come directly from the building's gym, she was wearing full makeup, including pale pink lipstick and rose shadow above her brown eyes. She looked like a model for an exercise video.

"Miss Byrd." Mike extended a hand, "I'm Detective Stoneman, NYPD. This is Detective Dickson. Thank you for speaking with us." He gave the woman's semi-limp hand a soft shake. "May we come in?"

"Oh, please," the young woman replied, "don't call me *Miss Byrd* or I'll gag. It's Lori. Just Lori."

Lori stood aside, gesturing the detectives in. The apartment was a quarter the size of Kayleigh's high-floor palace. A single window in the narrow living room looked north over Riverside Park. The furniture was modest and slightly worn. Museum lithographs in mass-market frames adorned the walls, along with pressboard bookcases stuffed with trinkets from travel destinations, photos, and a few actual books. Mike guessed that Lori had lived in this apartment for several years.

Mike found his way to a maroon sofa, where Jason joined him. Stafford asked the young woman if she wanted him to stay, but she dismissed him with a wave and took a seat in an overstuffed lounge chair opposite the two detectives. She crossed her legs, clasped her hands in her lap, and said, "How can I help?"

Jason leaned forward. "First, we want to offer our condolences on the passing of your friend. It must be a shock to lose someone so young."

"It sucks," she said in a throaty but even voice. "But I can't say I'm totally shocked. I mean, she did a *lot* of drugs. And she was always trying crazy new things. But she always just got high and happy. I wish I knew who gave her whatever it was she OD'd on. I'd like to kick their ass. It was probably Brock, although he almost never paid for anything. You should talk to him for sure. And Vickki and Sherwood. He always has sketchy shit. It had to be after she did the Montezuma thing. Kayleigh was so trusting. People were always ready to dance and drink Kayleigh's booze and who cares if somebody fucking dies?"

Mike and Jason were happy to let Lori talk. Getting it all out seemed to be cathartic for her. When she took a breath and looked at Jason, he asked, "What time did you leave the party Monday night?"

She tipped her head back and stared at the ceiling, then pulled out her phone.

"What are you looking for?" Mike asked.

"My last Insta from Monday," she replied without disengaging from her screen. "OK, that was eleven-forty-two, and I left maybe fifteen minutes later, so, a little before midnight, I guess."

"Do you know what drugs Kayleigh took?"

"Not really. That creep, Sherwood, had some shit I didn't touch. And she was planning to do that Montezuma." Then Lori's eyes widened. "Hey, you're not going to hassle anybody about the drugs, are you? I'm not ratting out my friends."

"You're not ratting out anybody. We're homicide detectives. We're investigating whether there's any chance that your friend might have been murdered. We're not concerned with anyone's drug use."

"Murdered? What do you mean? I saw her — I mean in the bedroom, when she was ... dead. She wasn't shot or stabbed or anything."

Jason grimaced involuntarily, wondering how to keep their witness from freaking out. "We are not saying it happened. It's a tragedy no matter what. But it's possible somebody slipped something into her drink or into the drugs she was taking, maybe accidentally. We're not sure. Our job is to check out all the possibilities." When Lori seemed to understand, he continued. "Do you know Sherwood's last name? Or Brock's?"

"No. I mean, not Sherwood. Maybe somebody told me, but I don't know. He's not in my phone." Lori put the device down on the arm of her chair.

"What about Vikki, the woman you mentioned? Was she there with Sherwood?"

Lori's voice took a higher pitch. "Vikki is *they*. Their name is Vikki Crawford. You can find them on Insta, @Vikkistrong."

Jason made eye contact with Mike, partly to make sure he was following the conversation. Mike took the hint. "Miss Byrd, I'm an old fart and don't have an Instagram account. Do you have a phone number for Vikki?"

"Don't call me that. My name is Lori." She grabbed her phone and swiped a few times, then read off the number so Jason could record it in his notebook.

"What about the other guy — person — you mentioned," Mike asked. "Brock. Do you know his last name?"

"Sure. Kayleigh's been with him for a while. It's Brock Taylor. He's an actor."

Mike immediately swiveled his head toward Jason, holding his eye contact with a raised eyebrow. "What do you mean, Kayleigh was *with* Brock Taylor?"

"He's, like, kind of her boyfriend. He comes to her parties and she goes to his shows and hangs out with him. Search for them on Insta and you'll get a million hits. I think it was Brock who got her into that crazy Pharmacist dude."

"Alright. We'll certainly look at him, also." Mike saw Jason writing in his notebook. "Do you know of anyone who might have wanted to harm Kayleigh?"

"Harm? You mean, like, on purpose?" Lori pulled her head back, as if wanting to distance herself from the question. "No. Of course not. Kayleigh was, like, the nicest person. That's why she let me hang out with her. Everybody loved her. She gave away shit and hosted everyone. Ever since she moved in, we've been friends. Nobody would — I mean, who?" Lori closed her eyes and choked back her emotions.

"OK." Mike tried to soothe the woman, who was clearly becoming agitated by the discussion. "We're putting together a list of everyone who was at the party. Would you mind helping us verify the names and match them against pictures?"

"Um, I guess so. I can try. But you'd be better off just looking at Kayleigh's texts. Anyone who was there will be on the group chat."

"Can you share that with us?" Jason asked. He knew they already had access to the texts on Kayleigh's iPhone, but wanted to compare them to another member of the group.

"Sure," Lori's phone was instantly in her hand again. "Can you scan?"

Jason placed his phone next to Lori's, then confirmed that he had received her text message.

Mike leaned back into the sofa, crossing his legs and attempting to appear casual. "We saw a video Kayleigh made around a quarter past midnight, so perhaps shortly after you left. Jason can show it to you in a minute—"

"I saw it, obviously," Lori said, scolding the senior detective without any hint of being intimidated by him.

"Of course," Mike acknowledged. "She mentioned The Pharmacist. You did, too. Can you tell us anything about him?"

"He's insane," Lori immediately replied.

"So, you know him?"

Lori scrunched up her face. "I don't like, *know* him. I mean, I've never partied with him. But Kayleigh follows his vlog. I mean, *followed*. She loved him. She was always trying his crazy cocktails. Her and Brock, and—"

"I'm sorry," Mike interrupted. "Forgive me for being slow and old. How would Kayleigh get connected with this person?"

"Everybody knows him." Lori looked at Mike like he'd asked whether water was wet. "He's like a guru for people's drug menus. He has a YouTube channel with, like, thousands of subscribers. He's always giving advice about what to take with what and how to combine pills with coke or weed and OTC to get a quirky high and shit. We all follow him because he's hilarious. He's like this hippie from olden times, but he's cool, too."

Mike flashed a skeptical glance at Jason. "You ever hear of this guy?"

"No. Youth drug culture is not really my thing. Or Rachel's."

"He sounds like the Rock 'n' Roll doctor."

"Who's that?" It was Jason's turn to cast a puzzled glance.

"Doctor Demento. Travesty, Limited." Mike stared at his partner's blank face, showing not the slightest glimmer of recognition. "Oh, lord. I am that old. Trust me, it was funny. It was a comedy record about a guy who gave drug advice over the telephone during his radio show. You know radio, right? It came before YouTube."

"I've heard that!" Lori shouted. "It's hilarious."

"See," Mike scoffed. "Cultured people understand fine nostalgic comedy."

Jason crossed his arms with disbelief etched on his face. "Are you suggesting this Pharmacist could have encouraged Kayleigh to spike her cocaine with something that killed her?"

"No!" Lori immediately responded. "He would never recommend something dangerous. And Kayleigh would never take something dangerous."

"Maybe not dangerous to most people," Mike said, "but maybe she had a bad reaction. We'll know soon enough when we get the toxicology report. For now, we want to try to rule out somebody doing something intentional. Can you think of anyone at the party last night who could have wanted to harm Kayleigh?"

She paused, then shook her head, causing a drop of sweat to spin off her forehead and splash into the hardwood. "No. Nobody."

In the hallway, after concluding their interview, both detectives agreed that Lori had been forthcoming and honest. She was certainly not a suspect. They had a growing list of additional witnesses to contact, and two persons of interest in Sherwood and Brock Taylor.

"It has to be the same guy, right?" Mike said as they waited for the elevator. "There can't be more than one actor named Brock Taylor."

"Probably," Jason agreed. "We'll track him down easily either way. Actors want to be found online."

As they left the building through the breezeway exit, avoiding the press, Jason said, "This one is starting to remind me of the Ballet Murder."

"Yeah. I was thinking the same thing. The night Alex Bishop went down at the ballet, we all figured it was a heart attack. We didn't think it could have been a homicide until we got the tox report. This one is pretty much the same. If the tox comes back showing an overdose, will there be any reason to put on a full court press?"

"I hope not. Maybe the media hounds will focus their attention on the drug users at the party and The Pharmacist and leave us alone. But I still want to talk to Brock Taylor."

Chapter 12
What's Missing?

AT ONE-THIRTY ON WEDNESDAY, Jason carried a small pizza box from Pietro's on Columbus Avenue into the bullpen conference room. Mike sat on the far side, a translucent blue plastic storage container in front of him resting on a white napkin.

"What did Michelle send you with today?" Jason set his box down opposite Mike's, next to his laptop computer.

"I haven't opened it yet, but I'm pretty sure it's grilled chicken breast and broccoli. Leftovers from last night."

"It's great that she has you eating a healthier diet." Jason lifted his lid, exposing a golden brown calzone half the size of a football. After he sawed in with a plastic knife it bled marinara sauce from its open wound. A moment later, ricotta and mozzarella dripped from Jason's plastic fork.

Mike watched the gooey mass disappear into Jason's satisfied mouth. "Do you have to eat that in front of me?"

"It's good for you," Jason mumbled between chews. "Think of it as a willpower exercise."

A few minutes later, Mike speared a square of his chicken and held it aloft, his elbow resting on the table. "I am resigned to the reality of my cholesterol levels. Enjoy that calzone while you can, my friend. One day it will catch up with you, too."

Mike cleared his lunch remnants and wiped his mouth before tossing a spent napkin into the corner trash can.

Jason carried his empty pizza box to the trash and poured himself a coffee. "You think the tox report will give us something other than a straight drug overdose?"

Before Mike could answer, his phone rang. "Stoneman . . . Hey, Keith . . . Yeah, we know. Good luck. When do you think you'll need us? . . . Sure. We'll be ready . . . Yeah. I'll tell him. Thanks."

"When does he want us?" Jason immediately asked.

"Friday morning."

"Friday?" Jason raised an eyebrow. "Did he say who would go first?"

"He wants you to do the heavy lifting, so you'll go first. I'll clean up the mess if you leave one." Mike kept his poker face in place.

"Great. I'll probably need it." Jason looked down at some of the notes from the Ballet Murder case file, but couldn't focus. "Mike, when I was downstairs yesterday talking to Sophie, she gave me her usual paranoid schtick about not trusting the computers. But she said something that's sticking in my head. She said, sometimes, the most important evidence is what's *not* there."

"What did the old girl mean by that?"

Jason slowly shook his head. "I'm not sure. I think she was talking about her evidence records; if somebody tried to alter the information in the computer, she still would have a record in her book. But she's got me thinking about the laptop records from the director."

"Yeah, I know. Like the PI said, it was all too easy. He made the exact searches he needed, found that digoxin would have a potentially fatal interaction, and that was it. So, what do you think is missing?"

"I don't know." Jason paced around the cramped space, finally settling into his chair. "Maybe nothing."

For the next hour, Mike and Jason poured over the physical files, prepping for their upcoming testimony. They were also waiting for a call from the officers working on The Influencer case, letting them know they had secured an interview for them with one of the potential witnesses. Before they got a call, Officer Robyn Konopka returned to their conference room door.

Mike asked, "What can you tell us about this character, The Pharmacist?"

"Oh, he's all over her phone," Konopka quickly responded. "She has seven of the guy's YouTube videos downloaded. I sent you the hyperlinks in an email, along with the labels she put on them. There are also two text message threads talking about drug combinations and there are references that are, I think, to some of his videos. I can't be sure who sent those texts. There are a few other text threads with burner phones, so I couldn't identify all her contacts."

"Does that seem unusual to you?" Mike asked. "That she had so many text threads with burner phones? Is that normal for someone like her?"

"I can't say, Sir. She's a major-league influencer and has hundreds of contacts. It seems like most of them text her, so I suppose there are bound to be some burner phones involved. Lots of high-profile people don't like to be identified in texts, just in case something leaks to TMZ or whatever. It didn't feel suspicious to me."

"Good work, Konopka." Mike beamed at the officer as if she had correctly answered a difficult question in one of his classes. "I marvel at how you young people use those phones. We're fortunate to have your expertise on this. Keep at it and let us know immediately if you find anything specific about what drugs she might have been taking, especially if you notice something called Montezuma's Revenge."

"Montezuma's Delight," Jason corrected.

"Oh, yeah. Delight. I guess that's a better marketing name for it."

Officer Konopka hustled away. Mike and Jason both pulled out their phones and opened the email she had sent a few minutes before arriving for her report. They clicked away at the links. Jason popped in a Bluetooth earbud so he could listen to a YouTube video. Mike scrolled through copies of text message threads. After twenty minutes of relative silence, Jason got Mike's attention.

"This Pharmacist is a piece of work. He interacts with his YouTube watchers in real time and talks about what drugs they're taking. He gives them advice, makes jokes, and tells stories about being at this party or that party with celebrities he says he can't name. It's like he's a one-man infomercial for dope."

"Like I said, he's the Rock 'n' Roll Doctor."

"You need to give that up, Mike. Nobody but you knows what it means."

Mike chuckled. "The dead girl's friend knew about it, and she's younger than you. So I think it's just you who's woefully ignorant of classic comedy."

"How about we ask Rachel and see what she says?"

"Only if we also ask Michelle," Mike parried.

"We need a tiebreaker." Jason poked his head out of the conference room door and scanned the bullpen. "Hey, Mariana!"

"No!" Mike feigned indignity. "That's not a fair choice."

"Why, Mike? Because she's Latina?"

"Of course not!" Mike protested, as detective Mariana Vega appeared in the doorway.

"What's up, gentlemen?" Mariana asked. A light-skinned Dominican with slender legs and mysterious dark eyes, she looked like anything but a cop. After nine years on the force and four working homicide, the veteran beat cops had learned not to underestimate her small package. She took no shit and gave out plenty.

Jason held out an arm toward Mike, as if introducing him at an awards show. Mike took the imaginary microphone and turned to their colleague. "Mariana, sorry to bother you. Jason is sometimes ignorant of classic comedy and has never heard the famous bit by Travesty, Limited, The Rock 'n' Roll Doctor. Do you know it?"

Mariana immediately broke into a grin and laughed. "My dad loved that old stuff. I heard it a hundred times. Pretty funny, until you start pulling sheets off the heads of dead junkies, huh?" She looked at Jason and winked. Jason scowled and waved Mariana away. She laughed louder as she walked back to her desk while mimicking the comedy bit. "Hello? Hello-lo-lo?"

"I rest my case." Mike clasped his hands on the table.

Jason pursed his lips. "Whatever. What I was trying to tell you before is that this Pharmacist joker likes to cook up exotic cocktails of different drugs and other shit and recommends them to his followers."

"What kind of other shit?"

"You name it. Usually it's cocaine mixed with herbs, homeopathic powders, mushrooms, over-the-counter medicine, or different kinds of booze. He claims his mixtures give people a special kind of high. Some of it starts with other bases like edible cannabis. I've only listened to parts of three episodes. The guy's a lunatic."

"Great. It all comes down to the tox report, just like we figured. If the lab tells us the girl had some ridiculous combination of shit in her system, maybe we can reverse-engineer it back to something this clown recommended. Is there an index to his drug menu somewhere?"

"Maybe. He seems pretty popular. Maybe some of his fans keep track online somewhere. We'll find it. If it matters."

Chapter 13
It Was a Party

THURSDAY MORNING, Jason and Mike compared notes about information they had gathered off the clock about The Pharmacist and Kayleigh. Rachel had schooled Jason about her research on Kayleigh's social media reach and how The Pharmacist developed a following within internet drug culture. They doubted The Pharmacist was directly involved in Kayleigh's death. Until they knew the precise drugs in the girl's system when she died, their interest was purely conjectural. Meanwhile, the list of potential witnesses continued to expand like a water balloon in a carnival midway game as the video review team matched names and faces from the Monday night party.

Mike and Jason briefly turned their attention to Logan Summers, who owned the lavish apartment in which Kayleigh died. The Wall Street tycoon had a particularly high profile. Born into a wealthy family whose fortune was made in the shipping industry, Summers attended private school in New York City. Then he went off to Yale, followed by an MBA from the Wharton school. From there came an internship at Goldman Sacks and five years at Northrup Investments, an exclusive financial management company. At age thirty, trading on his family name and fortune, he opened his own hedge fund and quickly attracted investors. Since then, Summers had been riding high.

He was on his second wife, but the marriage was on the rocks, judging by the fact that she was seeking a divorce.

Summers had a short police record consisting of two drug-related arrests, neither of which resulted in a felony conviction or guilty plea. Both charges were reduced to misdemeanors and then dismissed.

"Rich white men don't do time for possession of cocaine," Jason grumbled. "Must be nice to have that kind of money and connections."

"It's a familiar story, partner, but let's focus on this case. If there is a case."

In Mike's mind, they were not yet conducting a murder investigation. They had no evidence that the apparent overdose involved any criminal activity other than illegal drug use. It wasn't likely they could charge The Pharmacist with manslaughter even if he did recommend a drug mixture that killed the girl. Still, they were planning for the possibility of interrogating anyone who might have been responsible for giving Kayleigh the Montezuma's Delight.

"You think the old guy, Summers, was banging Kayleigh in that high-priced love nest?" Jason asked.

"Seems likely. Why else would he be hanging around her parties? But so what? If he was sleeping with her, why would he kill her?"

Jason scratched under his left ear. "Maybe he stashed her in the apartment before his wife found out and filed for divorce. Maybe he needed her to disappear."

"Possible," Mike agreed, "but why do it in your apartment? If you were going to knock her off, wouldn't you do it somewhere else?"

"Not if you were going to make it look like an overdose."

Before they could continue the conversation, Mike's mobile phone rang. It was Michelle. Mike put her on speaker so Jason could hear.

"The cause of death is still cardiac arrest, induced by a drug overdose. The tox report shows cocaine at significant levels in her blood. She also had a high blood alcohol level of 0.14. There were two unusual substances in the report: fentanyl and carbamazepine, which is an anti-seizure medication. Both are odd, but the fentanyl is the key. That's the likely killer.

"The results on the samples taken from the apartment showed only cocaine, except for the residue collected from the countertop in the bathroom. That one had fentanyl too, along with carbamazepine. It's not unprecedented for drug users to mix cocaine and fentanyl. I can't say for sure the exact concentration of the fentanyl in the mixture from the powder residue, but the level in her blood was pretty high. Lots of fentanyl on the street has a high potency that the users often don't realize.

"I can't say whether the carbamazepine contributed to the fatal response, but the fentanyl by itself was enough to kill her. Opiates like fentanyl can have a bad interaction with anti-seizure medications, not to mention alcohol. It's not possible for me to say whether she took that combination knowingly or if somebody spiked her cocaine without her knowledge. All we can say for certain is that the fentanyl was likely what killed her and it was only present in the bathroom sample."

"Thanks, Michelle. At least we have more information now." Mike looked at Jason to make sure he had no questions, then ended the call.

"We've got Konopka researching The Pharmacist's YouTube videos," Jason said. He then sent her a text message relaying the information about the drugs found at the scene. He asked her to flag any videos in which the internet drug guru recommended mixing cocaine with carbamazepine or any other anti-seizure meds. He also wanted her to flag any mention of fentanyl, but he and Mike doubted that The Pharmacist would ever suggest his viewers use such a highly dangerous substance.

The information from the tox screen made murder more likely, but not a certainty. Few recreational drug users would knowingly take fentanyl, but it wasn't out of the question for the adventurous Kayleigh. If somebody wanted to kill her, sneaking some into a combo cocktail she was already planning to ingest would be a good method.

"Right now, we've got nobody in particular to focus on."

"What about our actor, Brock Taylor?" Jason asked. "We have some reason to suspect that he knows how to kill someone by using a drug interaction."

"It's quite a coincidence to have one person so close to two cases involving drug-induced heart attacks. But what's his motive?"

"I don't know. But I think we now have an investigation. Accidental overdose is still on the track, but it's not in the lead anymore."

Ten minutes later, Mike got a text from Janice Harris. She had lined up three witnesses who were available for interviews. "Let's go," Mike said, "we can get a slice at Ray's on the way."

* * *

MIKE AND JASON SPENT the afternoon crisscrossing Manhattan, interviewing people who attended the party at the dead girl's apartment. Two of them, Rich and Connie Kronish, lived in a building on 79th and Riverside Drive, near the Park Towers. They were a power couple in their mid-twenties. He was a lawyer working for an investment bank and she was a rising star at a midtown advertising firm. They were packing for a vacation to Aruba. Mike and Jason were lucky to catch them before they left town.

Both Connie and Rich were frequent guests of their favorite Instagram influencer. Connie met Kayleigh through one of her clients, who used Kayleigh for directed TikTok advertising and Instagram promos. Since they lived close by, Kayleigh invited them to parties frequently. They danced, took selfies, drank top-shelf liquor, and did a large amount of mind-altering substances Connie said were definitely not illegal. Connie volunteered to send Jason some photos.

"What do you know about Kayleigh's drug use at these parties?" Mike asked.

"There was pot, which is totally legal," Rich quickly admitted. "I'm sure some guests had pills and other things. Maybe mushrooms. I'm not saying that I ever saw anyone snort cocaine or use a needle for anything, but it wouldn't have shocked me."

"Did you ever witness Kayleigh getting into any kind of argument with any of her guests?" Mike asked.

"No. Never. Kayleigh was always cool at her parties. Everyone loved being there. Why wouldn't we?"

"Is there anyone you can think of who might have had a reason to harm Kayleigh?" Mike leaned forward and made eye contact with Connie.

She squirmed for a moment, turning her head toward her lawyer husband. Rich answered for them both. "No. Nobody."

They both knew about The Pharmacist, but had never met him or knew anyone who had. They said they had never ingested any of the pharmaceutical cocktails he recommended, but admitted Kayleigh and some other party guests probably had. They both said they — and Kayleigh — would certainly never take any fentanyl.

"That shit is dangerous," Connie said. "Kayleigh would know better."

They both knew who Brock Taylor was and admitted seeing him at some of Kayleigh's parties. They had no personal information about his relationship with Kayleigh, but acknowledged that they danced together and sometimes kissed.

On a whim, Jason asked Rich if he knew who Logan Summers was. He did, since Summers was a significant player in the financial community. When asked if he knew that Summers owned the apartment where Kayleigh lived, Rich seemed genuinely shocked.

"I guess that explains why he sometimes hung out with her," Connie said. She acknowledged seeing Summers at a few parties. Somebody had pointed him out as a very rich man. Neither Rich nor Connie could say for sure whether Summers was in attendance three nights earlier. Mike impressed on the couple the need to keep the details of the interview confidential. They both were the types not to want their names associated with the drug-culture parties at Kayleigh's apartment.

* * *

AFTER GRABBING A SLICE at The Real Original Ray's pizza, their next stop was another young woman who became familiar with Kayleigh via Instagram and got to know her by attending her parties. Jason remarked on how few of their witnesses seemed to have day jobs, but it made interviews easier.

Tina Anderson told a similar story. Her friends, a couple named Jake and Earnest, invited Tina to a party. Since she and Kayleigh started to follow each other online, she got on the invitation list. Tina was forthright enough to acknowledge that other party-goers used various drugs, but none whom she would identify. It was certainly not her, or Jake or Earnest. They drank plenty, but avoided the abundantly available drugs. Tina had no insight into who might have wanted to harm Kayleigh, or where she got her drugs. Mike and Jason were careful not to say that Kayleigh was murdered, or mention the specific drugs in her system. They expected that anything they said would end up on Tina's social media feed within moments of their departure, despite impressing upon her the need for confidentiality.

Like Rich and Connie, Tina knew about The Pharmacist. She knew that other people mixed drug cocktails as he instructed, then made videos of the resulting reactions. She also thought Kayleigh had posted such videos in the past. It was a revelation to Mike and Jason. It was a world to which they were oblivious. But they worked homicide, not narco. Tina promised to send Jason links to as many videos as she could find, even if they did not involve Kayleigh or any other guests.

Tina said Brock Taylor had been around a lot in the past several months, but claimed not to know what his relationship was to Kayleigh. She said she didn't know who Logan

Summers was, but when Jason showed her a photo, she admitted seeing him at a few parties with Kayleigh. "But he was the old guy in the room. Why would I talk to him?" Tina did not recall seeing Logan at the party on Monday night.

Tina also disclosed that Jake and Earnest were away on a cruise. They did video reviews of cruise ships, which they posted on YouTube and other social media. To Mike's amazement, they did this professionally. In any case, they would not be available for an interview until they returned the following Tuesday.

Next, Mike and Jason met with a very reluctant man named Sherwood. Lori Byrd had fingered Sherwood as somebody who supplied drugs. He was a friend of Vikki Osterman, who was out of the country and not available for an interview. Sherwood had a job at a marketing firm on Sixth Avenue and agreed to meet the detectives in the building lobby. He proved to be the least cooperative of all the witnesses, immediately demanding a lawyer and refusing to answer any questions other than confirming his name and that he knew someone named Vikki. Mike and Jason figured he was terrified about being busted for drug distribution. They were not able to convince him to talk.

By the end of these interviews, Mike and Jason had formed the definite impression that none of the witnesses had a close personal relationship with Kayleigh. In fact, none knew much about her aside from following her social media and attending her parties. Only Lori Byrd seemed to have much insight into Kayleigh's life.

By late afternoon, they decided to circle back to Lori. But first, they wanted to make a surprise visit to Brock Taylor.

Chapter 14
In the Spotlight

BROCK TAYLOR HAD NOT ANSWERED his cell phone when Officer Harris attempted to arrange an interview, but the actor was not difficult to locate. He wanted the entire English-speaking world to know exactly where and when he would be performing. Announcements were on his website, Instagram, Twitter, and Facebook pages. On this Thursday, Taylor would be on stage with three other singers at a club in the Hell's Kitchen neighborhood on Manhattan's West Side. There were two shows, at seven and ten-thirty p.m.

As soon as Jason got the information, he called Rachel. She reached out to one of her Broadway friends to ask when they would arrive at the venue for the first show. Rachel reported back that a performer would likely arrive by five o'clock in order to score a free dinner and eat far enough before the show to prepare.

Mike and Jason arrived at the Edge of Your Seat club at a quarter past five. The woman at the check-in podium, wearing a black body suit that emphasized all her curves, told them seating did not begin until five-thirty. When Mike flashed his badge and asked to speak to the house manager, she directed them to a harried woman named Sheila Montgomery who was holding a meeting with the wait staff inside. The detectives stood in the back of the cramped showroom until Montgomery sent the staff off to their pre-show preparations. The dimly lit room's center was filled with square tables crammed impossibly close together. The perimeter was lined with semi-circular booths. Electric candles on each table barely added to the ambient illumination.

Mike advanced toward the manager as soon as she ended the staff meeting. "Ms. Montgomery, I'm Mike Stoneman, NYPD." He flashed his badge and ID wallet. "We understand Brock Taylor is one of your performers tonight. We need to ask him a few questions. Is he here?"

"Oh, shit," Montgomery pressed her lips together. "Are you gonna take him in? I have two shows tonight."

"We're not here to arrest him. He's a potential witness in a case we're working on. We need to talk to him for a few minutes. Where can we find him?"

"He's probably in the kitchen. The talent eats in the back before the show." She gestured to a swinging double-door in the corner to the left of the stage. "Please don't keep him too long."

Mike led the way through the doors into the kitchen, which was bustling with activity. A tall man wearing a white chef's hat directed them toward two long picnic-style tables with benches. At one table, several waiters wearing black slacks, white shirts, and aprons ate and chatted over the din from the kitchen. At the other, two men and two women were also enjoying a meal. One woman wore a floral robe that might have been silk. Her companions sported jeans and t-shirts. They did not notice the approaching detectives.

"Brock Taylor?" Mike raised his voice to cut through the chatter. He recognized Taylor from the head shot, posted on his website. He would have been able to pick him out of this lineup easily, since the only other man at the table was a thick Black man with dreadlocks.

"Yeah?" Taylor turned his head, but did not stop chewing his ravioli.

"I'm Detective Mike Stoneman, NYPD. We need to talk with you for a moment. Can you step into the ballroom with us?"

Taylor hesitated. "What's this about?"

"I'd rather keep it confidential," Mike replied.

"Should I be asking for a lawyer?"

Jason jumped in. "We think you may be a witness, Mr. Taylor. You're not a suspect. If you would like to have a lawyer present, we can take you in to the station, but then you'll have to miss your performance."

Taylor scowled, took another forkful of ravioli, then got up. Still chewing, he picked up his plate and a fork, then pushed past the detectives. Inside the showroom, he sat at a table near the door and continued eating his pre-show meal. With a mouth full of pasta, he looked at Mike, who had caught up. "So, wha' can I help you wif?"

"I assume you heard about the death of Kayleigh Bronson?" Mike stood over Taylor rather than sitting at his table.

"Yeah." Taylor swallowed and dabbed his mouth with a napkin. "That's really a shock. She was a good kid. I heard it was an overdose."

"Where did you hear that?"

Taylor returned his attention to his food, spearing another ravioli. "It was all over Instagram."

"Don't believe everything you see on the internet," Mike said. "We understand you were at the party at Kayleigh's apartment Monday night. Is that true?"

"Sure." Taylor popped the morsel into his mouth. After a few chews, he added, "It was a good party, but I had to leave before it ended. I had a call the next morning."

"So, you weren't there when Kayleigh recorded her TikTok video about having done the Montezuma's Delight?" Mike glanced at Jason, giving him a subtle signal to jump into the questioning.

"No. I wasn't there. I saw it the next day, of course. It was fucking everywhere."

"Did you provide the drugs suggested by The Pharmacist?"

Taylor stopped chewing, then swallowed before responding. "No, man. I didn't."

"Who did?" Jason pressed.

"I wouldn't know, would I?"

"You might."

Taylor looked away from the detectives, back at his pasta. "I have an idea, but I don't really know."

"We're open to all ideas," Mike prompted.

Taylor looked up, locking eye contact with Mike. "You should talk to her sugar daddy, Logan. He's a complete junkie. Kayleigh told me he was getting her something special. He might know. I don't know."

"You have done drugs with Kayleigh, right?"

"I can't say." Taylor continued to hold Mike's gaze.

"You mean you won't say?"

"If you say so." Taylor looked down at his plate. Only one ravioli remained. He impaled it and held his fork in the air halfway to his mouth. "I'm not going to admit to any illegal drug use, so if that's what you want, you'll be disappointed."

"We don't give a damn about anybody's drug use. We want to know who might have had a motive to murder Kayleigh."

Mike and Jason watched carefully for Taylor's reaction to the question. He had none. He finished chewing and looked at them as if answering a question on a satisfaction survey about the quality of his food. "I can't help you there, gentlemen. As far as I know, everyone loved Kayleigh. She was cool, and a lot of fun. I'm going to miss her."

"It's a funny coincidence," Jason moved to a position directly across the tiny table, "how you just happened to be in such close proximity to two people who died from drug-induced heart attacks."

"I guess so," Taylor calmly responded.

Mike looked away from Taylor and spoke to Jason. "Makes me want to check into a person's alibi."

"This is all fascinating speculation, gentlemen, but I need to get ready for my show." Taylor rose, dropping his napkin onto the table. "Am I under arrest? Or can I go to the dressing room?"

Jason leaned in toward Taylor, putting his face only a few inches away. "You are free to go, for now. But I'm puzzled why you would not want to help us find someone who might have murdered your girlfriend."

"She wasn't my girlfriend, and I'm helping you as much as I can. I just don't know anything about that. If somebody killed Kayleigh, then I hope you find them. Right now, I need to go." Taylor pushed past Jason and disappeared beyond the kitchen doors.

Mike and Jason remained in the showroom. Jason said, "He's not being straight with us."

"Does that make him guilty?"

"I'm not sure," Mike said, still looking toward the kitchen. "He says Logan Summers is Kayleigh's sugar daddy?"

"Interesting, for sure," Jason said. "He's quick to point us toward somebody else. You think that's suspicious?"

"Not necessarily. But it makes him a suspect." Mike grabbed Jason's arm. "We need to talk to Lori Byrd again. We're past five o'clock, so Sully is going to have to deal with the overtime."

Chapter 15
Refreshed Recollections

LORI OPENED HER DOOR MOMENTS after the knock, obviously alerted by the front desk that the police were once again on their way up. Her stoic face suggested that she was not excited about another conversation with the detectives. "I already told you everything I know," she preempted the questioning.

"We have some new information," Jason said, stepping through the half-open door into the apartment without waiting for an invitation. "We'd like to get your impressions and see if it sparks any additional memories for you." Mike followed Jason inside, leaving Lori to close the door. By the time she reached the living room, the two detectives were already seated on the maroon sofa.

"I really can't tell you anything more." She stood with her arms crossed, as if sitting down would invite the cops to stay.

Jason once again took the lead. "Miss Byrd—" He stopped himself, seeing the young woman's reprobative stare. "Sorry, Lori. Did you ever know Kayleigh to use opioids?"

"You mean like heroin, or oxy? No. No. She never did that."

"What about fentanyl?" Jason pressed.

Lori put a hand to her mouth. "Oh, God no! What? Are you telling me . . . ?"

"We're not telling you anything, officially. Please do not post about this, or it might interfere with our investigation. Do you understand?"

Lori looked past Jason, unable to focus. "Um, sure."

"Where do you think she might have gotten hold of fentanyl to mix with her cocaine? Do you think this guy, The Pharmacist, could have recommended that?"

Lori slumped into the lounge chair opposite Mike and Jason, her hand still covering her mouth, her eyes wide. "Oh my God! What? No. No. No. Kayleigh would never do that. She was smarter than that. Even totally high, she would not put fentanyl in her. That's crazy!"

Mike was pleased that Lori was so worked up over the news. It was exactly what the detectives had hoped for. "It's looking more like somebody might have spiked your friend's cocaine cocktail with something she wasn't expecting — and it killed her. We can't prove it yet, but we're more suspicious now than we were yesterday. We've spoken to several people who were at the party. It seems like you may have known her better than anyone. Yesterday, when we asked whether you thought anyone might want to harm Kayleigh, you said you didn't know. What about Brock Taylor?"

"Brock? No. Why would he? He's a sponge. I mean, I never fell for his bullshit charmer act like Kayleigh. But no. I can't imagine." Lori looked past the detectives toward her north-facing window. The low sun cast long shadows from the Riverside park trees, their creeping black tentacles reaching toward the apartment buildings.

She was lost in thought until Jason asked his next question. "What about Logan Summers? What was his relationship like with Kayleigh?"

Lori looked back and forth between Jason and Mike, then down at the floor. She answered softly, "He's Kayleigh's sugar daddy. Not that she needed one. She's raking in the YouTube and TikTok money and she's got loads of advertising deals going for her Insta. But he, like, totally pampered her. He took her to Paris for a weekend, which was so romantic. He was crazy about her, which is why he let her have her totally fab apartment. He would never—"

"Did Summers know that Kayleigh was also sleeping with Taylor?" Jason interrupted.

Lori froze, her eyes wide, as if she had never considered the answer or its implications. "Probably not. Kayleigh was kind of juggling them. She didn't want Brock to act like he was her boyfriend if Logan was around. But it's not like Kayleigh and Logan were engaged or anything. He's married, I think. Kayleigh didn't have any obligations to him. And Brock was . . . well, let's just say I was hoping Kayleigh would get over him eventually. I don't think he loved her."

"Do you know whether Summers ever brought drugs for your friend?"

"Well, sure he did. I mean, he was totally into it. More than Kayleigh."

"What about Taylor?" Mike cut into the dialogue, forcing Lori to switch her attention. "Did Taylor ever give her drugs?"

Lori's face soured. "He did Kayleigh's drugs, for sure. He's an actor, he doesn't have much money. Kayleigh bought the stuff, or got it from Logan, and shared with Brock. He was into crazy shit. He's the one who got Kayleigh into The

Pharmacist's weird combos. But he never bought anything, as far as I could tell."

Jason asked the next question as the detective team worked to keep her off balance. "So you're saying that it was more likely Summers who would have brought Kayleigh the Montezuma's Delight mixture she took at the party. Is that right?"

"Wait — I'm not going to get him into trouble for — No, I mean, I don't know. I don't know anything." Lori clasped her hands in her lap and stiffly stared at the coffee table.

Jason attempted to thaw the sudden chill. "Lori, we're not interested in arresting anyone for drugs. I understand that there will be drug use at parties like the ones you attended. It's normal. At this point, it's practically legal. I give you my word that we will not arrest Summers, or you, or anyone else for drug use or drug possession. It's not our beat. We're trying to determine if somebody murdered your friend. I'd like to think you would want to help us do that. Don't you?"

The silence was palpable as Mike and Jason waited for Lori to speak, broken only by a distant siren. The detectives watched her eyes and facial expressions as she contemplated whether to open up to them. Mike imagined her on the other side of a poker table, and knew whatever she said next, she would not be bluffing.

Eventually, Lori looked at Jason with moist eyes and said, "Kayleigh told me she and Logan had to cool things down for a while because he was going through his divorce."

"What was Kayleigh's reaction?"

"She was kinda bummed out about it, I think."

"Did she love him?" Jason asked.

"Kayleigh loved everybody, but she had a connection with Logan. It wasn't like some daddy complex or anything. She loved how he was so enthusiastic around her. He was ready for anything. They went indoor skydiving. Can you believe that? She was like his fountain of youth."

"What about Taylor?"

"Brock is sexy and has cool friends and is fun to party with. But I don't think Kayleigh loved him."

"Did Taylor know that?" Mike asked.

"God, no!" Lori blurted. "I mean — I don't think so. He was kinda in his own world most of the time."

"Was Summers at the party Monday night?" Mike asked.

Lori hesitated. "I think so. I mean, I didn't see him, but I'm pretty sure. Monday was her anniversary in the apartment. Kayleigh was excited because somebody had scored something special from The Pharmacist. She wouldn't say who, but it had to be Logan."

"Was that the Montezuma's Delight?" Jason risked interrupting.

"Probably. That was just before I had to leave. She told me she was going to make a TikTok afterward."

"We saw the video," Jason said. "Do you know who filmed it?"

"No, I had left the party by then. I remember giving her a kiss and telling her to have fun. She said she was planning on it. That's the last thing she ever said to me." Lori lowered her head and tried to keep from crying.

"Thank you, Miss Byrd," Mike soothed, forgetting to address his young witness by her first name. "This has been very helpful information. We really appreciate it. But, to be clear, you did not actually see Logan Summers in the apartment Monday night?"

"Um . . . I guess I didn't. That's a little weird."

"Like he was trying to stay out of sight?" Jason asked.

Lori shrugged.

Mike stood and moved toward the door. "If we need to confirm any more information, we'll let you know."

"You promise nobody will get into trouble because of what I said?"

"Lori, as we said, we're not interested in drug use or possession. We're not arresting anyone for that. You have my word. But we do need you to keep this to yourself. If there is a killer out there, you don't want him to know you talked to us or that you have any information about what killed Kayleigh." Jason gave the woman a reassuring pat on the upper arm, then joined Mike at the door.

As soon as they were in the hallway, Mike said, "You think we have a possible motive now for Taylor?"

"Jealousy? I'm not sure about that. Kayleigh was his meal ticket and his drug supplier. He seems like the kind of guy who would string her along, maybe blackmail her by threatening to mess up her thing with Summers. Why kill her? And how would he get access to the Montezuma's Delight if it was Summers who brought it to the party?"

"Still. There's something there." Mike looked at his reflection in the big gilded mirror in the elevator lobby while Jason pushed the call button. "Taylor was evasive."

"I'm more interested in Summers. But if she was his fountain of youth and he was freely fucking her and taking her on trips, why would he spike her drugs with fentanyl?"

"Maybe it was all an act. Maybe he was more worried about the impact on his divorce if his wife found out about him and Kayleigh?"

"I'm thinking we might have enough now to go to Sully about interviewing Summers."

"And The Pharmacist, if we can track him down."

A soft ding announced their elevator's arrival. Mike stepped inside first, then faced the closing doors. "You think we've got a homicide?"

Jason stared at the lighted numbers indicating their progression toward the lobby. "Unless we find a video of this Pharmacist nut prescribing fentanyl, I'd say it's more likely than not that somebody slipped it to her. Unless somebody else turns up, her sugar daddy—who brings her drugs and is going through a divorce—is the most likely suspect."

"Yeah. Seems right. You don't suppose the guy left incriminating evidence on his laptop, do you?"

Jason let out a deep guffaw. "We'll check, but I doubt we'll get that lucky again."

* * *

AS SOON AS THEY STEPPED into the lobby, Officer Harris waved them toward her. She was outside the building's security office where she had spent the day reviewing video camera images. She ushered them into the tiny room filled with small monitors and a control console. She sat to make room for the detectives.

"We identified somebody exiting the building through the breezeway door late Monday night. Actually, twelve forty-one Tuesday morning."

"Do you have an ID?" Mike asked.

"No, and there's no way to get one. Here, let me show you." Harris tapped the shoulder of a building staff member who had been assisting her. An image sprang to life on the ten-inch monitor. Mike and Jason recognized it as the security camera at the service entrance. It was focused on the large vehicular door, but included some of the interior roadway and the pedestrian exit. Two figures came into frame, moving toward the door. The heads and upper bodies of both people were obscured by a large umbrella, unfurled inside the breezeway, obviously for the specific purpose of shielding them from the security camera. Blue pants with a gold stripe identified the person holding the umbrella as a building doorman. The other person was obscured except for their lower legs, encased in dark slacks and wearing dark men's dress shoes. The visitor left through the door. The doorman, umbrella still engaged, walked back the way he came until out of frame.

"I see what you mean," Mike said. "No chance of a positive ID there. Do you know whether he arrived through the breezeway, and when?"

"Yes." Harris bounced from her chair. "It looks like the same man entered through that door at eleven twenty-four, using the same umbrella maneuver to avoid the camera. Nobody else went in or out in between."

"We should grill the doormen," Jason said. "That man's identity could be important."

"I already did that," Harris said. "The crew here now is the same as Monday night. None of them will admit to being the doorman holding the umbrella. The senior guy on the desk, Mr. Jimenez, says the people who get that kind of clandestine service usually tip extremely well. The doormen aren't going to rat them out."

"Yeah?" Mike grunted. "Maybe we'll have to test that theory if it becomes important. Good work, Harris. Are you about done with your shift?"

"I'm into a little overtime, Sir," Harris replied. "I thought you would want to see this today. Should I not put in for it?"

"Put in for it. Sully has us chasing this and the commissioner won't mind. But you can knock off for the night now."

As they made their way toward the subway and their own trips home, Jason said, "The man in the video might not have been at Kayleigh's party."

"True. And if he was, he might not have had anything to do with her drug ingestion. But, then again, he might have. Like I said, we'll see if it becomes important."

Chapter 16
On the Hunt

STERLING WRIGHT SPUN his index finger around the rim of a nearly empty tumbler of scotch. In the dim glow of the tiny table light meant to mimic a candle, the Club Cabana looked fashionably antique rather than merely rundown and dingy. The team of waiters scurried through narrow aisles with trays of drinks while the performers were in between sets. Sterling knew that Brock Taylor had two numbers in the second act and would not be leaving the club. He scanned the area to the right of the stage, where a few cast members were chatting with friends at the front-row tables. If his target made an appearance, he wanted to monitor any interactions. Nathan's trial was underway. A breakthrough that would change the defense's strategy was unlikely, but Sterling had no better options.

Across the table, a woman in a form-fitting red dress twirled the stem of her empty martini glass. Sterling thought she looked like a young Diana Ross. Judging from the lascivious looks she was getting from the other men in the club, including the waiters, her dress was a hit. Sterling raised his glass in her direction, then drained the dregs of his scotch. They had already ordered another round. His date made a half-hearted attempt to return the toast with her empty glass.

Rhonda was the sister of Sterling's best friend. He had brought her out for the evening so he wouldn't be conspicuously sitting alone, and so he wouldn't have to deal with flirty single women. Rhonda was promised free drinks and decent entertainment. He was there to work.

Waiting for their server, Sterling's thoughts drifted to the path that had brought him to this state of affairs. In 2021, the newly minted detective marched in civilian clothes in a Black Lives Matter demonstration. The crowd got rowdy and some trouble-makers started throwing rocks at store windows along the parade route. Sterling tried to get them under control before the demonstration turned into a riot. He was wrestling with two men attempting to vandalize a storefront when two uniformed officers arrived. One of them recognized him. The next day, he was summoned to his captain's office. His presence in the demonstration was a violation of departmental policy, and his participation in the destruction of property was an offense that could get him fired. He told his side of the story, but it fell on deaf ears. Sterling received a reprimand after the police union came to his defense, but he was blackballed after the incident.

After another incident, where Sterling lodged a formal internal complaint of racism, he was given an option to be fired and fight it in court, or take a settlement, sign a confidentiality agreement, and leave quietly. He took the deal, like he had much choice. His plan was to set himself up as a private investigator with the seed money from the settlement. The problem was that most ex-cops who went private got their business off the ground based on referrals and references from their former colleagues. He got a few referrals from the Black cops, but not many. As a result, his business struggled as he burned through the settlement money on office space and advertising.

Then the Ballet Murder happened in the spring of 2022. A cousin who worked as a stagehand on *Godfather: The Musical* connected him to the lawyer representing Nathan Matthews. Sterling agreed to a big discount on his usual fee in exchange for a percentage of any future civil settlement. Mostly, he wanted the publicity. He hoped being connected to such a high-profile case would lead to more business. But the case dragged. Nathan ran out of money to pay his lawyers. Sterling stayed on. Nathan insisted he was innocent and Sterling believed him. He was, effectively, betting his business on his ability to help prove it.

He realized that his personal stake in the outcome compromised his objectivity. He didn't care. He couldn't care. For the past few months, Sterling had focused on Brock Taylor. He had the opportunity, at least in theory, to plant the evidence. Sterling was sure Taylor was their man. He needed to prove it. That was why he was in the club where Taylor was performing.

"What are you watching for so carefully?" Rhonda's question snapped Sterling from his reminiscing.

"Oh, I — I'm watching for Brock Taylor."

"Watching for what? You think he's gonna confess from the stage?"

Sterling handed his empty glass to their waitress, who had arrived mid-question. After they both had fresh drinks and Sterling had taken the first sip of his second Johnny Walker Red Label, he said, "I'm looking to see if he talks to anyone or meets with anyone who might be a lead for me. I have no jurisdiction to question him or search him. But if I can find somebody else who I can squeeze, I might be able to find an angle."

"Does that mean you don't want me to distract you from your surveillance?" Sterling felt Rhonda's toe slide up the length of his calf under the table. She had been wearing three-inch heels, but this was definitely a bare foot.

He leaned forward, nearly knocking over the faux candle as he pulled his legs backward. "Rhonda, you know Chris would wring my neck."

"Well, I'm not going to tell him. Are you? I'm not that awkward fifteen-year-old anymore. I get to make my own choices. I'm not here as a favor to Chris. I'm here because I've always had a crush on you." Rhonda's index finger traced a path from her chin, past the ruby-colored jewel hanging on a gold chain around her neck, to the satin fabric between the curves of her breasts.

Sterling watched, mesmerized. Then he shook his head and blinked, sitting back in his chair. He reached for his scotch glass, contemplating his next move, when a flash of gold caught his eye.

Now his attention snapped fully to the figure standing in the archway separating the backstage area from the audience at the front of the room. Brock Taylor leaned one arm against the wall, his flamboyant 1970s disco costume sparkling under the dim overhead lights. He looked ready to take the stage again at any moment. Sterling understood the man's appeal as an actor. With a solid six-foot frame and toned muscles, a slim waist, and a dancer's legs, he had a powerful voice and cat-like movements on stage. His face was narrow, sloping to a thin chin that allowed him to use makeup to give the impression of masculine or feminine features. To Sterling, his face was weak, but he understood how some might find it beautifully vulnerable.

"No comment at all?" Rhonda pouted.

"Not now!" Sterling hissed. "There he is."

Rhonda turned to watch what was taking Sterling's attention away from her. Taylor leaned in close to the face of the figure he was talking to, whose back was to the watchers. They wore jeans and a sequined denim jacket. Their short, dark hair gave no conclusive evidence as to gender. Taylor seemed to be having an intimate conversation, his mouth inches from the person's ear. Then, he suddenly grabbed his companion's sleeve and pulled them forward, toward the stage door and into the shadows.

"Shouldn't you follow them?" Rhonda asked.

"No. They're not going anywhere. If I charge over there it would let him know I'm watching him. No, let's see who that other guy is when they come back."

"You think it's a guy?"

"Probably. The women in this place are dressed much better. Like you." Sterling turned back to Rhonda, making a concerted effort to keep his eyes on hers, rather than on her necklace area. "I noticed that you're not the scrawny teenager I met when Chris and I were both beat cops. It's impossible not to notice. For tonight, though, I need to focus on—"

His attention swung back to the front of the house, where Denim Jacket strode quickly away from the archway. As he came toward them, Sterling could see he was male, and he was angry. Sterling and Rhonda watched the man breeze past them without a glance. He took a seat at the bar and motioned to the bartender, who turned away and began preparing a drink as if the order was something familiar.

"Whatcha gonna do next?" Rhonda asked in an excited whisper.

Without taking his eyes off Denim Jacket, Sterling replied, "I'm going to watch that guy and try to figure out who he is. I don't recognize him, but he had a rather heated conversation with Taylor. Maybe, when he leaves, I can talk to the bartender, who seems to know him. Then — Hey!" Sterling reached out toward Rhonda, who had left her chair and was sauntering to the bar. In a loud whisper, he hissed "Where are you going?"

Rhonda craned her neck around to say, "I'm helping out," without stopping.

She continued to the bar, squeezing into the space next to Denim Jacket. She leaned far over the polished wooden surface and quickly attracted the bartender's attention. While she waited for her order, she swayed her hips to *Livin' La Vida Loca*, playing in the background. Sterling watched in a panic, wondering what Rhonda was doing, but not wanting to rush to her side and expose himself to the target. There might be a time in the future where he would need to confront the man and would not want to be recognized.

Rhonda's head turned toward Denim Jacket. Sterling saw her smile and brush a strand of hair behind her ear. Three minutes later, when his drink arrived, the man turned away and walked back to a table near the front of the house. Rhonda returned to Sterling's table with two drinks.

"What were you doing?" he snapped as soon as Rhonda sat.

"Getting you information," she purred, handing him a tumbler of dark liquor.

"You shouldn't have—"

"His name is Lawrence Teel. He's an actor and he has a website: Lawrence Teel Performances dot com. You're welcome." Rhonda flashed a satisfied smile.

"How?" Sterling blurted.

"You men are all alike." Rhonda sipped her new martini. "You can't not try to impress a sexy woman."

Sterling pulled out his phone and entered the website.

A pouting Rhonda watched her putative date devote his entire attention to his screen, leaving none for her. She picked up her martini and scanned the room. "Um, Sterling?"

"What?" he said without disengaging from his screen.

"That man you were watching, he's over there with Mr. Teel." Rhonda pointed subtly with her index finger, which was pressed against the table top.

Sterling slowly turned his head. Sure enough, Taylor and Teel were engaged in another intense conversation near the stage, their heads pushed closed together. Teel pulled back, shaking his head. Taylor pressed a finger into Teel's chest. Teel slapped his hand away, spun around, and stalked toward the club's entrance. Taylor followed Teel.

"Wait here." Sterling was already out of his chair. He approached the bar, then veered to the exit door as soon as Taylor passed through. Outside, the September night was warm but had the damp smell of a recent shower. The slick sidewalk to the west was sparsely populated, with no figures resembling Teel or Taylor. To the east, toward a cluster of bars and restaurants, the pavement was thick with pedestrians. He saw a tall figure dart from the flow to the left, between the club's building and an adjoining establishment. He wasn't sure it was Taylor, but he hurried forward.

Rounding the brick corner, Sterling looked down a thin alley with recessed doorways on both sides, likely emergency exits. Shadows from the two adjoining buildings nearly blotted out the ambient light. A circular metal light fixture protruded from one wall, casting a pale cone of light in which two figures stood close together. Neither man noticed Sterling's arrival.

"You do *not* want to screw me over on this!" spat Taylor's angry voice.

"Why are you so worried, dude?" Teel's voice was less animated.

"It's just that — There's some shit going down. Her husband will have me whacked, and you, too, for helping me. So you need to keep your mouth shut."

"I got you. Don't worry. Just don't push me. I'm not your flunky." Teel stretched out his right arm, nudging Taylor farther away.

"This is serious!" Taylor pushed back with both arms, sending Teel sprawling backward against the wet bricks.

"Fuck you!" Teel shouted. He pushed off the wall and lunged forward, throwing his arms around Taylor's shoulders. The two men fell into the opposite brick barrier.

Taylor grunted as his back impacted against the immovable object. He then snapped his head forward, slamming his forehead into Teel's. As Teel wobbled backward, Taylor threw a roundhouse left, connecting with a slapping squish against Teel's face.

As Teel fell to the ground and Taylor stood over him, Sterling leapt toward the fray. He didn't announce himself but planted a right hook into Taylor's kidney from behind.

Taylor grunted in pain and crumpled to his hands and knees on the asphalt. Sterling clenched his hands together into a hammer fist, which he crashed down on the back of

Taylor's neck. Taylor slumped to the pavement on his stomach with another deep grunt.

Sterling reached a hand out for Teel, who was still on his butt on the wet alley. "Are you alright?"

"Thanks, man, but I didn't need any help."

"It looked like that guy was attacking you." Sterling wiggled his hand, encouraging Teel to accept the invitation for a help up. Teel grasped Sterling's hand and allowed the PI to lever him to his feet. Taylor moaned and put his palms on the ground, as if preparing to push himself up.

Teel disengaged from Sterling's hand. "I got it from here. He's a friend of mine. We had a little disagreement."

"What were you arguing about?" Sterling asked, hoping to catch Teel both off-guard and in a grateful mood.

"Nothing that concerns you, man. Thanks again. We're cool."

Taylor had managed to get to all fours. Sterling glanced down. "You want me to put him down again?"

"No. No. Thanks. We're good. You didn't need to slam him like that. You a cop or something?"

Sterling hesitated, but he wanted this man to trust him. So, he told the truth. "I used to be."

Taylor, gasping for breath, croaked out, "He's working for *him*."

"Hey, hang on—" Sterling held out his hands, palms up.

"Why were you spying on us?" Teel yelled.

"I wasn't—"

Sterling didn't get a chance to finish the sentence. Teel lurched forward, encircling Sterling in his arms and pinning his hands. Sterling kicked out one wing-tip toward Teel's shin. Teel squealed in pain, but maintained his bear hug.

While Sterling strained to extricate himself, Taylor struggled to his feet. His sequined outfit was streaked with grime and wet stains. He reared back and plowed his right fist into the small of Sterling's back. Not being a trained fighter, he missed the kidney, but the blow to Sterling's spine sent spikes of pain shooting toward his neck.

"I'm trying to help you!" Sterling grunted into Teel's ear.

"Fuck you, asshole!" Teel released his hug and shoved Sterling with both hands. He fell against the wall, scraping his forehead against the rough bricks. Teel planted a roundhouse kick into Sterling's side, sending him to the ground. His back screamed as his tail bone impacted the pavement.

It was two against one and he was already injured, so Sterling made the instant decision that flight was the superior option. He rolled to his left, pushing up with his arm as he scrambled for traction on the smooth leather soles of his loafers. He was two limping strides toward the street by the time Teel and Taylor realized he was running.

"Fuck you!" Teel shouted, not moving to chase.

Sterling rounded the corner back toward the club, slowly getting past the back pain. He did not see any sign of pursuit. Staggering inside the club's door, he looked exactly like a man who had been mugged in the alley.

The usher, to whom he had waved on his way out so the guy would remember to let him back in, gave him a side-eye before asking, "You need some help?"

"I'm good." Sterling waved, pushing into the club's interior. He attempted to hide his injuries while resuming his chair opposite Rhonda.

"What happened to your forehead?" Rhonda reached out to gently touch the bleeding scrape. "Sterling, you need at least a Band-Aid." She scooted across to a kneeling position, digging into her purse for a tissue, which she dabbed on Sterling's wound. "What happened?"

"I'm not sure, but I think I struck a nerve."

Chapter 17
On the Stand

ON FRIDAY MORNING, Mike and Jason sat on an uncomfortable wooden bench in the hallway outside the fourth-floor courtroom at the New York State criminal court building in Foley Square. As witnesses, they were not allowed inside during the trial. They were not allowed to know anything said by other witnesses before they took the stand. Keith Harris had prepped them well, and they were ready for the boredom of waiting. They each brought reading material.

After fifty-six dull minutes in the corridor, the padded courtroom door opened. Michelle walked out, wearing the blue-and-white business suit she nearly always chose for testimony days. She smiled at Mike and Jason. "It went pretty much according to prep," was all she would say as she breezed by. Harris had warned them against having any conversation about the testimony.

The bailiff motioned to Jason, who walked toward the courtroom. Mike was left to twiddle his thumbs alone. He pulled out his copy of *Resurrection Walk* by Michael Connelly and settled in.

When Jason pushed through the padded door ninety minutes later, the court officer motioned to Mike that it was now his turn. Jason whispered, "Take your time with this guy," as he took his seat back on the bench. He had promised Mike to wait so that they could leave the building together.

Mike walked calmly into the crowded room, where the judge and the jury were absent. The trial was on a recess. The media and curiosity seekers filled every seat in the gallery. Mike swung open the rail separating the audience from the lawyers, jury, and courtroom personnel, the barrier known as "the bar," and strode comfortably to the witness box. He noticed the courtroom sketch artist staring at him while frantically scratching on her pad.

When court resumed, the bailiff brought out a bible and Mike looked directly at the jury as he swore to tell the truth. Keith Harris rose behind the prosecution table, looked down at his notes, and began the questioning.

Mike told the jury how the investigation went, beginning with the first interviews with staff at the ballet. Then, he and Jason interviewed the witnesses at the theater, who described the acrimonious relationship Alex Bishop had with Nathan Matthews, the defendant. Mike described how he instructed the uniformed officers to confiscate the director's laptop and identified his initials on an evidence tag attached to the machine. Mike had not done the forensic analysis of the computer and could not testify about what was found there, but the computer tech had already done so. The direct examination went exactly as they had prepped it.

When Keith said, "No more questions, Your Honor," Mike focused his attention on the defense attorney, Kevin O'Beaney. Mike expected a broad-shouldered man with manicured nails and carefully styled hair. Instead, the lawyer was shorter than Mike, with brown, wavy hair that appeared not to have been combed in weeks. He wore a plain blue suit with shiny patches on both thighs. Nevertheless, Keith had warned his witnesses that the man would be aggressive, combative, and disrespectful toward the government's witnesses. Mike steeled himself, adopting his best blank poker face.

"Detective Stoneman, you've been on the force for nearly thirty years, haven't you?"

Mike paused, as every ADA who had ever questioned him in court had coached him. The mantra was drilled into him. One: Think about whether you understand the question. If you don't, ask for clarification. Two: Think about whether you know the answer to the question. If you don't, say that you don't know. Three: If you understand the question and know the answer, think about how to answer in the most direct way, using simple language that the jury will understand. Face the jury, not the attorney, and confidently state your answer. He made eye contact with the man in jury seat number one, who was paying close attention even to this simple question. "Twenty-eight years next month," Mike said, without sounding arrogant or regretful.

"You've been a homicide detective for how many of those years?"

Pause. "Almost twenty-two."

"And you're the most senior homicide detective in the entire NYPD, isn't that right, Detective Stoneman?"

"Yes, I am." Mike mentally kicked himself for not pausing, but it wasn't a question to which Keith was going to object. One of the reasons for the pause was so that the prosecutor could raise an objection before the witness blurted out an answer.

"And, in over twenty years as a homicide detective, how many cases have you investigated?"

Pause. "Oh, I wouldn't know exactly how many. I don't keep track." Mike smiled at the attorney, which was his way of silently adding, *You prick*.

"Well, Detective, can we say that the number is at least more than two hundred? That would be an average of ten per year."

Pause. "Yes, I would say my average number of cases per year has been more than ten."

"And, Detective, in all those hundreds of cases over your long career, can you think of any other case, besides this one, where the evidence pointed at one suspect so quickly and so clearly, and where your investigation was as clean and simple as this one?"

Pause.

Keith was on his feet immediately. "Objection — It's a compound question."

The judge turned to Mike, looking down from the bench. "Detective Stoneman, do you understand the question as phrased?"

Mike stole a quick glance at Keith. He didn't want to seem evasive or stupid in the eyes of the jury. It was not that complex a question. Mike suspected that Keith had objected as much to force Mike to take his time and think as to induce a favorable ruling from the judge. "I think I do, Your Honor."

"The objection is overruled. The witness can answer the question." The judge nodded at Mike.

"Sure," Mike again smiled, making eye contact with the woman in seat number six. "I recall a case where a woman was shot. Her husband was lying on the floor next to her with a knife wound in his gut. He was still holding the gun when the first officer arrived. That one was pretty easy." A chuckle rumbled softly through the courtroom and the jury box.

O'Beaney also laughed and held up both hands, as if in surrender. "OK, Detective. Sometimes an investigation is pretty easy. So, let me change the parameters a bit. Can you think of a case where you did not have a murder weapon, and where the suspect who was eventually arrested was not present at the murder scene, but where the evidence still pointed at one suspect so quickly and so clearly, and where your investigation was as easy as this one?"

Pause. This time, Harris did not bother with an objection. Instead he subtly lifted his hand off the table, showing Mike a peek of his palm. The signal reminded Mike to take his time. It was a complicated question. Mike could easily say he could not remember every investigation. However, saying he could not remember would confirm the lawyer's point. It was an ingenious question.

Mike cocked his head and brought a hand to his chin. "Well, that's a difficult question to answer. I've had a lot of cases, and some investigations resulted in fast arrests. I've certainly had a few where there was an eyewitness who immediately implicated a particular person, or where we had security video that immediately showed us the killer's face. Those are easy cases, like this one."

Harris gave Mike a subtle nod. It was a solid answer.

"But, Detective, would you place this case in that group — among the easiest and quickest investigations you have ever had?"

Pause. "I would say this one is near the top of the list of quickest and easiest. Sure."

"Now, Detective," the lawyer turned his back on Mike, facing the jury, "I'm sure you have had cases where there was evidence found on a computer belonging to the accused person, is that correct?"

Pause. "Sure. That happens."

"And have you had cases where the evidence included internet searches that the accused person allegedly conducted, and which were deemed to be suspicious?"

Pause. "Well, I'm sure there have been such cases, but I can't recall the specifics of every case on the spur of the moment."

"I'm sure that's true, Detective. Let me ask you this. Can you recall any such case where all the allegedly suspicious internet searches were conducted on one day, in the space of less than twenty minutes?"

Pause.

Less than twenty minutes? Mike did not recall Keith prepping him for this. The ADA was not objecting, which meant the twenty minutes had to be something already in evidence. Mike maintained an even composure, despite being knocked a bit off-balance by the question. "Again, Sir, I can't recall the specific details of every case I've ever worked."

The lawyer smiled. "Detective, is it fair to say that, at this moment, you cannot recall any such case — where all the allegedly suspicious internet searches were made on one day in the space of less than twenty minutes? Is that correct?"

Pause. Mike was stuck. He couldn't remember any such case. He couldn't say that there was one, or the lawyer would ask him for details, which he would not be able to give. He fell back on the final part of the mantra. Four: If the answer to the question is yes, just say yes and move on, without making the jury think that you are worried about it or think it's significant. Don't let the other lawyer leave the jury with the impression that your "yes" is a big point for the defense.

"Yes. At this moment, I can't recall one." Mike looked at the jury, making eye contact with an elderly woman in the back row in seat number eleven. His expression showed no concern.

"And, Detective, is it fair to say that you also cannot recall any other case where the critical internet searches occurred when there was no other action taken by the defendant? No other windows opened, no email checked, no other websites accessed? The computer was powered up, the critical searches conducted, and then the machine was powered off — is that correct?"

Is this true? Again, this was information about which Keith had not prepped Mike. Again, there was no objection. Mike glanced at Keith. He clenched his fist, signaling Mike to give a solid answer. This question was as complex as the last, but basically sought the same information. The lawyer had already made his point to the jury. "Yes," Mike said, wondering if the jury would even be able to follow what he was affirming.

"Detective, in a case where a killer was planning to poison someone by administering a drug that would have a fatal interaction with another drug, wouldn't you expect the killer to research the possible drugs they might use for more than a few minutes?"

Pause.

"Objection!" Keith was on his feet and moving around his table toward the judge. "Counsel is making an argument and asking the witness to speculate without any foundation!"

"Sustained," the judge quickly ruled, without waiting for an argument from O'Beaney.

He nodded at the judge and smiled at the jury. "Detective, in your professional opinion, is it possible that somebody other than Nathan Matthews could have run those internet searches on his laptop, leaving the evidence to frame Mr. Matthews for the murder?"

Pause. Mike was ready for this question. He and Keith expected it and had practiced the response. "Mr. O'Beaney, it's always possible to theorize that somebody else planted the data on Matthews' laptop, but I uncovered no evidence during my investigation to support such a theory."

"But, Detective, it is *possible,* correct?"

"It's possible that Harvey Weinstein broke out of prison, planted the evidence on the laptop, then broke back into prison so nobody would notice." Again, the courtroom broke out in restrained laughter. "I can't say with absolute certainty that didn't happen, but the likelihood is not significant enough to make me worry about it."

"How significant must a possibility be, Detective, before you would become worried about it?"

Pause. This question also had not been on the prep list. "It's not possible for me to answer that question, Sir. It would make me worried when it makes me worried. I can't quantify it."

"So, knowing that the information found on Mr. Matthews' laptop was so condensed, was so easy to find, and so obviously implicated him, does that not worry you, at least a little?"

Pause. This was another one Mike was expecting, but the specific search information was new. How had Mike not seen that in the forensics report? Was it even in there? He could not appear to be confused, and could not afford to let the jury think he didn't already know that information. "Mr. O'Beaney, I have learned over my many years never to underestimate how stupid and careless people can be. Criminals do dumb things all the time."

"No further questions."

Keith had no re-direct exam questions for Mike, who was dismissed with the court's thanks. As he walked toward the swinging gate to exit the courtroom, he looked the defense attorney in the eye. By then, O'Beaney was seated at his table, next to his client. With his back to the jury, Mike inclined his head a tiny bit and raised an eyebrow. It was a fair skirmish, which Mike had fought to pretty much a draw. But the lawyer had made his point. Mike acknowledged his adversary.

Mike also nodded to Keith, who cocked his head and raised one eyebrow. He was trying to say *I'm sorry* without tipping off the jury.

Walking toward the rear door, Mike replayed the lawyer's questions. He wracked his brain, trying to think of other cases involving computer evidence. He thought of several, but none were as clean as the Ballet Murder. None involved such a condensed series of searches in such a short period of time, assuming that information was correct. It had to be, or Keith would have objected. Maybe Matthews got lucky and found his answers quickly. Maybe he had done other searches on a different computer and was just double-checking. Maybe that was why he didn't do any other work on the machine. Maybe he was stupid and thought that by deleting his browsing history the evidence would be erased. Mike had seen plenty of dumber killers.

But Nathan Matthews was not a stupid man. He was meticulous and organized. Could somebody have set him up? Did Mike and Jason take the bait and arrest Matthews too quickly? Mike wouldn't admit it on the witness stand, but it bothered him. Did it worry him? He wasn't sure. And that also bothered him.

Chapter 18
Nagging Doubt

IT WAS LATE ENOUGH in the day when Mike and Jason left the courthouse that they decided to skip the trip back uptown to the precinct house. Mike suggested adjourning to a bar they enjoyed on Franklin Street. Over a pair of Balvenie 14 Caribbean Cask pours, they decided to have a full conversation about the Ballet Murder, now that their testimony was over. The high mirror behind rows of liquor bottles reflected Mike's and Jason's faces. At four-fifteen p.m., the place was sparsely populated. "Blue Bayou" by Linda Ronstadt played on the sound system.

"Did we miss that information in the forensics report from the techs? I don't remember seeing anything about how long the searches took or whether there was other activity on the machine. Am I crazy?" Mike sipped his scotch with one elbow on the bar. The smooth, polished walnut felt like an old friend.

Mike had repeated to Jason the sequence of questions Kevin O'Beaney threw at him on the witness stand. The lawyer had not asked them to Jason. As the more experienced homicide detective, Mike's answers to the points about the circumstances being so unusual had the maximum impact. It also prevented Jason from tipping off Mike about the coming questions.

Jason sipped his scotch, taking his time. "You're not crazy. I'm sure if we dug deep into the tech report, we would find that information. But it sure as hell wasn't in the summary. The techs missed it, or at least didn't think it was important enough to include. The big news was the on-point searches they found in the deleted history. Why did it matter how long he spent conducting the searches? I get why they missed it. But it was them, not us."

"Why doesn't that make me feel better?"

"Because it was our bust. We're responsible. But I have to tell you, Mike, what bothers me more is the other point, about there being no other activity."

"Why is that?"

Jason made eye contact with Mike in the mirror. "Think about it. If you're working on the computer at your desk, what do you do when you boot it up?"

"I don't know. If it's me, I guess I read my email and look for any messages from Michelle, then check the Mets website, read that day's *Faith and Fear in Flushing* blog and then I do whatever else I need to do."

"Exactly." Jason turned his head to look directly at his partner. "Anybody would do that. You wouldn't start up the machine, run six very targeted searches related to your plans to kill off your leading man, and then shut down without doing anything else. Right? It's like Sophie said, sometimes it's what's missing that matters. If there was no other activity at all on the laptop during that session, the theory that it was a plant becomes more plausible."

"Maybe," Mike hesitated, "but just because there's another possibility doesn't mean the guy we arrested isn't guilty."

"Using his own computer to search for a possible drug interaction isn't crazy." Jason picked up the thread of trying to convince himself to let his doubts go. "Maybe he wasn't really planning to kill Bishop, but found the magic drug interaction and got inspired. If it were me, I'd certainly delete the search history. Hell, I'd throw the whole laptop in the Hudson River, but deleting the data makes sense."

"It makes sense," Mike agreed. "It wasn't that hard. He got lucky, but he also found the most obvious interaction, the most often warned about. Not a surprise that it happened quickly. Plus, he could have done more research somewhere else. What they found on the laptop may not have been all the research he did. Maybe this was the one time he forgot to go into incognito mode." Mike made eye contact with Jason. His partner looked skeptical.

"Fine," Jason conceded. "Maybe he's guilty. Most of the time, the obvious explanation is the correct one. He could have been framed, but is that a more likely scenario?"

Mike tipped back his glass and drained the last drops of the precious liquid. At eighteen dollars per serving, he wasn't wasting any. "We don't know, and it's too late now."

"He was getting ready to head out to the Directors Guild dinner party. He was in a hurry. So, he pops into his office, he runs his searches, then deletes the results and then heads out. That's not so implausible."

"Sure, plausible. But why then? Why do it in such a rushed window right before you know you're going out to a dinner? Is that the time you would choose to start working on the research about your contemplated murder?"

"Look at it from the other side. How would somebody else have planted the evidence? The director was paranoid about security and privacy. You think he'd leave his laptop open in his office when he's not there?"

"I don't know," Jason said. "I agree it seems unlikely. But the one person who seems like a plausible suspect is Brock Taylor. The understudy. He was in the theater, so he had access."

"How does he know the password to the director's laptop?" Mike retorted. "And how does he get into the locked office?"

"I don't know, but as long as we're sliding down this rabbit hole, let's assume Taylor had the access. He had an alibi for the night of the Broadway Cares gala, but we never confirmed it."

"We never focused on anyone else's alibis except for Matthews. Was that tunnel vision?"

Jason shook his head. "I don't think so. It was just efficient."

"OK. So, in the end, Matthews is still the most likely killer. He's probably guilty."

Jason put his empty glass on the bar with a clack. "I know. But I also know that we didn't finish the investigation. We found the easy-to-find evidence and we stopped."

Mike pulled out two twenty-dollar bills and put the stacked glasses on top of them for their bartender. "It's up to the jury now. But what the lawyer said is bothering me more than it should."

"You said it's not our concern," Jason reminded Mike.

"Yeah. It's not. We need to let it go."

"We gonna do that?"

"Probably not. It's gonna keep bothering me. But we're not doing anything about it until after the trial."

Chapter 19
Scratching an Itch

OVER DINNER THAT NIGHT, Mike and Michelle each shared a recap of their testimonies and their impressions of the defense attorney. Michelle had faced few questions on cross-examination, since her testimony was mostly a summary and explanation of the toxicology report. There was not much to contest.

"It's funny," Michelle said in between bites of steamed fish fillets with ginger sauce, brown rice, and mixed veggies. "The lawyer didn't contest my testimony about how simple it would be for someone to spike Alex Bishop's drink before the ballet. In fact, he seemed to be making the point that it would be extremely easy for anyone to do it."

"Did he ask you about being present that night?"

"No. It didn't come up."

Mike scratched the side of his face. "Same for me and Jason. I know it's not relevant to anything, but I expected it to come up, to make it seem like we had some possible bias because we were there."

"Maybe," Michelle deftly used her chopsticks to raise a chunk of fish, leaving it suspended in front of her, "he wants to seem confident in his defense and not appear to be grasping at straws."

"If so, he's the first defense attorney ever to miss a chance to impeach a witness." Mike sipped his Chardonnay. He would have preferred a beer, but Michelle insisted that the white wine had fewer calories and was better for his heart. "I have to admit, the more Jason and I talk about it, the more the defense's argument bugs me. The evidence from the laptop is all the prosecution has. Aside from motive and opportunity, there is nothing else that implicates Matthews. It does seem strange that Matthews would run those searches so quickly, without any dead ends or false leads, in such a short time, and then power down his computer without doing any other work. I hate to admit it, but the facts are consistent with somebody else getting access to the machine, then running the incriminating searches and getting out."

"So, do you think the jury will acquit him?"

Mike grimaced. "Probably not. As much as the lawyer may spin up the planted evidence theory, it's just a theory. There's nothing pointing at anybody else. If it wasn't the director, then who? Who else can they prove had motive and opportunity? Without being able to point a finger at a plausible alternate killer, the jury has to act based on the evidence they have."

"Did you identify any other possible suspects during your investigation?"

"No." Mike dropped his chopsticks and picked up his fork. His pride was not getting in the way of securing every last scrap of carbohydrate from his plate. The diet Michelle had him following when they ate together left his tummy rumbling throughout the evening. "The director was the first person who came up. We got the evidence from his laptop, arrested him, and never dug into any other possible suspects."

"If it was a set-up, then somebody did a good job, huh?"

"Yeah. A hell of a job. You have to admire such cunning."

"Or, maybe the director really did it and he thought deleting his search history was all he needed to do to cover his tracks."

Mike gathered his dishes. "Right. Occam's Razor. The obvious answer is usually the correct answer. So, why is it bothering me so much?"

Michelle loaded their plates into the dishwasher. "Probably because he has been protesting his innocence for over a year. Most guilty people who are caught with this much damning evidence take a plea deal and don't demand a trial. He's acting like somebody who got framed, which makes you tend to believe the possibility. But, really, you're blaming yourself for not noticing the unusual information in the forensics report and not doing a more complete investigation. Why do you think that was?"

Mike picked up a dirty dish towel, which was bound for the laundry hamper, and squeezed it harder than necessary. "I've been thinking on that. There was a lot of media pressure because of the high-profile actor getting snuffed. The commissioner's office was hounding Sully every day. We also had another case running at the same time. Maybe we were distracted. When we announced that we had arrested the director, the press was all over it. The commissioner was thrilled. Nobody wanted to keep the case open. We were all happy to wrap it up. Seems like the definition of tunnel vision."

Michelle started the dishwasher. She slid her arms around Mike's neck and kissed him. "The real question is, what are you going to do about it?"

"There's not much we can do." Mike slumped against the kitchen counter. "We've been looking at the evidence we have, but most of the boxes got shipped to the DA. We don't have any authority to start re-investigating the case, and the arrest is more than a year old. There's not much chance that we'll find the real killer after all this time."

"You're saying the chances are slim, the evidence is cold, and it would be a difficult investigation?"

"Yeah."

"When has that ever stopped you before?"

* * *

AFTER DINNER, Mike and Michelle watched the local news coverage of the trial. The courtroom sketch artist had captured Michelle's testimony, which the reporter characterized as "powerful" proof of a murder based on the fatal drug interaction. The reporter, doing a live report from the steps of the now-empty courthouse in a driving rain, closed by stating that Matthews continued to maintain his innocence. She noted that the prosecution's case would continue on Monday and was expected to conclude by the end of the following week.

Mike was ready to switch the TV to the Mets pre-game show when the next story caught his attention. It was Kayleigh's death, which was reported as a "likely" drug overdose. The broadcast noted that a police investigation was still ongoing. Before the news went to commercial, there was a teaser for the following program, the network's daily entertainment and gossip news from Hollywood. The teaser was all about Kayleigh's death. The promo said the circumstances of the drug overdose were "suspicious" and promised to provide details about who *might* be under investigation for murder.

"How does this little girl I've never heard of get so much coverage?" Mike mumbled.

"She's a young woman," Michelle scolded, "and she's a major social media influencer. Millions of people follow her every move. She's a celebrity, even if *you've* never heard of her."

"Oh, like you have?"

"No," Michelle admitted. "I haven't, either. But just because *we* aren't familiar with her doesn't mean she's a nobody."

"How does that even happen?" Mike threw up his arms. "How does a young woman like her, who's not a movie star or a singer or the daughter of a celebrity, get millions of followers on Instagram and TikTok? What did she ever do to become famous?"

Michelle slumped her shoulders. "I have no idea. The young people are addicted to content on their phones. They'll watch seemingly anything. Once something becomes a thing, everybody jumps on. We should really ask Star. She's a lot more plugged into this sort of thing than either of us."

"OK. The next time she comes over for dinner, we'll pick her brain. That should be pretty soon, at the rate you've been inviting her."

"Do you have a problem with having Star over for dinner?" Michelle's voice took on a sharp edge.

"No. Of course not. She's fine. It just seems like you're, well, hovering a bit with her."

Now Michelle was fully offended, standing with her hands on her slender hips. "I am not!"

"What I mean is that you need to let her be a college student. She's only been at school a few weeks, and it seems like she's eaten dinner with us more than with her classmates."

"I promised my sister I'd look after her. And she has had dinner here *three* times. That's not hovering."

Mike, realizing he was in an unwinnable argument, chose to backtrack. "I exaggerated. I'm sorry." He decided not to mention that they had also taken Star out to dinner twice. "I like her. She's a great girl."

"Woman," Michelle corrected.

"Right." Mike took a deep breath. "She's a great young woman. I like having her around. And I'd be very interested in letting her inform me about how these viral internet celebrities come to exist. I can probably learn a thing or two. You should invite her over Sunday night, when Jason and Rachel will be here." He raised his eyebrows and held out his palms, looking like an oversized Basset Hound who had been caught peeing on the carpet.

Michelle relented and softened her expression. "Good. See, you *can* be taught." She returned to her seat next to Mike on the sofa. "Shall we watch the segment about Kayleigh?"

"Sure. We can call it case research."

Mike settled in, putting an arm around his wife and sometimes teacher. He knew Michelle liked watching the celebrity gossip and Hollywood entertainment news. She loved movies and was a student of pop culture. Mike could watch the game later. The Mets' season was a lost cause. Management had traded away many of their top veterans for young prospects. They were playing out the string. Mike wondered if Nathan Matthews' lawyer felt the same way about his ongoing trial.

Chapter 20
Dim Sum

ON SATURDAY, JASON CALLED Mike and asked him to come to a meet-up with Nathan Matthews' PI, who said he had some new information. When Mike asked Michelle if she minded, she punched him in the arm and shooed him out the door. Mike and Jason were on their own time. Anything they did regarding the Ballet Murder case on the weekend could not get them in trouble, at least not much. Their trial testimony was done. What could it hurt?

Jason and Mike took different subways to lower Manhattan, meeting Sterling Wright at one of Mike's favorite restaurants, the Nom Wa Tea House on Doyers Street. Chinatown was always an interesting place to explore and Mike often brought out-of-town visitors to the Tea House for a unique meal. The place was not as informal and unknown as when Mike's uncle took him there thirty years earlier, but Wilson Tang still had a smile for the detective and whisked him to a table in the back corner. Jason arrived shortly after and they ordered a round of steamed pork buns while they waited for their third wheel.

When Sterling walked in, he looked uncomfortable and lost. There were few Black patrons in the place, but he saw

Jason waving from the back corner and made his way through the labyrinth of small tables to their booth.

He took a seat next to Jason and opposite Mike, then immediately launched into what appeared to be a prepared speech. "Thank you both for meeting with me. I know it's crazy to be talking about this while the trial is still going, but I finally have a lead on Brock Taylor. Thursday night I was at a club and I saw him meeting with another actor named Lawrence Teel. They had some kind of argument. Then, they had a fight in an alley. I'm thinking—"

"Wait a minute," Mike interrupted. "You're a little ahead of me. Let's take it slowly."

"I'm sorry." Sterling put both palms down on the table and took a deep breath. "I've been living this case for a year, along with Nathan, so I sometimes forget that you have been away from it for a while."

Before Sterling could continue, a waiter rolled up a metal cart filled with plates carrying steaming dumplings, wicker steamers containing buns with a variety of fillings, and other dim sum delicacies. Mike expertly selected dishes for the table and thanked the server.

While plucking dim sum items from his plate with chopsticks, Mike said, "Let me say that both Jason and I are here on our own time. We're not working this case. We worked it already. We both testified and supported the DA, who's trying to convict the guy. We're not doing anything to mess up his case. We're not working with you."

Mike paused. Sterling was paying attention without trying to interrupt.

"But we're both a little bit bothered by what the lawyer — and you — said about how easy the evidence was to find. How it seems to not make sense that the internet searches would be so clean and quick. I'm willing to entertain the idea, in theory, that there could have been another killer. This hypothetical other killer would have had access to Matthews' laptop, would have had a motive to kill Alex Bishop, and would have been able to either spike the guy's drink or get somebody else to do it. That's a lot of what-ifs. But it's possible our investigation wrapped up too soon, and that bothers me. We're not making any promises, but we're willing to talk. So, Brock Taylor. The understudy."

"Yeah," Sterling said, withdrawing his hands from the table and engaging his chopsticks. "Nathan has been doing nothing but think about this for the past year. Brock had his own issues with Alex, and also with Nathan. He had the best motive — at least after Max Bloom, who we already ruled out."

While they ate their dim sum, Sterling explained. Early on, Matthews thought the most likely person to have framed him for the murder was his business partner, Bloom. He suspected that Bloom wanted to sink the show and collect the insurance money once the early reviews came in. It was ironic, since Bloom had insisted on hiring Bishop as a "big name" for the show. Matthews and Bloom, along with several minor investors, were worried when the reviews were scathing and Bishop was singled out as a major problem. They figured the show was doomed. Pre-sales would take them only so far. The Tony Award nominations were perfunctory. There were only three new musicals still open when the nominations came out. They had to be nominated. They were giving out discounted seats and running daily lotteries to keep the theater full, but they anticipated closing after the awards show. Unless they miraculously won Best Musical, they were done. Even if they won, it would be a struggle.

Bloom was going to lose a lot of money, as was Matthews. But they had insurance on Bishop, because of his heart condition. And they took out separate business interruption insurance against the inability of their star to perform. The insurance money could save the producers from financial ruin if Bishop was unable to appear. If he died, they would recover twice. Bloom had become increasingly hostile toward Bishop during private conversations with Matthews, ranting about how it was going to be such a waste of his dead wife's estate money. Bloom had the motive and the opportunity to poison the guy's drink, although how he would have gotten the damning data on the laptop was the hole in the theory. Sterling never found evidence linking Bloom to the laptop. After nine months of fruitless investigation, Sterling gave up on Bloom and turned his attention to Taylor. By then, the trial was approaching.

"We know Max Bloom," Jason said. "We agree with your assessment; he's not smart enough to pull off the murder." Mike couldn't suppress a laugh while Jason continued. "It sounds like your client also had a motive to kill off his leading actor — same as Bloom or any other producer. The insurance angle only makes Matthews look more guilty. If Bloom were involved, I would immediately suspect that he had help, and your client would top the list."

"I know. That was always a problem. Of course, when Nathan got arrested, Boyds of Britain refused to pay off on the policy. When the show closed, all the producers took a bath on the investment. We knew the insurance policy would not pay off if Bloom was the killer, since he was also a producer. Nathan didn't care. He just wanted to find the real killer and save his ass from prison. But if Taylor was the killer, then Boyds would have to pay off."

"Which means your client has a built-in reason to accuse Taylor, both to save himself and to collect the money," Jason pointed out. "That makes him — and you — a pretty unreliable source."

"OK," Mike said through a mouthful of shrimp dumpling, "aside from wanting to get the show's leading man out of the way so he could be the star, what other motive would Taylor have for murdering Bishop?"

Sterling finished chewing a bite of pork bun and sipped from a tiny tea cup before speaking. "Taylor's girlfriend was also in *Godfather*. She dumped him and started sleeping with Nathan."

"And you think that gave him a particular motive to frame the director?" Jason picked up on the mental thread.

"Exactly!" Sterling stabbed a shrimp dumpling with a chopstick.

"That's another stretch," Mike said. "It's one thing to take out the guy in front of you in the pecking order, but doing it and framing the director? He gets the leading role *and* gets his girlfriend back at the same time, assuming she wants him back? And by doing that, he gives the police a ready-made suspect that takes suspicion off him? That's some kind of master criminal shit. You think he's that smart?"

"I don't know how smart he is. But he could have done it, and it all makes sense. You have to understand the whole story. Before Bishop came on, Taylor was supposed to play the part. It would have been his big Broadway break. He's been a supporting actor and singer in a bunch of shows, but never the lead. Then, the producers decided they needed a big name and brought in Bishop. All through rehearsals, Taylor told anybody who would listen that he could play the part much better."

"That could be every understudy on every show on Broadway, couldn't it?" Jason asked.

"Fair point, but Taylor was particularly pissed off. Bishop arrived late for one show. They said he was sick, so it was Taylor's chance to do a Saturday night performance. Then, Bishop waltzed in a few minutes before showtime and demanded that they delay the curtain so he could get ready. The director made Taylor go out in front of the curtain to inform the audience about the delay. It was so unprofessional and had Taylor all steamed up. That was three weeks before somebody poisoned Bishop."

"We heard all about that incident during the investigation," Jason said. "It was part of Matthews' motive. So, it points at him as much as anyone else."

Sterling nodded somberly. "I get it. But Taylor did end up back with Ginny before the show closed. I'll share with you, confidentially, that Nathan got her a better part in the show while Ginny was sleeping with him. He's not proud of it, but it's the truth. It's possible she was still seeing Taylor. She might even have been involved, somehow. I only know that I'm convinced Taylor is the guy."

Mike, who had been eating throughout, said, "It's all speculation. You have nothing but a theory. Plus, it would make just as much sense that the two of them — Matthews and Taylor — were working together toward the common goal of getting rid of Bishop."

Sterling sat back and dropped his hands. "You never investigated him, because you had your suspect. If we did a proper investigation now, we might find something."

Jason put a hand on Sterling's arm. "Taylor was one of the cast members who told us about how Matthews and Bishop had been fighting. He wasn't the only one, but I remember him being pretty specific. Almost like he wanted us to treat Matthews as a suspect."

Mike waved to a waiter passing near them with a tray of new dim sum offerings. He then pointed his non-chopstick hand toward Sterling. "What you may not realize, is that we did question the other members of the cast. Jason and I were reviewing our case notes in preparation for the trial. Taylor had an alibi for the night of the gala. He was performing in a drag revue at a club in Jersey that night. He gave us the name of the house manager. We never ran down the alibi after we focused in on Matthews, but it seems like a pretty solid story. And it could be discredited easily if it weren't true."

"Exactly!" Sterling sat forward in his chair. "It might have been a bald-faced lie, but you never checked it."

"Sure, it's possible." Jason tapped his chopstick on a water glass. "But it's a pretty specific story, and easy to verify. Let's assume it's legit. Does that take him out of play as a suspect?"

Sterling pointed his right index finger at Jason. "He could have had somebody else spike the drink at the cocktail hour."

"I know," Mike said soothingly, taking on his professorial voice. "The reality, however, is that most people don't have a ready supply of henchmen available to commit murder for them. A mob boss, maybe, but a struggling actor? It's highly unlikely a guy like Taylor would farm out the project in order to establish an alibi. My experience is that an amateur like this would do it himself, if he would do it at all. And if he had an accomplice, the most likely person is Nathan Matthews."

"Sure. I get it," Sterling reluctantly agreed. "But you said you never verified the alibi. You could do that now. If it doesn't check out, then you would have grounds to dig deeper. Will you at least do that?" He turned to look at Jason as he finished the plea.

Jason said, "We'll think about it."

"Anyway, what was it you were telling us about Taylor getting into a fight?" Mike sipped his tea from a tiny porcelain cup.

Sterling took a breath, switching mental gears. "I've been watching Taylor, to see if he did anything suspicious or gave me any opening to corner him and question him. I can't just barge into his home and I can't get a warrant like you. Anyway, I was watching him perform at a club in the Village Thursday night. He met with another actor named Lawrence Teel. They left the club together and I followed them into the alley. They had an argument and got into a fight. I tried to help Teel and dropped Taylor, but then Teel came after me and the two of them were on me. I decided I didn't want to kill anybody, so I got out."

"Does that explain the shiner on your forehead?" Jason pointed.

"Oh, yeah." Sterling touched the bump on his head. "I fell into a wall. I heard them talking before the fighting started. Taylor said he was worried about something, and Teel didn't understand why Taylor was so worried."

"About what?" Mike asked.

"I don't know. They didn't say. When I told them I was an ex-cop, Taylor said he thought I was working for *him*."

"Who's *him*?" Jason put down his chopsticks.

"I don't know. I doubt he could know that I'm working for Nathan."

"You're that good?" Mike said. "You think the guy is a super-villain and plotted out this elaborate murder. If that's true, why couldn't he know you're Matthews' PI?"

Sterling's shoulders slumped. "I guess it's not impossible. But I think there's somebody else."

"Like maybe Logan Summers?" Mike speculated. "Kayleigh was trying to avoid letting Logan know that she was sleeping with Taylor. Taylor might think Logan would hire a PI to follow him."

"What?" Sterling looked at his two brunch companions. "Are you talking about a different investigation?"

"We can't talk about that," Mike said. "You understand."

"I'm not sure what's happening in your other investigation. But you should definitely talk to Ginny Healey. She was practically living with Nathan in those few months. She hasn't come to visit Nathan, and refused to talk to me. I suspect she believes Nathan is guilty, but you should talk to her. She's currently in the chorus of *Hadestown*."

Mike nodded while sipping his tea. "Virginia Healey. Jason, wasn't she also among the witnesses who told us about Matthews' conflict with Bishop?"

"Yes. She was. I remember we knew she was romantically involved with Nathan. We viewed that as making her more credible. I don't remember anyone telling us that she had been involved with Taylor, but I doubt we ever asked. Something else we missed."

"Listen, Sterling," Mike wiped his mouth with the napkin he had plucked from his belt, "I understand you are fully invested in this case. You may be a little too invested. Too close to it. You're grasping at any straw you can, and you're getting into fights with suspects and witnesses. I get it. Am I right that you've got some money riding on it? Like you'll get a big payday if you can figure a way to get your client exonerated?"

"Sure," Sterling admitted. "That's true. I have a lot riding on this case, I won't lie. But I'm also a cop, like you. I know when something smells bad, and this whole case is a bag of July garbage rotting in the sun."

"You should be a poet," Jason quipped.

"Sure. Everybody needs a little side-hustle." Sterling nearly cracked a smile. "You're right that I've spent a lot of time thinking about this case. But that's why I'm so sure about it."

"OK." Mike wiped his hands and glanced down at his empty plate. "You've said your piece and given us a lot to think about. Give us a few days and we'll let you know if we find anything that supports a further investigation."

"So, you're going to look into the alibi?"

"I'm not promising anything," Mike said. "We have no jurisdiction and no open case file to work. I'm sure we'd never get authorization to re-open the investigation of a case at trial. But I'm willing to do a little off-the-books digging — just to see if there's anything there. To satisfy myself that we had a clean bust."

"Thank you, Detective." The PI reached across the table and grabbed Mike's hand awkwardly. "I respect you as a cop. I know you want to do the right thing."

"Sure," Mike said, retracting his hand.

"I appreciate you listening to me. I usually have trouble getting cops to give me the time of day."

"I know," Jason said. "I looked you up. I know about the run-in with your captain over the Black Lives Matter protest. The computer records don't say much about the incident that got you fired, but I assume there was some kind of mutual agreement. Am I right?"

Sterling pursed his lips in a pained expression. "Detective Dickson, nothing in the world would make me happier than to tell you the whole damned story. But I'm working under the terms of a confidentiality agreement and I am not allowed to give out any of those details. I'm sure you understand." Sterling then locked eye contact with Jason. "So I'm sure you'll be able to say I did not tell you anything about a bust where the perp was boosting a flat screen. Or how, when I told him to drop the TV, he threw it at me. Now, you might think it's reasonable to fire your weapon at a guy who may have been drawing a gun while you dodged the chunk of hardware. Others might consider it to be excessive force. Let's just say that when the cop involved is already in the doghouse for other reasons, something like that can become a firing offense. And, yeah, such situations often result in mutual separation agreements, especially after the detective involved accuses the department of racial bias. But you didn't hear it from me."

"We understand," Mike said. "I'll assume you made detective because you deserved it and you're smart. That's enough for me to go on. Until proven otherwise. Who knows? Maybe your guy will get acquitted, then it won't matter."

"That would be nice, but it won't bring back the sixteen months of his life Nathan has spent as an accused killer."

"He'll get the insurance money, though, won't he?" Jason pointed out.

"Maybe. I haven't even thought about that. I guess we'll see."

The three men all tossed bills onto the table to cover their food. Mike suggested that Sterling leave first, so they would not be seen walking together on the street. "I'm not paranoid,"

Mike chuckled, "but I like to assume somebody is always watching me."

After waiting three minutes while they chatted with Mr. Tang about his post-pandemic business, Mike and Jason walked into the shadows of Doyers Street. It was a narrow canyon of buildings that did not permit the sun to penetrate except at its zenith. They walked together in silence down Canal Street, past bustling storefronts, tables on the sidewalk strewn with goods, fish and produce markets, and jewelry stores.

When they got to the subway entrance where Mike would head back uptown, Jason pulled him aside into a quiet doorway. "We don't need to borrow trouble by investigating this guy's theories. Are you sure you're OK poking our noses back into this case? Sully will have a meltdown."

Mike looked into his partner's eyes. "I need to satisfy myself that there's not something here we missed the first time around. Maybe it won't take long. Maybe we'll be able to avoid even telling Sully what we're doing. I agree that we need to keep it under the table, at least for now. I assume you're on board and that you trust this guy?"

"Yes. I do."

"Not just because he's Black and got railroaded off the force?"

"No. It's not relevant."

"It is if we're doing this for him and not for ourselves." Mike cocked his head, inviting Jason to take the exit ramp if he wanted to.

"No. It's not for him. I mean, sure, I feel sorry for him. I can understand why cops go private. In his case, he didn't seem to have a choice. But it's the facts here that are itching at me. I won't sleep well at night unless we at least take another look."

"Good. I feel the same way. Go home and play with JJ and Rachel. You have class tonight, right?"

"True," Jason said.

"When do you get that master's in bullshit?"

"Master of Public Administration, as you well know, asshole."

"Oh, yeah. I seem to recall." Mike smiled.

"The graduation at Marist is in May. I should get the degree then. I'm looking forward to taking Rachel and JJ up the Hudson for it. It's beautiful, I hear. I figure even taking courses online I should get to wear a cap and gown and be there in person for it."

"Sounds nice. When the mayor makes you police commissioner, I guess I'll have to call you *Sir*, huh?"

"I'll insist on it." It was Jason's turn to smile.

"We'll see all three of you for dinner tomorrow night, right?"

"Yes. Rachel is looking forward to having some time with Michelle."

"Great. See you then. Monday morning we still have The Influencer case to work, but I think we'll find a few free minutes for some other research."

* * *

AFTER WATCHING MIKE DESCEND into the maw of the New York Subway system, Jason turned to walk back along Canal Street toward his train to Brooklyn. Before he took his second stride, Sterling fell into step with him.

"Thank you for supporting me," Sterling said. "I haven't had many cops on my side the last few years."

"We're not on your side, dude. We're doing this for ourselves. You're just a third-party beneficiary. Be glad you're private and you don't have to answer to the brass on this."

Sterling stopped in the middle of the sidewalk. When Jason had skidded to a stop a few feet ahead, Sterling said, "I thought it would be so easy, going private. It's been crazy hard. I'm in debt. All my settlement money is gone. If I can't get Nathan off, I'm not sure where the next client is coming from. I'll end up working night shift security somewhere."

"You'll do fine." Jason nudged Sterling into the alcove of a doorway, out of the flow of pedestrians. "Lots of police forces out there in the world if you want to move to Billings or Duluth."

"I'm not leaving New York. My whole family is here."

"OK. Then stay. Plenty of crime and fraud to go around." Jason laughed and merged back into the pedestrian stream. "Mike and I will let you know if we find anything. If we don't, then you and your client will be out of luck. We're not making this our life's work. But you have our attention."

"That's all I can ask for. Thank you."

"Don't thank me yet. I haven't done anything."

"Yes, you have. You've stuck your neck out, even a little bit, for me. It's been a while since that happened. I appreciate it."

"Fine. Now get away from me before somebody sees us talking." Jason pushed Sterling toward the curb, but smiled and waved as he ducked down the stairway into the subway to Brooklyn.

Chapter 21
A Third Opinion

AFTER A MORNING STROLL in Central Park and a bagel from Zabar's on Sunday, Mike and Michelle circled back to the apartment. Michelle busied herself in the kitchen, preparing food for their upcoming dinner party with the Dicksons. She had run across Broadway to get chicken nuggets for JJ and cod fillets for the adults, along with fresh veggies and a loaf of Italian bread.

Mike wanted to catch the end of the Mets game on TV. The team was in the crapper, but he was curious to see the new rookie sensation, Ronny Mauricio. Looking forward to the young players' future careers was about all that was left for Mets fans in the waning days of the season. During a commercial break, Mike ducked into the bathroom next to the guest bedroom, which served as the study, exercise room, and all-purpose storage closet.

Suddenly, Mike bellowed from the other side of the apartment, "Michelle? What the hell is this?"

"What, dear?" she called back calmly as she applied a coating of breadcrumbs and spices to the cod fillets.

Mike appeared in the archway separating the kitchen from the dining alcove, holding a gold-colored plastic bottle of hand soap. "When did we start using this junk in the bathroom? It smells like crap."

"I got it on sale at Bath & Body Works. It's called Sweet Cinnamon Pumpkin." Michelle did not look up from the fish, splayed on a baking sheet on the counter. Topsy sat at attention on a dining room chair, hoping for a scrap.

"Cinnamon pumpkin? Are you kidding me? I don't want this all over me. What happened to the regular anti-bacterial hand soap we've always had?"

Now Michelle looked at her husband. "We finally finished that big jug of liquid soap you must have bought back in the 90s. It was truly vile, Mike. It smelled like hemorrhoid ointment. Besides, you almost never use that bathroom. You still have your soap on your side of the sink in *our* bathroom, so you can use that if you don't like the good soap."

"It's not a question of good or bad," Mike fumed. "Don't you think I should be consulted before you put something with this kind of awful smell in the bathroom?"

"It's not awful. I like it. It's nice. It's welcoming to guests. It gives an autumn scent to the room, which is nice this time of year."

Mike held up the bottle, waving it toward the dining nook window as if contemplating tossing it to the pigeons. "It's just — I mean — there have to be better scents than this."

Michelle wiped off her hands on a tea towel hanging from her apron, branded with the logo of the New York City PBS station. She slipped her arms around Mike's waist, pulling him into a gentle hug and resting her face against his neck. "I know it hasn't been easy for you, living together in one place. For the record, I had the same soap in my bathroom in the 23rd Street apartment for years. You never complained about it there. But I get it. I'll make sure to invite you to come with me next time I go to Bath & Body Works."

Mike set the bottle on the dining table, then put his arms around Michelle. He gently massaged her back and laughed. "I did *not* say I want to go soap shopping with you."

"Well, if you want some say, then you have to come along. It's only fair."

Mike pulled back his head so he could look Michelle in the eye. "I just want some things to stay the same."

"Sorry, bub. Nothing stays the same. You're a hard man to change, but little by little I'm going to make you into a modern human."

"What was I before?"

"A cop." She swung her tea towel and brushed Mike's face. "Oh, and remember, I invited Star to join us for dinner.

Mike pulled Michelle's head gently back to his shoulder. "She and Rachel love each other. And Topsy adores her. That cat loves everyone but me."

* * *

DINNER WAS A CACOPHONOUS AFFAIR for the first hour and a half, with much cooing and fussing over JJ from both Michelle and Star. Then there was a period of shrieking when JJ was not happy with the quality of his chicken nuggets.

Star and Rachel dominated the dinner-table conversation with a lengthy discussion of the merits of different Broadway shows. Despite her youth, Star was an aficionado of soundtracks for shows she had never seen live. Rachel was thrilled to have a companion who shared her love of theater.

When Michelle brought out the coffee, JJ was happily playing with Topsy in the living room. Rachel grabbed her phone and spent three minutes taking photos of her son's happy face. When she showed Michelle and Star the shots, they both marveled at how good they were.

"He may not like looking at the camera, but he loves looking at Topsy," Star observed.

When everyone had made a sufficient fuss over the photos, Mike and Jason told the ladies about their discussion with Sterling Wright. With their trial testimony over, they had no concerns about maintaining confidentiality. However, they made sure Rachel knew they were strictly off the record, as far as her pals at ACN might be concerned.

"We'll check out the understudy's alibi for the night of the ballet gala," Mike said. "But we already looked at the security tapes to see if we could identify anyone serving Bishop a spiked drink. We weren't specifically looking for Taylor, but I'm guessing we would have recognized him if he had been there."

"Oh, Uncle Mike," Star spoke up in a disappointed voice. "I mean, c'mon. The guy's an *actor*. It's the oldest trick in the theater book. If I were an actor and wanted to be there to kill Alex Bishop, I would come in a disguise. He had access to professional makeup and costumes. It would be easy."

"The girl has a point," Rachel agreed.

"It's certainly possible," Jason agreed, "but he still says he was somewhere else. We'll be able to pin that down one way or the other."

Mike held out his hand across the table to get the group's attention. "If I'm remembering right, Taylor's alibi is that he was performing in a club in Jersey, in a drag show. Do you have the same memory?"

"Yeah, Mike. That sounds right."

"Wait!" Rachel exclaimed. "If it was a drag show, maybe Jackie can give you a lead." Rachel's younger brother, Jackie, was a professional drag performer. He had relocated back to New York from Las Vegas after Rachel and Jason's wedding there in early 2020. Since he came back home, there had been none of the excitement that the wedding party experienced in Vegas. They all appreciated the relative calm.

Mike pulled back his hand. "I wasn't even thinking about that. I presume we can talk to the show's producer, or director, or the venue, and get the record of who got paid for that night's performance. That will tell us whether he was there or not."

"Uncle Mike," Star broke in, "you're still not thinking like an actor. If he was supposed to be in the drag revue and he wanted to have a good alibi, he would have somebody else perform in his place. In a drag costume, you'd never know it wasn't him."

Mike pondered Star's observation. "You have a devious mind, Star. Are you sure you're not a master criminal?"

After everyone stopped laughing, Rachel said, "I'm not sure you're right, Star. Drag performers have very specific costumes and makeup, not to mention performance style. It wouldn't be easy for Taylor to send in an imposter. His fans would know it wasn't him."

Star dropped her head. "I guess I have some things to learn."

"Of course you do," Michelle put an arm around her niece's shoulder. "That's why you're at NYU. When you graduate, then you can be a master criminal."

Star laughed. "I certainly hope to be a master of something on Broadway one day."

"It's a tough road," Rachel said, "but you're young and full of energy, so you go for it. If it doesn't work out, let it not be because you didn't give it your best shot."

"It's all still speculation and hypotheticals," Mike said, bringing the discussion back on track. "We'll need some actual evidence. But we can start by checking out the alibi and go from there. We can also try to talk with Miss Healey, although that will be a little harder, because we have no actual case to investigate."

Michelle pressed some bread into her plate, sopping up the last bits of garlic and lemon juice. "Since when has having no authorization stopped you? I recall a completely unauthorized undercover operation in a Brooklyn hotel—"

"Alright," Mike waved for Michelle to stop, tilting his head toward Star. "Point taken. But I didn't have much of a choice with . . . what was her name?"

"Steph," Jason offered, flashing a satisfied look at Mike.

"Sure. Steph Bettger. She was going with us or without us, as you recall. And it was *you* who couldn't keep her under control when she ran away—"

"Alright, fine. Maybe not the best example. The point is that you have never let the absence of permission stop you from following a lead or doing what you thought was right. I also recall a cruise where you were told specifically that you didn't have any jurisdiction and were forbidden to conduct an unauthorized investigation. So don't tell me the problem now is that Sully won't let you."

Mike gave a guttural *hrummpff* as he slumped back into his chair. "At this point, the trail is so cold, it's not likely that we'll be able to find the real killer. If there even is one."

"Mike, what do you want me to say, huh?" Michelle asked. "You want me to give you permission to forget about it?

What if Nathan Matthews gets convicted? Are you going to let the guy rot in prison? Fine. I give you permission. It's not your problem. If you can sleep at night and forget about it, then go ahead."

Mike rose from his chair, letting out a soft groan, then stretched his back from side to side. "It's been a nice dinner. I'm sure I'll sleep fine tonight."

Fifteen minutes later, the guests exchanged hugs and kisses as they departed the apartment. Michelle prepared a doggy bag of leftovers for Star to take back to NYU.

While they were doing the clean-up, Mike said, "Your niece is pretty sharp."

"Don't underestimate the women in my family," Michelle replied. "We're not big, strong, and mean, but we pack a punch when we need to and we don't get fooled by men."

"I'll have to watch out, then." Mike grabbed a white garbage bag and headed out to the trash chute.

Chapter 22
Missing Links

ON MONDAY, MIKE AND JASON were back on The Influencer case. The media coverage and internet speculation had only grown six days out from Kayleigh's death. Sully was getting daily inquiries from the commissioner's media director, asking for updates. Unfortunately, the detectives had only questions.

"We got the forensics back on the girl's laptop." Jason held up his phone, as if Mike would be able to read it.

"Anything helpful?"

"Not really. Plenty of videos featuring The Pharmacist, but nothing we didn't already know about or have on her phone. A bunch of TikTok video drafts and edits, but nothing relevant."

"I guess we don't always get critical evidence from the laptop." Mike turned back to the file their research team had prepared over the weekend on Logan Summers. They had instructed Officer Konopka to add references to Summers to her search of the dead girl's social media accounts.

The more they looked into the voluminous publicly available information on the Wall Street tycoon, the more they disliked him. He contributed millions to charitable causes, which seemed mostly organized by his wives. But his business reputation was that of a bully. Over his three employers, no fewer than six lawsuits named him as a defendant. The allegations ranged from securities violations to financial fraud to sexual harassment. All the filed suits had been resolved through confidential settlements. Mike and Jason speculated that, for every suit filed, several were settled before litigation. His reviews as a boss on two internet crowd-sourcing sites were decidedly negative.

In his personal life, Summers' current wife had filed for divorce four months earlier. The power couple was known enough that their marital strife was covered on Page Six of *The New York Post*, and in other society gossip sources. She alleged that Summers had multiple extra-marital affairs, that he had abused her physically and emotionally, and that he had used illegal drugs in the presence of his children. It was messy. Oddly, however, the gossip pages did not identify Kayleigh as one of the women with whom Summers was sexually involved.

"Maybe they just haven't found out yet," Jason suggested.

"They didn't seem to be trying to keep it a secret," Mike observed. "All those kids knew about it."

"You think his wife knew?"

"Probably," Mike said. "We'll have to talk to him at some point, but I'd still like to have a better idea of how much of a suspect he really is."

Jason tapped his finger on the table. "He might be trying to hide the whole thing from his wife."

"True, although it sounds like she has plenty of dirt on him already." Mike leaned back, stretching. When his cell buzzed, Mike answered before the second ring. "What have you got, Officer Konopka?" After thirty seconds, Mike switched to speaker for Jason.

"I've been scouring the information on her phone, but I haven't found a single real reference to Logan Summers. There are lots of references to her 'squeeze' and her 'honey bear,' but nothing with the guy's name. It's like she knew he didn't want to be outed, so she was careful."

"That tracks with the information we have. I'll give you ten to one that's our Logan."

"Sure. Now, what do we do with it?" Jason asked.

"We don't have any evidence yet that he gave Kayleigh fentanyl without her knowledge, even assuming he was there and brought her the Montezuma's Delight."

Jason pulled out his wallet and placed a five-dollar bill on Mike's desk. "Five bucks says he was there. He was probably the guy we saw on the video hiding behind the umbrella."

"I won't take that bet," Mike chuckled. "Maybe he did it, but she knew about it and consented, like it was another crazy drug combo she wanted to try. Regardless, unless we can put the fentanyl in Summers' hand, we've got a big hole in our theory."

"You're probably right. Remember what Sophie said. Sometimes it's what's missing that's important."

Mike shrugged. "The problem is figuring out what's missing."

Chapter 23
This Meeting Never Happened

MIKE AND JASON MET with Captain Sullivan about their plan to pay a surprise visit to Logan Summers' office. Sully agreed that the information they had accumulated warranted an interview, even if the guy was likely to immediately lawyer up and not answer any questions. But, since Summers was such a high-profile member of the community and was so well connected to local politicians, Sully asked his detectives to put off the visit until later in the day. That way he could alert the commissioner in case the shit hit the fan.

"That works for us, Cap," Mike quickly agreed.

"It does?" Sully furrowed his brow, immediately skeptical. "You're usually gung ho to catch your witness — or maybe suspect — off guard. Aren't you worried that somebody will give the creep a heads up and take away your element of surprise?"

"I am, Sully, of course. But charging ahead without clearing the political decks usually gets me in trouble, and puts you in a tough spot. Michelle is trying to teach me discretion, and I'm trying to learn."

Sully turned to Jason. "You agree, Dickson?"

"Absolutely, Sir. We have a few other things to chase down today."

"OK, then." Sully still looked bothered by the absence of objection. "Get out of here. I'll call you when I've got clearance from the commissioner."

Back in the bullpen, Jason quietly said, "You were right. I owe you five dollars."

"Let's jump," Mike replied, "before something else comes in needing official attention."

They exited the precinct and turned left toward Columbus Avenue. At Broadway and 96th, they hopped the express #3 train downtown and were at the Times Square stop in six minutes. "When the subway works, it's amazingly efficient," Mike remarked as they walked north toward 48th street and the Walter Kerr theater, home of the Tony Award-winning musical *Hadestown.*

Inside the main lobby, a flash of their badges convinced the teenager behind the ticket window to buzz them through the cast door into the backstage area. The space was quiet at nine-thirty on a Monday morning. Two stagehands confronted the detectives, but pointed them to the stage manager's office once they identified themselves.

The stage manager was a woman whom Mike could only say was somewhere between thirty and sixty-five. Her face was made up with care. Her red hair, a color unlikely to be natural, was styled to resemble Lucille Ball's. She wore a cream-colored, tailored blouse with an open collar, displaying a huge red gemstone dangling on a delicate gold chain. Her lower body was concealed behind a large desk made of dark, polished wood. The office itself was dingy, appearing not to have been modernized since the theater was built in the 1930s.

In a thick accent Mike thought was likely Queens or Long Island, she said, "Can I help you?" She did not seem intimidated by the appearance of two cops.

"I'm Detective Stoneman, NYPD. This is my partner, Detective Dickson. We're interested in having a conversation with one of your cast members, Virginia Healey."

"Is she in trouble?"

"No," Jason said, "she's a witness. We can't discuss the case. She's not in trouble. Can you give us a cell phone number or tell us how to get in touch with her?"

"She'll be right here in a half-hour. There's a dance team rehearsal 'cause we got two new dancers and they gotta do a run-through with the choreographer. She'll probably be here early, 'cause they know if they're late they'll get reamed out for it. You can talk to her as long as she's on stage at ten. She'll probably be hanging out on the side stage. You gonna recognize her?"

"Thanks." Mike motioned to Jason to leave the office. "We know what she looks like."

They followed a narrow corridor until it opened up to the area between the dressing rooms and the stage, segmented by thick, black curtains hanging from the high ceiling that shielded activity offstage from the audience. Several young men and women wearing tights, leotards, and sweat pants were stretching on the hardwood or congregating in small clusters. They scrutinized the faces, looking for their actress.

Within a few minutes, their quarry appeared, walking casually toward them. She wore a baggy gray sweatshirt with a Hunter College logo and black yoga pants. Her blonde hair was pulled back into a ponytail. She wasn't wearing any makeup, but her smooth skin and the heart-shaped face below blue eyes made her stand out in any crowd.

Jason intercepted her before she reached her castmates. "Miss Healey?"

"Yes?" she responded, curious, but not hostile. For all she knew, Jason was a casting director looking for actresses.

Jason flashed his badge. "I'm Detective Dickson, NYPD, I know you have a ten o'clock rehearsal, but can we talk to you for just a few minutes?"

"About what?" Ginny turned off her actress-available-for-hire demeanor and seemed nervous.

"I'd rather not say out here where other people can hear," Jason said in a hushed voice. "Let's step over to the wings." He gestured toward an area near the edge of the stage, between two curtains that would mute any conversation. Mike joined him and flanked the actress as they escorted her away from prying ears.

Knowing they were up against a deadline, Jason got right to the point. "Miss Healey, we're doing a follow-up investigation concerning the murder of Alex Bishop last year, when you were in the cast of *Godfather*. You're not a suspect, but we need some information and hope you can help us."

"Wait," Ginny said, "Nathan Matthews did it. He's on trial."

"That's right," Mike jumped in, "but we believe there were others involved. You were, well, friendly with Mr. Matthews before the whole thing happened, right?"

"I was sleeping with him. Everybody knows that." The woman did not seem offended by the question, nor embarrassed by it.

"I realize it was a long time ago, but you may remember that, on the night of May 7, 2022, somebody ran some internet searches on Matthews' laptop computer. We understand he kept the laptop in his office and that the office was generally locked. Is that right?"

"Yes. I told all this to the officers who talked to me last year. Wait, weren't you the same ones?"

"Detectives. Yes, we are. And thank you for your cooperation then. Nathan Matthews' story was that he attended a Directors Guild dinner and left the office around six o'clock, a half-hour before the searches happened. Do you recall confirming those facts last year?"

"Yes. I did."

"But you didn't go to the dinner with him."

"No."

Mike snuck a glance at Jason, then continued. "Who in the cast and crew would have had access to the director's office that night, when he wasn't there?"

"Anybody would, if he left the door unlocked. The theater is pretty secure, but anyone who had backstage access could have gotten in."

"He didn't lock the office when he wasn't there?"

Ginny paused for a moment. "He usually did, but I don't know that he did every night, or on that particular night." She looked out at the main stage, where a few of her colleagues were milling about. "But, even if somebody got into the office, his laptop had a password."

Jason asked, "Did you know the password?"

"No," Ginny immediately responded.

"Who did know?"

"I'm not sure. Probably Rich, the stage manager. He needed to input cast assignments on the master schedule when there were switches. Maybe the choreographer. I'm really not sure. Listen, I need to stretch and get ready for rehearsal."

"We know," Jason said. "Just a few more things. We need to talk to some other cast members that we're having trouble finding. Do you know how we might contact Brock Taylor?"

Ginny pursed her lips as if she'd done a shot of sour tequila without a lime. "I haven't seen him in a year."

Jason raised an eyebrow. "Really? We heard that, after Matthews was arrested, you and Mr. Taylor got back together."

"Well, alright, fine. Yes, we hooked back up for a while after the whole shit show, but that was ages ago. I haven't seen the asshole in months."

"Why is he an asshole?" Mike stepped in, causing Ginny to turn her head.

"He's just a jerk sometimes," she said. "And he's bi, so it was crazy being with him when he was hitting on some guy right in front of me. I got fed up with it and after the show closed, we split."

"One more thing," Mike said. "Do you know if Taylor was a drug user?"

"Ha!" she burst out. "That I will gladly tell you. Brock was crazy into drugs. He did everything. It's amazing he could hold it together for performances. He was into a YouTuber called The Pharmacist who cooked up weird combinations. Brock was always trying these cocktails of pills and coke and shit to see what happened, when he could afford it. I was not a fan. He had a medicine cabinet in his place filled with pill bottles. You can get him for drug possession any time you want."

"I'm glad you're not protecting the asshole," Mike quipped.

"He can kiss my ass," Ginny said, then turned to Mike with pleading eyes. "Look, I've told you all I know. I gotta go." She looked back and forth at the two detectives. When neither tried to stop her, she dashed away onto the stage, shedding her sweatshirt and tossing it into the front-row seats.

Mike and Jason exited the theater and paused outside the stage door. Mike said, "She absolutely knew the password. She was too quick saying that she didn't know. Like she had thought about it. Nothing we can prove, but it's suspicious."

"You think she might have given it to the asshole?"

Mike paused. "I would not say never. They were together, then she dumped him to fuck her way to a better part. She may have still been seeing Taylor on the side. Before she decided he was an asshole, she might have helped him get access to the laptop. Maybe she didn't know what he was going to do. Hell, maybe he wasn't doing anything. We're still only speculating that Taylor planted the evidence. He still has an alibi. So, it's a huge maybe."

"We'll have Sterling ask Matthews if he ever shared his password with Ginny." Jason already had his phone out to send a text. When he finished, he looked up. "Off to Jersey?"

Chapter 24
The Stress Factory

THE STRESS FACTORY WAS AN ALL-PURPOSE VENUE, with food, a full bar, tables and waiters, and a small stage at the front of the room. The venue hosted mostly stand-up comedy, but the owner, comedian Vinny Brand, filled in slow nights with music and drag shows. Mike and Jason stood in the empty hostess area inside the main entrance waiting to speak with Vinny or his house manager.

When Mike's phone buzzed, he listened intently for thirty seconds after answering, then hung up without speaking another word. "That was Sully. He says we have clearance to interview Summers."

"Great," Jason replied while studying his own text messages. "He doesn't know we're in Jersey, right?"

"Right," Mike confirmed. "Hopefully this won't take too long."

Mike noticed a large poster on the wall listing the upcoming dates and acts. Monday appeared to be drag night. The show scheduled for that evening was titled "Drag Jeopardy," with host Trinity K. Bonet, a former winner on *RuPaul's Drag Race.*

"I should let Jackie know about this. He loves that queen," Jason remarked. "Remember, from Vegas?"

Before Mike could confirm or deny his memory of the Vegas drag show at Senor Frog's, a concerned-looking middle-aged man wearing a tan sport jacket emerged through a camouflaged doorway next to the hostess station. "I'm the venue manager, Jerry Kauff," the man said, extending a hand in the general direction of both detectives. "How can I help you?"

Jason reached for the hand and gave it a firm shake. "I'm Detective Jason Dickson. This is my partner, Mike Stoneman. NYPD." Jason pulled out his badge and ID, which Kauff glanced at. "We're looking for someone who can help us verify a performance that took place last May."

Kauff didn't seem phased by the request. "May I inquire what this is about?"

Jason exchanged a quick glance with Mike. "It involves a homicide investigation. We're not at liberty to give you many details. I'm sure you understand. The information is not confidential, but it will help us verify a few things. We are hoping to get your cooperation without needing a subpoena."

"Of course," Kauff replied. The owners of businesses tended to be cooperative, unless they were mob fronts or otherwise involved in criminal activity. A legitimate businessperson was more worried about the prospect of losing a day's revenue if the cops closed them down during an investigation, or scared away their customers with an obvious police presence. Although Mike and Jason had no jurisdiction in New Jersey, they could solicit cooperation from the local police. Cooperation and a quick exit from the cops was far preferable to protecting someone's privacy. "Can you tell me what information you need, before I agree?"

"We're looking to verify the names of the performers who were on stage on the twenty-third of May last year. Our notes say the show was a Broadway drag revue. Does that sound familiar?"

Kauff nodded. "We do those shows several times a year. They're quite popular. We have drag shows most Mondays. I can't say I remember that show in particular, but I'm sure we have records. What exactly are you looking for?"

"Let's start with payment records," Jason suggested. "Do you have a list of the performers you paid for that gig?"

"I'm sure I do, back in my office. Would you gentlemen care to wait here, or accompany me?"

"We'll tag along," Mike said, falling into line behind Kauff and Jason.

Through the hidden doorway, a dimly lit corridor snaked through the bowels of the building. At the end of a narrow hallway, Kauff stopped and opened a door labeled "Manager."

"Sorry about the mess. Have a seat and I'll see what I can find for you." He gestured toward two stocky chairs opposite a desk piled so high with papers and other debris that Mike could not say whether the surface was wood or metal. Overhead fluorescent lights brightly lit the space. Framed photos hung on most of the wall space, depicting performers who had graced the club's stage. Kauff sat at his desk and began clicking his computer mouse while staring at a large monitor, the contents of which neither detective could see. "May 23, 2022, right?"

"Right," Jason replied.

"OK. Here we go. We did have a Broadway drag revue that night, so you got that part right. Eight o'clock."

"Sure," Jason said. "We're interested in the show performers."

"Anyone in particular?"

"I'd rather not say. If you can give us the full list, that would be best." Jason crossed his legs, as if settling in to stay as long as necessary. He wanted to make it clear to Kauff that they were not leaving until they got what they wanted. If he intended to do any other work, he needed to get them out by providing the records.

"That's probably fine. But there's some personal information here — social security numbers and phone numbers and such. Also the amount of money each performer got paid. Would you mind if I hide that data?"

"We don't need social security numbers." Jason wanted to be conciliatory. "But please leave in the phone numbers in case we need to contact any of them. Also, can you tell me how you paid the talent? Was it a check, or cash, or a bank deposit?"

"Checks," Kauff answered. "We have a service that cuts and mails the checks."

"Great." Jason winked at Mike. A check was helpful because it could provide information about what bank account it was deposited to and sometimes an example of a signature. They didn't know whether that information would be needed, but it was good to have available. "Please print us out the names of the performers who were paid."

"The names on the checks won't match their stage names, mostly," Kauff said.

"That's OK. We need the real names."

Kauff clicked his mouse a few more times. A cube-shaped printer in the corner sprang to life and spit out two pages into a plastic tray. Kauff handed one copy to each detective. "This is the list, one for each of you. The performance date and title of the show are listed. Is that all you need?"

Mike and Jason both scanned the list. Brock Taylor's name was listed alphabetically with the other performers. Mike said, "Not a surprise."

"What's not a surprise?" Kauff inquired.

"Oh, no, that wasn't a question," Mike stiffly replied. "We expected to see one of the names. I don't suppose there is anyone here who would have a specific memory of that night's performance? Someone who could verify whether one particular performer was really here?"

"I doubt it," Kauff said. "Of course, if somebody didn't show up for their slot, then we wouldn't pay 'em. Anyone on that list was certainly here. We're not in the habit of paying no-shows."

Jason folded the paper and inserted it into his jacket pocket. "It's as solid as we thought," he said to Mike.

"What about what Star said?" Mike leaned toward Jason, speaking quietly, "About Taylor maybe getting somebody else to cover for him?"

"Do you mean a substitute performer?" Kauff asked.

"Good ears," Mike said, raising his voice back to normal volume. "Yeah. Somebody suggested to us that a performer could get a sub to fill in for him at the last minute, which would make it look like he was here when he really wasn't."

"Well, I've never known a performer to let somebody else get paid for their gig. The people who got paid are almost certainly the people who performed. If a substitute showed up, we would make sure to pay them and not the no-show. Of course, if you wanted to check, you could look at the tape."

"Tape?" Mike and Jason said together.

"We record all the shows," Kauff said matter-of-factly. "I think we may erase the files after a few years, but I'm pretty sure we'd still have this one."

Mike gave Jason a weary look; they should have thought to ask for video of the performance in the first place. "A copy of the video would be helpful."

Five minutes later, with a thumb drive in his pocket containing an mp4 file of the performance, Mike exited the Stress Factory with Jason on his heels. While standing on the platform, waiting for the NJ Transit train back to Manhattan, Mike said, "We can't use a uniformed officer to review this for us, so we'll have to do it ourselves."

"Why not have Rachel do it? She's tuned into this stuff. She'd love it. I bet Jackie would even help."

"Great idea. Have Rachel watch the video and confirm that Taylor was really there performing." Mike held out the portable storage device.

Jason pocketed the drive. "Sure. It will make her happy."

"Alright. We can't say for sure whether the video will support the alibi, but the payroll records certainly confirm it. If he's on the video, then he's out as a suspect, unless you can think of any way he could have been in both places at once."

"Agreed. And I'm still bothered by Ginny Healey's evasiveness. Something's going on there."

"We'll see." Mike consulted his watch. "We need to get to Wall Street."

Chapter 25
Following the Money

THE OFFICES OF GOLD STAR INVESTMENTS, LLC were as opulent and impressive as Mike and Jason expected from a big-money Wall Street hedge fund. Any clients coming to this office would be worth millions and would expect their investment advisors to exude the same wealth and status. The rich and powerful were at ease when surrounded by the bold and beautiful. It made them more comfortable when they didn't have to feel guilty about their affluence.

The two homicide detectives were out of place in this environment, which was a corollary intention of the interior designers. Anyone who did not belong should feel intimidated and uncomfortable. But Mike and Jason had taken down rich criminals before and were not worried about being on Logan Summers' home turf. They wanted him to feel invincible and untouchable so that he might accidentally volunteer something useful. If they dragged him to the precinct and put him in an interrogation room, he would demand a lawyer and clam up tighter than a nun's knickers.

They met building security in the lobby and identified themselves to the receptionist. She scanned their ID cards and badges, then called up to the 57th floor to inquire whether the detectives should be admitted. They identified Summers as the person they were there to see without an appointment. After a five-minute wait, the lobby attendant gave them laminated temporary ID cards that would get them past the turnstiles guarding access to the elevator bank. Once on the Gold Star floor, a brightly dressed receptionist asked them what their business was with Mr. Summers.

"Tell him we're investigating the death of a young woman with whom Mr. Summers is acquainted, and that we assume he would prefer we not give out any additional information," Mike said politely.

They waited on a plush sofa with a Hudson River view, wondering whether Summers would agree to speak. Mike hoped his message via the receptionist would convey a willingness to be discreet, which would make him more inclined.

After five minutes, a woman in a tight-fitting black skirt and matching jacket walked into the waiting area on stiletto heels. "Detectives?" Mike and Jason stood, not sure whether they were being admitted or asked to leave. "Mr. Summers will see you now. Please follow me." She strode down a carpeted hallway with remarkable speed, given her precarious footwear. Mike and Jason hurried after.

At the threshold of a room with a smoked glass exterior, she halted and beckoned them forward with an outstretched arm, like Vanna White inviting them to the stage. Mike entered first and, despite himself, was impressed by the view of the Jersey City skyline across the river. The sun glinted off the windows of recently constructed office towers. The room seemed larger than its square footage because of the floor-to-ceiling windows. At a conference table topped with a dark red wood, two men made eye contact without standing. They had positioned themselves on the far side of the table, so their guests would have to squint toward the bright windows during any conversation.

It was an intentional power play. Mike suspected that the windows either had hidden shades that could drop down to shield the sun or were coated with a surface that could be turned opaque at the touch of a button. He did not ask for such consideration, happy to let their host have every perception of a home-field advantage.

Mike recognized Summers from all the photos of him they had been scrutinizing. He was a large man, both in height and girth, with a shock of black hair slicked back from his forehead in a way that Mike suspected was hiding a bald patch. He had wide eyes with an exceptionally large amount of white showing around brown irises. His square chin was slightly out of place on his bloatedly round face. The other man was older, with graying hair on both sides of his gaunt cheeks, wire-rimmed spectacles, and a dark gray pinstriped suit with a paisley maroon tie.

It was the older man who spoke first. "Detective Stoneman. Detective Dickson. My name is Marvin Powell. I am the general counsel for Gold Star Investments. In that capacity I am here as counsel for the company and I am, for now, serving as personal counsel for Mr. Summers. I will insist that any questioning happen in my presence, but Mr. Summers wants to cooperate with your investigation and has agreed to speak with you. Are you going to read him his Miranda rights?"

Mike chuckled. "No, Mr. Powell. Mr. Summers is not under arrest, and since he already has you here as his attorney, I don't think it's necessary to advise him of his rights. I'm sure you have already done that."

"I have," the lawyer replied flatly. "We presume you are here to talk about the unfortunate death of Ms. Kayleigh Bronson?"

"That's right." Mike turned away from the lawyer and addressed his questions directly to Summers. "Mr. Summers, can you confirm that you are the owner of the apartment in the Park Towers where Miss Bronson died?"

"Yes," Summers said, clearly expecting the question and showing no inclination to provide any further information. He likely had been instructed by his counsel to say no more than absolutely necessary.

"Can you also confirm that you were present at a party in the apartment last Monday night?"

"I was."

Mike pegged Summers as someone who had been deposed in multiple litigations. He fixed his eyes on Mike as he spoke each answer, letting the detective know that he was not the least bit intimidated and was fully in control. His facial expressions provided no hint of deception. Mike thought it would be interesting to play poker with this man.

"What time did you arrive?"

For the first time, Summers hesitated before answering. "It was late. Probably after eleven o'clock, but I'm not sure."

"When did you leave?"

For this answer, Summers seemed prepped. "Shortly after midnight."

"Can you tell us what your relationship was with Ms. Bronson?"

"Detective, I presume you have done your homework. You know I am going through a very public divorce at the moment. As you can imagine, such questions are a bit sensitive because they imply something that is simply not there. I identified this young woman as an up-and-coming influencer on social media. People like her have a growing, well, *influence* on a wide variety of issues. Mostly, they can move markets and affect product sales merely by mentioning things in their videos. I decided to befriend her and help her with her finances. She may be a major client of this firm someday. She also can help me subtly plug a stock or talk about an industry group in a way that will influence her followers to invest — or sell. All well within FTC regulations and approved by international regulators."

"And that business relationship includes putting her up in your swanky apartment?"

"Correct. It's an investment."

"So, you're telling us you are not involved with her in a sexual relationship?"

"That's correct."

"So, you didn't take her on a trip to Paris?"

Summers' eyes flashed a hint of surprise, but he maintained his general composure. "I had a marketing trip to Paris and invited Ms. Bronson to come along. I introduced her to several people in France who might be future clients of hers as well as mine. It was a business trip."

Mike gave Jason a subtle signal to jump in. He did. "Listen, Sir, we don't give a rat's ass where you stick your dick. It's none of our business and we're not interested in providing information to your wife's divorce lawyer. But we need you to be straight with us if we're going to find her killer."

"Killer!?" Summers' voice shot up a half-octave and filled the room with his surprise and alarm. His lawyer put a hand gently on his arm, a reminder to keep quiet and only answer the questions asked. Summers, however, was not easily controlled. "I understood that her death was an accidental overdose."

Mike resumed the lead. "It might have been. Do you know who provided her cocaine Monday night?"

"No," came the terse response, again feeling rehearsed.

"Did you share any of her cocaine at the party?"

"No." Summers was back to minimalist mode.

"We have information from several party-goers that there was a large amount of drug use. Did you witness that?"

"No. I did not see anyone consuming illegal drugs."

"What about at other parties you have attended at the apartment since Kayleigh moved in?" Mike fell into the familiar use of Kayleigh's first name.

"I have not been to many such parties, Detective, and I can't say that I recall."

Mike decided to change gears. "Are you familiar with a personality on YouTube called The Pharmacist?"

Summers' eyes darted to the ceiling momentarily, a small chink in the man's poker face. He again hesitated. Mike figured the financial whiz was calculating how much trouble he could get himself into if he lied. "The name rings a bell, but I don't recall."

"Let me help you, Sir. He recommends drugs and drug combinations to his followers, encouraging them to mix things like cocaine with over-the-counter drugs and herbal supplements and such. The goal is achieving a special kind of high. Does that help you ring your mental bell?"

"I do recall some people talking about this," Summers said slowly, thinking while he spoke. "Do you think that the poor girl died from a reaction to some drug combination recommended by this, um, Pharmacist person?"

"It's one of the theories we're following," Jason cut back in. "Another possibility is that somebody spiked her cocaine with a substance that had a bad interaction and killed her, either accidentally or intentionally. If it was intentional, it would be murder. Would you know anyone who was at the party who might have done that?"

"No, Detective. I would not."

"Were you ever in her bathroom, in the master suite, during the party Monday?" Jason followed up.

"I recall using the bathroom, Detective, but I don't recall whether it was the master bath or the guest bath."

"So, you could have possibly gone into the master bathroom?"

Summers looked annoyed. "Detective, may I remind you that I own the apartment. If I choose to use the master bathroom, that's my prerogative."

"So, that would explain your fingerprints being there?"

"Yes," Summers said quickly, a glimmer of a smile touching the edges of his lips, then vanishing.

"But," Jason pressed, "when you were in the master bathroom, you did not see any lines of cocaine laid out on the granite countertop, or any bags or bottles of drugs?"

"No."

"I understand that this party was on the date of Kayleigh's one-year anniversary of living in the apartment. Did you know that?"

"Yes. That's the reason I showed up, to mark the occasion. As I said, I had been grooming her to be an asset to my business."

"What present did you bring her?" Jason snapped back.

"I'm sorry?" For the first time, Summers seemed off balance.

"It was her anniversary. *Your* anniversary, of sorts — one year of her living in your glorious apartment. So, knowing this was the occasion, I'm sure you brought her a nice gift to mark it. What did you bring her?"

Summers regained his equilibrium and answered confidently, "I did not bring her anything. Living in my apartment was quite enough of a gift."

"So, you did not bring her a special present from The Pharmacist?"

"No," the tycoon said firmly.

"You didn't score her the Montezuma's Delight?"

"I don't know what you're talking about."

"That's interesting," Mike said. He looked at the lawyer, as if he might be particularly interested. "So, you're telling us that, after Ms. Bronson's death in your apartment, you didn't watch her last TikTok video? She said she had just done a hit of the Montezuma's Delight."

Summers stiffened. "Gentlemen, I'm very sorry but you came without an appointment and I really do need to move on to an important meeting." He stood. "Mr. Powell will call for the receptionist to show you out. I'm sorry to be so abrupt, but I am already late. You will excuse me." With that, Summers whisked out the conference room door, leaving the other three men behind.

"I'll fetch the receptionist," Powell said.

When they exited the elevator and cleared the turnstiles into the expansive lobby, Mike took a seat on a padded bench, with Jason next to him. "You think he's lying only about not sleeping with the girl and about not knowing what a Montezuma's Delight is, or about everything?"

"Everything." Jason leaned forward, putting his elbows on his knees. "His reaction to the idea that it could have been murder was way over the top for someone who was not romantically involved with her, and someone who shouldn't care that much why she's dead. He also didn't ask what drugs she had in her system or what killed her. Most people would be more curious, unless they already knew."

"I agree. He's lying about not knowing about the drug use, and he's lying about not knowing The Pharmacist. We didn't get his prints, but he admitted being in the bathroom. He knew better than to try to lie about it. I'd say there is plenty of smoke here, but nothing we can take to the DA as evidence."

"You think he brought the junk recommended by The Pharmacist, right?"

Mike nodded. "Yep. The question is whether he spiked it himself, or if somebody else did. Or if Kayleigh did it on her own. Proving that one way or the other will problematic."

"But let's not make assumptions." Jason moved toward the exit door. "I doubt that Brock Taylor had any real opportunity to spike the cocktail if Summers brought it for her. And I can't see his motive for killing her. But let's not rule anything — or anyone — out until we're finished. No tunnel vision this time. Right?"

"Roger that." Mike pushed through the glass doors into the September sunshine.

Chapter 26
The Pharmacist

LATER ON MONDAY, while they waited to hear about what happened in the courtroom downtown, Mike and Jason went to pay a visit to The Pharmacist. He had been hard to find, despite his wildly popular YouTube channel. Their subpoena to YouTube's parent company, issued on Friday, was met with resistance. The Google legal team cited privacy concerns and refused to provide the contact information for the channel's owner.

It was Rachel who came up with an interesting strategy over the weekend. She posted a comment on one of The Pharmacist's videos, identifying herself as an EMT. She said she was dealing with an adverse drug reaction for somebody who took a drug cocktail recommended by The Pharmacist. She requested he reach out to her by email. The Pharmacist sent an email within a few hours and then called to talk about drug interactions and treatments. The NYPD's connections with the local utility and cable companies provided a match for the phone number, along with the specific address.

Mike and Jason arrived at the four-story walk-up on 9th Street in the West Village. The Pharmacist lived on the first floor in the rear, overlooking a tiny courtyard. They lacked a search warrant, but convinced the building's superintendent to show them to the YouTube star's unit and knock on the door for them while standing in front of the peep hole.

The Pharmacist attempted to close the door as soon as he saw the two detectives. Jason inserted his foot into the jamb and held it open. "Hang on, Sir. NYPD. We just want to talk to you."

"Like hell! I do not give you permission to enter my home." The Pharmacist looked the part of a counter-culture hippie, with long, stringy hair, ripped bell-bottom jeans, a woven headband, and a graying goatee. He stood defiantly in his half-open doorway, glaring at the two cops.

Mike held out his badge, allowing The Pharmacist to hold it and scrutinize it. "I'm Homicide Detective Mike Stoneman. This is my partner, Detective Jason Dickson. We're not here to hassle you, Sir. We're investigating the death of Kayleigh Bronson and we need your help."

"Kayleigh . . ." the man's angry face softened. Then he snapped back to attention. "I had nothing to do with that. Kayleigh was a friend and a supporter. I don't know anything about her overdose."

Jason tried to calm him. "We're not here to accuse you. We think somebody might have spiked Kayleigh's Montezuma's Delight. We don't care who used it or sold it to her or whatever. We're trying to find a killer. We'd like you to help us. Will you do that?"

The man stroked his gray ponytail while he scrutinized the detectives. He then pulled out his cell phone and punched two icons. "I'm recording this conversation. You two cops have told me that I'm not under arrest or under suspicion and you have not read me my Miranda rights. That's correct, right?"

Mike looked at Jason and shrugged. "That's correct. We would like your voluntary cooperation."

"Fine. You can come in, but you have to agree to leave and stop questioning me if I tell you to. Do you agree?"

"Sure," Mike confirmed.

The Pharmacist turned and went inside, leaving the door ajar. The apartment was simple and modern, without any sign of drug paraphernalia. The unit had a loft bedroom and a tiny kitchen. In his YouTube videos The Pharmacist smoked a perpetual joint, but his home had no odor of weed. He was sitting in a rocking chair by the time Mike and Jason entered the single sitting room. His cell phone was prominently placed on a wooden coffee table, ornamented with a lace-fringed runner topped by a wooden Buddha.

"The electric company tells us your name is Craig Goldstein," Mike said. "Is that correct?"

"Damned Big Brother," the man muttered. "Yeah. Sure. That doesn't matter."

"Did you know Kayleigh?"

"I never met her," he said in a subtly twangy accent. Mike figured somewhere in Texas. "But I'm sad that she's dead. I watched some of her content and she was pretty cool. She had a future. I was happy to have her mentioning me. Her followers were subscribing to my channel. I'll be sorry to lose the cross-pollination."

"Did you supply the drugs and other substances that you recommended in your videos?" Mike asked, trying not to imply that an affirmative answer might get the man arrested.

"Let me make this clear, Detective. I do not supply illegal drugs to my followers. My shows recommend drug combinations, based on my own experiences and on the suggestions of colleagues and viewers. I always include a disclaimer that people should consult with their own doctors before taking anything and that any drug can have an adverse interaction with other drugs and/or alcohol. If you've watched any of my shows, and I'm sure you have, you'll know this. I even provide specific warnings about known drug interactions when they apply. My followers should be careful and ingest drugs at their own risk."

"We understand," Jason said. "Like I said outside, we're not here to hassle you about drug use. You posted a video in which you talked about something you called a Montezuma's Delight. We're working under the impression that this particular cocktail included the anti-seizure drug carbamazepine. Does that sound familiar?"

"Sure. I remember that. The mix is cocaine, mezcal, and carbamazepine. It is an anti-seizure med, but it's safe for that use and that combination. I put warnings on that video about some interactions folks need to be careful about. I'm not hiding anything."

"We appreciate that," Jason said. "Kayleigh made a video the night she died saying that she had taken the Montezuma's Delight. It turns out she had exactly those drugs in her system, along with fentanyl."

"Wait! Whoa! Hold on, Detective. I have never recommended that anyone take fentanyl. That shit is poison. I don't recommend any opioids. They have too many interaction risks. I never told anyone to use fentanyl!"

"We know," Mike calmed him. "We're not accusing you of causing the overdose. But we need to know whether you provided the carbamazepine to anyone who might have put together the cocktail for Kayleigh. If we can identify the person who brought her the mixture, it might help us."

"How should I know?" Goldstein flipped back a loose string of hair from his face like a stray cobweb.

"Because you're a doctor, somehow," Jason said. "You talk about it all the time on your show. You prescribe drugs that are not controlled substances — the extra ingredients for your cocktails. You write those scripts as long as the requester says that they suffer from whatever malady it is the drug normally treats, but I'm guessing you don't ask for any verification. I get it. It's a business. We're not here to revoke your license or arrest you for trafficking in herbs and spices. Nobody will blink an eye at your little operation. You're an old white dude with money. You're bullet-proof. I get it. But can you tell us whether you wrote any scripts for carbamazepine in the past two months?"

"I probably did," The Pharmacist said matter-of-factly. "When I run those shows, I expect that viewers will want to experiment. If they need supplies, I'm happy to supply them, for a small fee. I don't keep track of who they go to."

"You don't keep any records of the prescriptions you write?" Mike was incredulous. "Isn't that contrary to standard medical procedures?"

"I wouldn't know," he said, looking away. "I want my followers to stay alive. They don't pay me if they're dead. If word gets around that people who follow my advice are dying from overdoses, that's bad for my business. It would also be bad if word got around that I was ratting out my customers to the cops. Don't you think?"

"Well, Sir, I think we actually have a mutual interest in finding the person who spiked one of your concoctions with fentanyl. Then we can clear your name and let everyone know the girl died not because of your advice, but because somebody slipped her something. Don't you agree?"

The Pharmacist pulled at his ponytail and took a deep breath. "Look, I almost never know who is actually asking for shit from me. People come to me through intermediaries. They set up brand-new email accounts and tell me they are suffering from exactly the symptoms that would warrant the prescription they want. I write the script and take their money. What they do with the drug is their business, not mine. I'm acting in good faith here."

Mike sighed. "Sir, I'm pretty sure you're savvy enough that if we try to arrest you and haul you into the station for interrogation, you're gonna have a lawyer meet us there and we'll get zip from you. Is that about right?"

"You're a smart man, Detective Stoneman."

"Don't flatter me. I know it's bullshit. But I'm also a pragmatist. I think you may still be able to help us. I'm betting that, when the time comes, you will. But we have some work to do first. We will come visit you again, when we have a more specific question to ask."

"Suit yourself." The man leaned back in his chair, making no moves toward escorting the detectives from his home. Mike stood, as did Jason. The interview was clearly over.

Jason then put a hand on Mike's shoulder to stop him. "Sir, on a completely unrelated matter. Do you recall last spring recommending any combination cocktail that included digoxin? Or writing a prescription for it?"

The Pharmacist thought about it for a moment, not seeming bothered. "No. I don't think so."

"OK. Thank you," Mike said. "We'll be in touch."

On the street outside the apartment, Jason said, "You saw where I was going there at the end, right?"

"Sure. It was a long shot, but worth a try. He said 'no' awfully fast. You would think a guy who has recommended hundreds of drugs over the years would not be so sure."

"Maybe he recognized the drug, but was sure he would never prescribe it?"

"Maybe. On the other hand, he seems willing to write any script for anyone who asks, whether or not it's a drug he's recommended. If somebody contacted him, asked for a specific drug, and knew the right symptoms, how's he going to remember?"

"We should have Konopka add digoxin to her list of search words for his videos, and expand the search back to the start of 2022," Jason said.

"That's a big stretch, and a use of resources on this case that might be questioned."

"But probably not. Who's going to ask questions about what Konopka is searching for?"

"You're probably right," Mike conceded. "Let's tell her and see what comes up. It's a shot in the dark, but it can't hurt."

Mike walked east, toward the nearest subway station. "We need some proof, but I'm starting to believe that our Wall Street tycoon may have decided his young mistress was a liability in his divorce and decided to taint her cocaine cocktail. It's just a suspicion, but it fits with the facts we have so far."

"So far." Jason held out a hand at an approaching car as he J-walked across 8th Street. "But we haven't seized his laptop yet."

Chapter 27
Supply and Demand

LATE THAT AFTERNOON, Mike got a call from Keith Harris to let him know that the presentation of evidence in the Ballet Murder case was over. Both Mike and Jason were off the hook as far as any additional testimony.

"That was fast," Michelle said as soon as Mike arrived home. She had received a similar call.

Keith told them both that, after the prosecution rested its case, O'Beaney put on a criminology expert, who testified about tunnel vision. The expert criticized the police investigation for failing to look at any suspects besides Matthews once they had the laptop data. He explained that the internet search data was suspicious because of the short duration and the absence of any other activity on the laptop during the session. He gave his expert opinion that it was "highly likely" someone planted the evidence on Matthews' laptop. After the expert finished, O'Beaney announced that the defense would have no other witnesses and moved for a directed verdict, which was denied.

"They'll do closing arguments tomorrow," Mike said, "then the jury will get the case."

After a dinner of spiced tofu and steamed vegetables, Mike and Michelle watched the trial coverage on the local news. The field reporter was also surprised that the defense chose to put on only the one witness. After a year of protesting his innocence, Nathan Matthews did not take the stand in his own defense. The reporter pledged to be back in court tomorrow for the trial's closing arguments.

"Did not see that coming," Mike said. "You?"

"Not in a million years. I didn't think he would try to argue that the digoxin wasn't the murder weapon, or that it was an accidental poisoning. But I expected him to call character witnesses to say that he's not the kind of person who would murder his leading actor, or some witnesses to verify his alibi."

"Yeah," Mike said slowly, thinking of something different. "But, in a way, it may be a good strategy. The lawyer has two ways to win this case. One is to provide the jury with an alternative killer to create doubt. He hasn't got that. The other is to create enough doubt about the prosecution's case that they don't need a specific alternate killer. The prosecution only has the laptop, along with motive and opportunity. But anyone could have poisoned Bishop's drink or hired somebody to do it. And as for motive, he's an actor. There must be dozens of jealous colleagues or disgruntled rivals who would want to snuff him."

"Just because there might be other people with a motive doesn't make a defense." Michelle enjoyed sparring with Mike over legal issues. "But having a motive and having specific evidence is totally different."

"Exactly. The real case is the computer evidence. The defense attorney's closing argument is going to be all about that — how it makes no logical sense that Matthews would run only those searches in that short window of time with no other activity. Just like his expert testified. If the jury believes it was a frame-job, then he walks. Otherwise, he's dead meat, no matter what other evidence he might have tried to put in. By not putting on any other witnesses, he makes it look like he's supremely confident in the deficiency of the prosecution's case. He keeps it clean. We'll see if it works."

"You sound like you want him to be acquitted." Michelle pulled her head from its resting place on Mike's shoulder and stroked Topsy, who had assumed her favorite position on Michelle's throw pillow.

"I don't even know what I want. I'm pissed off that this dopey criminologist is criticizing me and Jason for having tunnel vision."

"Hasn't that ever happened before?"

"It has," Mike said, "but this is the first time it might be true. And that's killing me." Mike reached around Michelle's shoulder and drew her back to him, prompting a meow of protest.

"What about the new case?" Michelle changed the subject. "Is there anything the girl's sugar daddy said that would give you probable cause to get a search warrant?"

"No. He's savvy. We're pretty sure he's lying, but that's just our opinion. He didn't say anything incriminating. Until we have some actual evidence, no judge will let us search his home or look through his financial records. He's got lawyers, so if we arrest him, he'll refuse to talk. We need something more than our suspicion."

"Is there anybody else with a motive to kill her?"

"Not that we've uncovered so far. It's a weird coincidence that Brock Taylor is connected to Kayleigh, but we can't figure any way he could have spiked her drugs, or why he would want to kill her. Hell, we still can't say for sure that she didn't take the fentanyl on purpose."

"What about people around Summers? Have you thought about talking to his friends or neighbors?"

Mike set down his after-dinner scotch on a glass-topped end table that had come over from Michelle's place. "We thought about that, but the party guests are more likely to rat him out than his neighbors or business associates. We don't have anything incriminating yet. We still have more people to speak to. We're having the uniforms track down the rest of the list, now that we have more of a focus."

Michelle's face brightened. "What about his wife?"

"What about her?"

"Mike, he's involved in a messy divorce. If you think he wanted to get rid of the girl because of how it would damage his settlement, then the best person to talk to is his wife. She probably knows about the girl and the love nest. She might be totally willing to give you information about things he said to her. Maybe he promised to get rid of her or something."

"But she's his wife. She doesn't have to talk to us."

"But what if she *wants* to talk to you? It's her choice. His lawyers can't prevent her from talking."

"Did I ever tell you that you're a genius?" Mike softly grasped Michelle's hand. "I'll take full credit for the idea, of course, with Jason. I can't let him know it was you."

Michelle nudged Topsy off her pillow, then used it to bop Mike in the head.

Chapter 28
Motive Deficiency

IN BROOKLYN, JASON READ *Goodnight Moon* to JJ, who for the past two weeks wanted that bedtime story. Every night. Jason had been juggling his regular work with his master's program studies, but this night was a welcome opportunity to have quiet time before bed with JJ, followed by dinner with Rachel.

Jason summarized the day's interviews, then presented the thumb drive and explained the assignment he hoped Rachel would help with. He had to physically hold her at the dining table. "I can start right now!" She was more animated about watching the drag show video than about any of her assignments for the cable news network.

"There will be time," Jason assured her, returning to his half-eaten dinner. To combat his wife's pouting face, he talked about The Influencer case. "Summers, the Wall Street guy, is lying about his relationship with Kayleigh. He may have had a motive to kill her to avoid her becoming an issue in his divorce."

"I'm not sure about that," Rachel said. "The guy is a total scumbag. He's probably had a dozen lovers. Why would he be so worried about this girl that he'd risk murdering her? Are we sure she wasn't pregnant? Maybe she was blackmailing him. If he's the killer, there has to be something more than just being worried about his divorce settlement."

"The autopsy didn't show her to be pregnant, so that's not it. I like the blackmail idea, but he was taking care of her and paying for her home. Why would she risk ruining that?"

"Unless the whole apartment arrangement was some kind of blackmail payoff."

Jason spun his empty wine glass by its stem. "I suppose it's possible. Did I ever tell you that you have a devious mind? But what about everybody else who had access to her? There must be competition and jealousy among these influencers. What would cause one of them to want to ice her?"

"I think you've got it wrong, honey. These girls are all friends. They cross-promote each other. If one of them has a million followers and another has half a million, they are better off if they can both have 1.5 million. They're young. They get some money out of the deal, from ads and deals with companies that want them to promote their products, but it's not millions. They're loving life and having fun. They're not trying to knock each other off."

"What about a disgruntled sponsor?"

"Not likely. If a sponsor isn't happy, they dump the influencer, just like any other client. Of course, it could have actually been an accident. She could have decided to take the fentanyl and maybe got a bad batch or took too much."

"I know. But, somehow, that doesn't feel right. She posted a video after she said she took the Montezuma's Delight cocktail. She said it was based on a recommendation from The Pharmacist. Don't you think she would have mentioned it if she added fentanyl to the mix? It just doesn't figure to have been an accident." Jason drained his wine glass and slumped back in his chair.

"At least this one isn't keeping you out on a stakeout all night," Rachel sighed. "It's nice having you home with JJ and me."

"I know. It's nice. Remember when you were working the night EMT shift?"

"Oh, yes. It's amazing we ever had time to make a baby, the way I was out on the streets and you were working your cop hours." Rachel left her place and sat on Jason's lap, putting her arms around his neck and leaning down for a gentle kiss. "Now that I'm on ACN hours, we can afford to give JJ a little sister."

"Or brother."

"Sure. Or brother. Having two is going to be tough, with you still working cop hours. Have you talked to Gil about the corporate security job with UBS?"

"I did. He's getting me some information. I'll have it in a week or so. But I don't know if I can leave Mike."

"You're not leaving Mike. He and Michelle will still be our best friends. They're godparents to JJ. They are not going anywhere." She stroked Jason's face. "I know you owe Mike a lot, but you have to think about me, and JJ, and the baby. When I go back to work after maternity leave, we'll need daycare for JJ — and the baby — and my mom can't do that forever. We have to make some decisions."

"How was JJ tonight?"

Rachel blew out a slow breath. "He was fussy. What's new? He didn't want to let me comb his hair again so I let it go. He gets so agitated right before bed if I force it."

"I know. He'll grow out of it. I promise." They shared another kiss. Then Jason leaned his head back. "This Ballet Murder case is still bugging the hell out of me. I know we don't always catch the bad guys, but if we're doing such a crappy job that we're arresting innocent people, then do I really want to keep doing it?"

Rachel pulled Jason's head into her chest. "You get like this whenever you're on a tough case. Get these done and then you'll have a clear mind. You and Mike will get there."

They rocked gently in the chair for several minutes without talking. The house was quiet, which was rare. The moment ended when JJ's cry from the bedroom jarred them back to reality.

Jason lifted Rachel easily into the air. "I'll get him. You've got a video to watch."

Chapter 29
It's Good to Be the Queen

TUESDAY MORNING, IT WAS RAINING. Mike woke early, putting in thirty minutes on the treadmill in the combination study and exercise room while Michelle showered and changed for work. When Mike exited the building, the September air had taken a chilly turn, warning that autumn was actually coming soon. After a hot summer where rain came mostly in the form of thunder storms that barely reduced the swelter level, a chilly, steady rain was a shock to Mike's system. He had not thought to wear a raincoat. He had an umbrella, which kept the rain off his head, but left his shoes, lower legs, and hands both damp and cold.

He met Jason under the awning at the front door of the Empire Suites apartment tower on Central Park South. Jason's London Fog raincoat was dappled with beaded water drops. He removed his leather gloves inside the lobby. A carpet runner was laid down over the marble floor to prevent guests from slipping. The uniformed doorman offered to stow their wet umbrellas in a giant porcelain vase near the door.

The front desk attendants greeted the two detectives with skeptical questions and carefully scrutinized their NYPD identification cards. Even then, they refused to allow them into the building without calling up to get Mrs. Summers' permission. The desk man, sporting a thin moustache that made him look more like a butler than a security guard, seemed surprised when she consented to a visit from the police.

While they rode in the plush elevator, Mike speculated that their presence in the building would be a topic of gossip among the staff. They had been directed to use the east elevator bank. When the doors opened, they understood why. The tiny lobby area on the 34th floor provided access to only three apartment doors.

Mrs. Evalyn Winston Summers stood in the open threshold of the far left unit, the one facing north with views of Central Park. Of course. Evalyn was dressed as if she were hosting a high society luncheon. Her purple dress had a conservatively cut neckline and hem, but flowed and shimmered even in the dim foyer lighting. Her dark auburn hair was piled into an elaborate design of swirling curls above a face that looked too young for her forty-six years. Expertly applied makeup accented her cheekbones and brought out the color of her light brown eyes. A string of pearls and two gold rings with large diamonds were her only accessories.

"You are the detectives," she announced, rather than asking.

"We are," Mike replied, extending a hand. "I'm Detective Stoneman. This is Detective Dickson. Thank you for agreeing to speak to us. May we come inside?"

The elegant woman turned and led the way into the apartment, leaving Jason as the last one through to close the door. The interior opened up from the relatively small foyer to an expansive living room featuring a spectacular view of the park through four picture windows. A dining alcove, home to a formal table with ten chairs, had its own window with an east-facing view. Mike assumed there was a kitchen somewhere, but its existence was hidden. A hallway stretched away from each side of the main room, presumably containing bedrooms and baths. It was easily the largest apartment space Mike had ever seen in New York.

The walls were adorned with original artwork, the colors of which complemented the furniture. Black pedestals supported statuary of both classical and modern design. Rich maroon rugs with intricate designs covered much of the floor, absorbing the sounds of footsteps as the detectives swiveled their necks to take in the tasteful opulence.

"This is quite a wonderful place." Mike wanted to break the ice with their potential witness, but he was also genuinely impressed.

Mrs. Summers directed them to a leather sofa the color of cappuccino foam. She took a seat opposite them in an identically colored easy chair. A cup of tea sat in a Delft China saucer on a coffee table between them. "It's Amelia's day off or I would have her offer you tea. I hope you don't mind."

"It's fine," Mike responded. "I understand you have two grown children. So, is it just you here now?"

"The children are from Logan's first marriage," she replied in a calm voice. "But yes, they are off on their own. Logan and I are both here, along with our housekeeper." Her accent carried a hint of affected British, as if she might have studied abroad.

"We don't want to take too much of your time. But — I'm sorry." Mike was puzzled. "I thought you and your husband were divorcing."

"We are," she responded simply. "But, as you may imagine, the apartment is a rather important component of the marital assets and neither one of us is keen on moving out yet. So, we are both still here. Logan stays in the west wing and I'm in the east. There is plenty of space for both of us without requiring much interaction. We have a summer home in East Hampton, but the commute is far too much for Logan to stay there regularly. I understand we own another apartment in the city that may be available for him in the near future," she raised an eyebrow, "but I presume Logan will want to stay until the property division is settled so that he can claim he still lives here."

"That's very . . . mature of you both," Mike said.

"Yes. Well, we've lived together for twelve years and have barely spoken for the last three. So, why should the fact that we're divorcing change much? He keeps out of my way and I've stopped caring about his affairs. So, you see, it's the best for everyone."

"I understand." Not finding a natural opening for his questions, Mike forced them forward. "We're here because we need to ask you about your husband's relationship with Kayleigh Bronson. Are you willing to talk to us about it?"

"Of course. Why else would I have agreed to meet with you?"

"So, you know about her? You mentioned the other apartment, so you know about that also?"

Their host tilted her head to the side. She seemed annoyed by the questions. "Naturally, I know everything, Detective. When I first met Logan, he was married to Margot, his first wife. At that time, I was the other woman. I wasn't the first, or the last. But I was the one who made him love me enough to marry me. I thought I could change him."

"How long have you known that your husband owned the apartment in the Park Towers?"

"Since the beginning. He said it was an investment property and that he was getting a great deal on it from his friend, Woody O'Meara. He told me it was being rented out. When I hired a private investigator to look into his behavior and to find out what our total assets really are, I found out he has been using it as a love nest. We're not actually collecting rent, although my investigator says there is still net value there if we sell it. I found out specifically about the little girl he's been hiding up there about six months ago. God, she's ten years younger than I was when he started fucking me, so you can imagine how that makes me feel."

Mike turned his head toward Jason. They had worked out several contingency plans for how to handle the interview if the wife refused to admit what she knew. Those plans were not needed, since Evalyn was happy to talk about everything. The plan was to have Jason handle the questioning about drug use, and now was the time.

"Mrs. Summers, excuse me," Jason cleared his throat.

"Oh, please call me Evalyn. I'm trying to lose the *Mrs. Summers* thing."

"Fine, Evalyn, I need to ask you whether you were aware that your husband used illegal drugs."

"Of course I am. It's the main reason why we're getting divorced. Logan always drank and smoked the occasional joint, but several years ago it got much worse. He was high more often than not, and when he drank and did the drugs, he got angry and violent. He started taking all kinds of pills and snorting coke on top of everything else. It got to be too much. I asked him to stop, but he just laughed at me. He said he was the king of the world and he would snort or smoke or pop whatever he damn well wanted. And he'd fuck whatever lovely young things he could find because life is short. He wanted to live every moment like it was his last. A philosopher, he is."

"Do you know where he got his cocaine?"

"Not specifically. He has a business contact in Colombia who visits New York every few months and brings Logan a fresh supply. If you'd like, I can let you know the next time he's planning to be here. You can catch them red-handed and throw my no-good husband in jail. It will help my settlement posture."

"Evalyn, we're homicide detectives. We don't handle drug cases. It's unlikely that purchasing a small amount of cocaine for personal use would result in any significant punishment."

"Believe me, Detective, Logan never does anything in small amounts."

"What about heroin or other opioids like OxyContin?" Mike watched the woman's eyes while Jason asked the question. He saw no flicker of concern or surprise. "Did he ever use those?"

Evalyn shrugged. "It's not like I was cataloging his drug use, Detective. But no, I can't say that I ever saw or heard about him using heroin. He took a lot of pills, so anything is possible. I never saw any track marks on him, or needles lying around the apartment. And I would have noticed."

Jason sat forward in his chair for the next question. "Have you ever heard of a person known as The Pharmacist?"

Evalyn furrowed her brows. "You mean Floyd, the pharmacist at the Duane Reed around the corner?"

"No. I'm talking about a guy with an online show who recommends exotic drug combinations. He encourages his followers to try them to get a special kind of high. Did your husband ever mention him, or something like that?"

Evalyn shook her head. "No. I've never heard that name. I have never wanted to be part of Logan's drug culture, so it's not a surprise to me that he never mentioned it. Why? Is it important?"

"Probably not." Jason sat back. "Did he know that you knew about him and the girl, Kayleigh?"

"I don't know. My investigator is discreet. We certainly didn't discuss it. I've barely spoken to him in the past four months, since the filing."

Jason exchanged a knowing glance with Mike. "Aside from maybe wanting to keep the information from you because of the divorce, can you think of any other reason why your husband might have wanted to kill Kayleigh Bronson?"

"I've been thinking about that." Evalyn reached for the cup of tea on a polished table next to her chair. "Logan has been through many young lovers over the years. When he tires of them, he dumps them. One threatened to go to the gossip columnist for *The Post* and expose him, so he paid her off. I doubt it would have been a big story, even then, but that was his decision. He told me about it at the time. He has no shame. He said he made a mistake. That the girl could have come back asking for more, like blackmail. He said he should have made sure he held something over her head that he could have pulled back if she broke her confidentiality agreement. Suing people for breach is a messy prospect, you know. He also once said he should have had her killed, to make sure she never carried out her threat."

Mike's right eyebrow raised involuntarily. "Do you recall the girl's name?"

"Sure. It was Monica Rexroad. She lived in Brooklyn Heights somewhere."

Jason made a note to check into her whereabouts — and safety. "To your knowledge, has your husband ever actually carried out such a threat to have someone killed?"

"I can't say that, Detective. He confided in me in the earlier years of our marriage, but once he started openly sleeping around, he was less forthcoming. But, if I had any evidence of such criminal behavior, I would certainly tell you."

Mike resumed the lead. "You said you had a private investigator looking into your husband's behavior. Did he ever tell you anything about Logan being blackmailed, by Kayleigh or by somebody else? Like, maybe the girl knew about some crime or fraud he was involved with and threatened to turn him in?"

Evalyn pondered the question for a moment. "I can't say for sure. My investigator told me he was working on a lead, but didn't have any corroboration for it."

"What was the lead?"

"That Logan was making plans to repossess the apartment. He had made some inquiries about renting it out. He may have been planning to evict the little tramp. Perhaps she didn't want to go quietly."

"Would you be willing to give us the name of your private investigator?"

"I'd rather not, Detective. It's my private matter and it's important for my divorce action. I don't want Logan finding out who he is, so I will decline to provide that information unless I am compelled to." Evalyn relaxed in her chair, as if they were chatting about what color fabric to buy for reupholstering the dining chairs.

Mike stood, signaling that the interview was over.

"Would you like me to show you where he keeps his secret stash of drugs in the house?" Evalyn smiled sweetly, as if offering cookies.

Mike consulted with Jason. They agreed that they should get a warrant first, even if Summers' wife was volunteering. The evidence, if they found any, could be tainted. It also seemed unlikely that Summers would have a fentanyl supply mixed in with his personal drug stash. He wasn't likely that much of an idiot. After thanking Evalyn for her candor and cooperation, Mike handed her a business card, asking her to call if she had any additional thoughts or information that might be relevant.

"Are you going to arrest him?" she asked as they were at the front door.

"I can't tell you that," Mike said, "but if we do, it won't be very soon unless other evidence comes to light."

Back in the lobby, the two detectives compared notes. "Summers has to expect that she has a PI following him around, right?" Jason grabbed his umbrella from the vase in the corner.

"I would guess so," Mike agreed. "His lawyer probably has one following her, too. It's not like he has been so secretive about his affair with the girl. Attending parties with dozens of her friends is not exactly clandestine."

"You think she was shaking him down?" Jason mused. "And if you're going to kill her, why do it in the apartment you own? The guy has money and connections. If he wanted to have her killed, he probably could. But why not just dump her and kick her out of the apartment? She must have had something on him, but the idea of killing her himself seems out of character."

"I know. I'm not sure where we are. By the way, what did you think of the wife?"

Jason laughed. "I'm glad I'm not married to her. She's one tough cookie. She's not worried about spilling all the beans on him. That works in our favor."

"Did you notice," Mike paused to make sure Jason was looking at him, "how she wasn't surprised that we were talking about Kayleigh's death as a murder investigation and that her husband might be a suspect. Does that strike you as odd?"

"Her PI probably keeps her fully briefed. Plus, Kayleigh's death in the apartment he owned figures to generate police interest. She'd probably be happy if we charged him with murder. It would help her divorce action."

"Yeah." Mike shrugged. Jason opened his umbrella and led the way out onto the street, heading west toward the Columbus Circle subway.

Chapter 30
Verdict

THE REST OF THE DAY on Tuesday, Mike and Jason debriefed the uniformed officers who had completed all the remaining interviews with partygoers. They were a week out from the night when the young influencer succumbed to her toxic drug cocktail. Between the passage of time, the guests' general reluctance to admit to illegal drug use, and their focus being on themselves rather than on any other participants, none of the witnesses provided any new or helpful information.

Nobody saw Kayleigh take her Montezuma's Delight. Nobody knew who brought the ingredients. They all agreed that Kayleigh would never intentionally take fentanyl. Only a few admitted knowing that Kayleigh and Brock were romantically involved. None said they knew about a sexual relationship between Kayleigh and Logan, although several admitted seeing Logan at prior parties. Nobody saw Logan on Labor Day.

Officer Martin reported back that Monica Rexroad, Logan Summers' former girlfriend whom Evalyn Summers said her husband had threatened to have killed, was alive and well and making soft-core porn videos. That angle of the investigation was another dead end.

By the day's end, the two detectives made an unusual recommendation to their captain. "We think it's time to call it an accidental overdose," Mike said to Sully. "It will let the press put the story to bed and may make the killer — if there is one — more relaxed and therefore more likely to make a mistake."

"You think there's a killer?" Sully asked, then immediately said, "No. Don't even tell me."

"We do, Cap," Jason said.

"Dickson, I told you not to tell me that!"

"No, you told Mike."

Sully grabbed a foam ball from the edge of his desk and squeezed it vigorously in his left hand. "What are you planning to do with the file?"

"We're going to keep it open, for now," Jason answered. "If we come up with something in the next few days, we'll follow it. If not, then we'll close it just like we've announced, an accidental overdose. Either way, the heat will be off for a while."

"Fine!" Sully barked. "I'll back that with the commissioner. He'll be happy to get the press off his back. Anything else?"

"No, Captain. That's where we are on this one. We'll keep you posted about any new developments."

"I'll be happier if there aren't any." Sully picked up his phone, which was the universal signal for any lesser cops to get out. Mike and Jason didn't need more of a hint.

* * *

IN ORDER TO MAXIMIZE their available time working on the unauthorized Ballet Murder investigation, Jason suggested that he and Rachel come to Mike's apartment for dinner Tuesday. Rachel had been reviewing the video they got from the Stress Factory and wanted to share what she learned with everyone at once. It made sense to gather over take-out Chinese, while Olivia put JJ to bed in Brooklyn.

When Mike arrived home, Star greeted him at the door with an unexpected hug. "Hi, Uncle Mike!" She wrapped her arms around his back, squeezed once, then released, stepping back and beaming up with her best smile. "Aunt Michelle invited me over to have dinner and brainstorm about your investigation."

"She did, did she?" Mike dropped his keys loudly in the bowl by the door and made eye contact with Michelle.

She looked up at the sound while she was putting out place settings on the dinner table. "Rachel said she wanted to see Star again," Michelle called out. "Can you call in the Chinese order? Oh, and Jackie is also here."

Mike slowly walked to the bedroom, waving greetings to Rachel and her brother. Jason had not yet arrived. Returning without his jacket and with a menu from Szechuan Palace in his hand, he gave Michelle a soft kiss and whispered, "Shall I order a little extra for Star to take back to school with her?"

"Good idea!" Michelle responded, returning Mike's kiss.

"I was kidding," Mike muttered, putting the menu down on the counter and pulling out his phone.

Twenty minutes later, when he opened the door carrying two plastic bags laden with rice, chicken, eggplant, and Lo Mein, he could hear the excited chatter coming from the living room.

"Mike! Come here," Jason called, "the jury is back in the Ballet Murder."

Mike dumped the bag on the dining table. "That was fast. They only had closing arguments this morning. Did they let him off?"

"Don't know. The reporter is live outside the courthouse, waiting for word. They don't have cameras inside."

"Oh, right. Duh." Mike didn't sit down.

For five minutes, dinner preparations were on hold while all six of them sat glued to the television. The broadcast broke away from the courthouse to other stories, waiting for some actual news. When the coverage abruptly cut away from a video about a home in New Jersey where dozens of dogs were rescued from appalling conditions, the courthouse reporter's face flashed back on the screen. She was wearing a blue dress with a sloping neckline and a wide black collar. Mike thought it looked like a party gown more than the professional attire of a journalist.

"We have just been informed that the jury has convicted Broadway director Nathan Matthews for the murder of actor Alex Bishop last May."

Mike pressed the mute button and headed toward the kitchen. "It's not surprising that it happened fast. After putting on only his expert witness, the guy's lawyer was taking a risk. It figures that the jury would either acquit or convict pretty quickly. They either bought the argument, or they agreed with the DA that the evidence was damning and the argument that it was *too* damning wasn't a defense."

"You don't seem very happy about the conviction," Michelle said.

"I know. It's probably the first time I was kinda hoping for an acquittal. At least my testimony didn't screw up the case for Keith."

As soon as everyone had settled into their chairs and the chopsticks were flying, Rachel and Jackie launched into a report on the video. Rachel had called in her own expert witness, her brother the drag performer. Since the case was not an official police investigation, Jason had not objected.

Jackie started off the presentation. "It makes sense that Brock Taylor would pick up a gig on a night when *Godfather* was dark. He was just the understudy. He was getting paid, but not enough to coast. Actors are always looking to score a few extra bucks. Rachel called me and I asked around among people I know about that show. It's a little unusual for someone like him to go slumming down to New Brunswick, but maybe he couldn't find anything in the city that night. The Stress Factory is a venue where you have to come dressed to perform because there is no backstage area and only one small dressing room. I found only one person in my circle who was at that gig. They didn't remember who else was there. It was a long time ago. But they did remember that it was a small house and the pay was shit."

"What about the video?" Mike asked.

Rachel answered. "About halfway through the set, Victoria LaCage performed. That's Taylor's usual drag name. Victoria performed the first act curtain-closer from *La Cage Aux Folles*. It looked like something that she'd done before, which is not surprising for a drag show. I mean, 'I Am What I Am' is an iconic drag anthem. Victoria's costume matched photos on Taylor's website. So, it would seem that the alibi is still solid."

"Don't worry, darling," Jason soothed. "You're not responsible for the content of the information. Every time we rule out one possibility, we get closer to the remaining options. Every piece is important to the investigation."

Star then piped up, "But the video doesn't prove that it was Taylor. It proves that somebody performed the song as Victoria."

"Sure," Mike said, "but—"

"Wait," Rachel cut Mike off. "This is where it gets interesting. There are a few things weird about that gig. The first is that he would even go to Jersey for a crappy show with a tiny paycheck."

"That's true," Michelle said. "Why would he go all the way to Jersey for a low-paying show?"

Jackie waved a well-manicured hand at their host. "I had the same thought. I had a show that night in the Village — since my big sister didn't invite me to the Broadway Cares gala. I know for a fact there was room in our lineup, so why go to Jersey?"

"So, I asked Star to do some digging for us." Rachel motioned for Star to take the floor.

"I scoured Brock Taylor's social media. When he performs in a drag show, he is obsessive about sending out notices to his fans to make sure he gets a good turnout. Every show he has done in the past two years got at least five tweets and four Instagram posts with photos. He links to the venue's website for the show announcements and always posts from the venue on the night of the show, telling his followers to get their asses down to the theater. Except for that Jersey show."

When Star paused for effect, Jason couldn't hold himself back. "I'll bite, Star. What was different about that Jersey show?"

"For that show, he was on radio silence. No posts. No tweets. Nothing on his website or his Facebook page. It's like he didn't want anyone to know about it. That's so out of character for him. We're thinking, either he booked the gig at the last minute and never had a chance to advertise it—"

"Or," Jackie jumped in, "he didn't want any of his fans to be there. It may be easy to step into somebody else's costume and wig and fool a stranger, but drag performers have some fanatical followers. The super fans would know if the queen on stage was an imposter. So, the best way to avoid that is to make sure none of your super fans are there to see. So you don't tell anyone about the gig. If Taylor had wanted to be in two places at once, he could have sent somebody there specifically to perform as Victoria LaCage, without telling anybody, in order to establish the perfect alibi."

Jackie, Rachel, and Star all looked at Mike, clearly proud of their research.

"That's a creative theory," Mike said, "but it's pure speculation. All we have for sure is a video of somebody that looks like Victoria LaCage performing and payroll records showing that Brock Taylor got paid for it. So, the alibi is solid and there's no evidence suggesting that it was all an elaborate hoax."

"Have we compared the video to other performances by the real Victoria LaCage?" Star asked, determined not to concede the argument.

"No," Rachel said. "I didn't, but what good would that do? No two performances are exactly the same. I've seen Jackie do his stuff as Belle de la Pomme dozens of times and it's always a little different."

"I know that." Star got even more animated. "But this is a big deal song for a drag artist, right? So Brock — Victoria — has probably done it a bunch of times. When somebody does the same performance over and over, they tend to have their own style, right?"

"Yes, that's true, honey," Jackie agreed, picking up some of Star's excitement. "If we had something to compare this to, we might be able to see differences, like Victoria's fans might have noticed if they had been there."

Star dropped her chopsticks with a clitter. "OK, so what we need is to find a video of Victoria LaCage performing that song when we're sure she's actually Taylor and compare them."

Jason, who had been working his phone during the discussion, smacked his hand on the table, causing his wine glass to wobble. "He's got one on his website!"

"What?" Mike asked.

"A video," Jason said. "On Brock Taylor's website, he has a bunch of videos of his performances. One of them is him performing 'I Am What I Am' as Victoria LaCage." He held out the phone, not that anyone around the table could read the tiny text on the screen.

"What are we waiting for?" Star bounced out of her seat. "Uncle Mike, can you connect your laptop to your TV?"

Five minutes later, the group was watching the video from the Stress Factory, and then the one from Brock Taylor's website. After the first run-through, they watched both again. Rachel, Jackie, and Star took notes. At the end, they paused one video on the television screen and paused the other at the same point on Michelle's laptop, which they propped up next to the TV so they could compare.

"They are very close, physically," Jackie said. "The height and build are about the same. The dress and wig are for sure the same. The makeup is a little different, but it could just be a bad night. The venue doesn't have a proper dressing room, so it could have been done in a bathroom."

"But the performances are definitely not the same," Rachel said. "They don't sound the same."

"She's right about that," Jackie agreed.

"They sound different to me," Mike said, "but I can't exactly describe why."

"Well, first off," Jackie said, "the Victoria from the Stress Factory show performed it a lot like George Hearn, the actor who originated the role on Broadway. He puts an emphasis on *bang* on the first instance of *bang my own drum*. He takes a big pause before *out loud*. He puts the emphasis on the word *deal* and puts a heavy diphthong on the word *deuces*. And he shouts the words, *Hey, world*! Those are specific and repeatable style points. On Brock's website, Victoria's emphasis is different on every one of those phrases. The real Victoria is more interested in showing off her pipes by singing the notes instead of speaking or shouting. As far as I'm concerned, it's not the same singer."

Mike and Jason were not fully convinced. They doubted that it would be deemed scientifically conclusive and hold up in court. But they agreed it might be enough to convince the DA that further investigation was warranted.

"There's still a big problem," Mike slumped back on the sofa. "The hypothesis that somebody did the Jersey show while impersonating Brock is plausible, but that would only prove the guy lied about his alibi. We would still need to place him at the Broadway Cares gala, where he would have had the opportunity to spike Alex Bishop's cocktail."

"We could pull the video from the gala and look more closely to see if Taylor was there, and served a drink to Bishop," Jason suggested.

"Sure. We should do that," Mike agreed. "But it won't be conclusive. Like Star pointed out already, if he was there, he would have been in disguise. Makeup and a wig and such. It would be impossible to prove that a waiter or a guest on a grainy security video was really a disguised Brock Taylor. Those images won't support facial recognition software."

"Do we have enough to go to the DA to get a search warrant for Taylor's apartment?" Jason asked. "Of course, if we run with this, we're going to have to tell Sully."

"Don't worry," Mike said. "I'll handle Sully."

Chapter 31
Requesting Permission

"FOR THE LOVE OF AUNT MILLIE, Stoneman, are you out of your damned mind? You want to re-open an investigation when the DA just got a conviction yesterday? Like you don't have enough fresh stiffs to work? You gotta dig up one that's two years old? I can't believe you're even asking!" The discussion with their captain Wednesday morning had gone pretty much the way Mike expected — badly.

When Sully took a breath and a tiny bit of the redness drained away from his face, Mike attempted to calm the situation. "Cap, we're not exactly re-opening the investigation. This guy may have been an accomplice. We're trying to finish an investigation that was never completed."

"Plus, he's still a person of interest in the Kayleigh Bronson murder," Jason added.

"And what the hell do I put on my case report, huh? I got a closed case with a successful prosecution outcome. I'm not re-opening that case file. Are you going to open a new one and say we're investigating this other actor to find another participant in the conspiracy? You're gonna put your name on that? Or you, Dickson?"

Jason, sitting placidly while watching Sully's fireworks, replied, "Sure. I'll be happy to put my name on the intake sheet. We have new evidence that warrants opening a new investigation."

"And where did this new evidence come from?" Sully's wrath was now directed at Jason, giving Mike a chance to regroup. "Please don't tell me you got a tip from the guilty director or his lawyer."

"No, Sully. We did not." Jason carefully navigated the narrow space between the whole truth and being dishonest with his captain. The original information came from Matthews' PI, not his lawyer, but since then they had done their own research. "We got a copy of the video from the show that was Taylor's alibi. Rachel, along with her brother and Mike's wife's niece, noticed that the performance didn't look the same as other performances of the same number on his personal website. So, that got us to thinking. Taylor went to a lot of trouble to establish a fake alibi for the night of the murder. We want to dig into that to see if he was involved." Nothing about what Jason said was untrue. He peeked at Mike in his peripheral vision and got a confirming nod.

"What the — Your wife? And Mike's niece?!" Sully's volume and the prominence of the protruding vein in his forehead were both on the rise. Mike chose not to correct his boss and point out that Star was not Mike's niece, but Michelle's. That wasn't going to help the argument. "Why would the DA want to re-start an investigation two years later for a new suspect?"

"It's only been eighteen months," Mike pointed out, unable to resist.

"Whatever! I don't care if it's two weeks. It's too damned long. You know that, Stoneman. The chances of you coming up with something worth chasing this long after the fact are zilch. It's a wild freakin' goose chase!"

"We know, Cap." Jason again tried to take down Sully's temperature. "It's our goose chase. We're going to work it in between other things, or after hours, off the clock. We won't put in any overtime because of this. If it doesn't pan out, we'll drop it. It's bugging us that there might be somebody else out there who was involved. It won't blow back on you. We promise."

"You two don't have a great track record of preventing things from blowing back on me," Sully fumed. "You get zero resources for this. No uniforms. No cars. You want to follow this, I'm not backing it and you're on your own getting the DA to authorize any warrants. Don't put it on your active case report. You get no credit for such nonsense. Clear?"

"Clear, Sir," Mike responded meekly.

"Now, get out of here and make sure you close the stupid internet girl case!"

Chapter 32
What's in a Name?

BY TEN O'CLOCK Wednesday morning, Mike and Jason were at the dingy corporate offices of Donald J. Stevens Food Services, Inc., the catering company that had worked the Broadway Cares benefit at the ballet the night Alex Bishop was murdered. Mike and Jason had met with the manager in charge of the gala event in May of 2022, immediately after the crime. Her name was Wanda Castillo. Today she greeted the detectives warmly, offering coffee, which they both accepted. In her tiny office inside the squat cinder-block building off of Twelfth Avenue, she was eager to help the police.

"We have a theory," Jason began. He explained the concept that the killer could have been posing as a waiter, and likely in disguise. There was a list of staff who had worked the event in the original case file, but Sophie had not received the files back from the DA's office after the trial. They needed to recreate it and hope for some connection to Brock Taylor, or maybe somebody else they had overlooked during the first investigation. "You have payroll records for everyone who worked the event, right?"

Wanda was a thin, wiry woman with dark hair pinned up above similarly dark eyes. She had the look of a veteran service worker who could probably heft a twenty-pound tray of drinks without blinking an eye, despite her slender arms. "I'm sure we have those records, Detective, but they would be with the corporate accounts payable office. For an event like that, all the servers are hired as contractors. We have their social security numbers and addresses for their tax forms, I'm sure, but I don't have access to that data from here. I can get it for you, though."

"Thank you. That would be helpful," Jason said, extending a business card. "You can email the data when you get it. In the meantime, how hard would it be for someone to show up for the event using a false name and work as a waiter?"

"Well, it would be pretty easy, actually," Wanda said. "It's pretty chaotic when we're getting ready for an event like that. The company sends out an email and text to all the servers on the list. The first ones who log in and sign up get the gig. We usually hire four or five more than we need because some of the dopes always back out at the last minute when they get a better offer. When they show up, they sign the roster sheet to record that they arrived, then they check in with their crew captain and off they go. It's not like we're checking IDs or anything."

"You ever have people show up who weren't on the list?" Mike asked.

"Once in a while. Usually it's just a mix-up or a glitch with our assignment system. It's no big deal. We'll usually let them work as long as we aren't way overstaffed."

"Don't you worry about whether the people are qualified? That they might steal your booze or harass the guests?" Jason asked.

"Worry? No. Does it happen? Sure. But we generally use actors and college students. They tend to be pretty reliable.

The actors have all worked as servers before and they know what they're doing. It's not rocket science, Detective. You walk around with a tray of hors d'oeuvres or glasses of wine and champagne and when your tray is empty, you go back to the kitchen to get more. We vet the bartenders a bit more to make sure they are trained to mix drinks, but the rest only need to know how to smile and carry a tray."

"What about guys subbing in for other people?" Mike asked. "Let's say somebody books themselves for the gig and then wants to skip out. Could they send in a different person and have them sign the first guy's name?"

"Sure. I suppose. If the second guy signed the first guy's name, then the first guy would get paid. It's all based on the information they have in our system when they log in. If somebody shows up and says they are subbing in, as long as they are on our roster, we'll swap them in and make sure the sub is the one who gets paid."

"Thank you, Miss Castillo," Mike said, standing. "Please send Jason that data when you can. We appreciate your cooperation."

Outside the building, the detectives discussed their next move. "So, like we figured," Mike said. "It's possible for Taylor to have been there, but we can't say for sure."

"We'll check the list, but I'm sure if Brock Taylor's name had been on the list when we checked it last May we would have noticed."

"But he could have signed somebody else's name."

"Sure," Jason said, "except that he would have had to know that somebody who was signed up to work the gala was not going to show up. If he signed somebody else's name on the roster, and then the real person showed up and saw that somebody else had already signed their name, they would probably say something, don't you think?"

"Another what-if," Mike scowled. "It's frustrating as hell. We'll get those records, but I don't expect much."

* * *

AT NOON, MIKE AND JASON CONVENED a meeting of all the officers who had been chasing down witnesses and video on The Influencer case. There were still a few potential witnesses who were out of town and more YouTube episodes of The Pharmacist's show to watch. These were necessary loose ends to tie up, but unlikely to produce meaningful leads. Officer Harris suggested making contact with the narcotics unit to see if they had any ideas about where the fentanyl might have come from and whether their lab report provided any clues as to its origin or connection to other deaths. Mike agreed to give it a try, but it was another longshot.

For most of the afternoon, the two detectives compiled their interview reports and evidence for the case file. Doing paperwork was every cop's least favorite part of the job. But having recently been through trial prep for the Ballet Murder, they knew that a well-organized case file was invaluable if the perp didn't take a plea. Of course, that assumed there was a perp, or even a suspect. For Kayleigh's murder, they had a strong suspicion about Logan Summers and a nagging doubt about Brock Taylor. They did not have probable cause to arrest either one.

At five o'clock, Mike stretched his arms over his head and sighed. "What's our next move?"

"I may have it here," Jason said, looking at his phone. "It's a message from Sterling. He says he went to Rikers Island

and spoke to Matthews. Virginia Healey absolutely knew the password for his laptop. Matthews says that, while they were together, he made the girl his de facto assistant. She regularly input show notes for him and helped him answer emails. If she said she didn't know, she's lying."

"Well, that's very interesting," Mike said. "We have nothing urgent on The Influencer for now. Let's go pay her another visit."

Chapter 33
Hell Hath No Fury

AT FIVE-THIRTY, Mike and Jason arrived back at the Walter Kerr theater, where the cast was in between the two Wednesday performances of *Hadestown*. The September weather had improved to the mid-70s. The sound of clopping on the pavement mixed with the pungent smell of horse as a carriage meandered by, filled with smiling tourists.

The detectives entered the theater through the wide-open doors without being challenged. As they lingered in the back of the house, an usher approached and asked who they were looking for. "We're here to speak with Virginia Healey," Jason said, flashing his badge.

"I don't know whether she's still here. Some of the cast is probably backstage hanging out, but most of 'em go out between shows. You can go backstage and ask."

The usher showed Mike and Jason where a doorway was hidden in the ornate wallpaper, leading to the backstage area. They wandered the dim hallways without challenge, asking the few cast members present whether they had seen Ginny. Nobody had. After patrolling the entire space, they found their way to the stage door.

Several cast members told the cops that anyone who had stepped out would certainly return through the door on a small alley separating the theater from an adjacent restaurant. Actors could duck in to avoid the crowds around the front of the house. A sleepy security guard sat in a chair to ensure nobody wandered in who didn't belong. Mike and Jason were confident that if they waited, the actress would return soon in order to prepare for the evening curtain.

"Miss Castillo came through," Jason said while checking his email.

"How so?"

"She sent over the list of the servers working the Broadway Cares gala. It's a spreadsheet, so hard to see on my phone, but we'll be able to look it over the next time we have a real computer."

Over the next fifteen minutes, six cast members returned from their between-show errands. Overhead, the Walter Kerr's ancient iron fire escapes zig-zagged down the building's side. Jason scanned 48th Street to the east, toward Broadway, while Mike monitored the western sidewalks, toward Eighth Avenue. A truck rumbled through the plywood entrance doors of a construction site on the south side of the street, obscuring his view of the sidewalk. When the truck passed by, Mike tapped Jason's arm.

"Hey. The blonde in the Columbia blue windbreaker coming this way on the south side. Is that her?"

"Could be," Jason squinted down the block.

As they watched, a male figure wearing a black hoodie stepped in front of the blonde in the windbreaker. The man had his back to the detectives. When he turned his head slightly, Mike could see wrap-around sunglasses covering his eyes under a black baseball cap. Ginny stepped to the side, toward the curb, as if trying to move past the man. He shuffled sideways like a basketball guard staying in front of a ballhandler. Ginny pulled up short, then took a step back, bobbing her head as if shouting at the man. He stepped forward, causing Ginny to jump back.

"Should we see whether she needs help?" Jason had already taken a stride toward Ginny. Mike fell in behind, not hurrying.

As Mike and Jason approached, the man reached out and grabbed the woman around the shoulders. The woman, who was definitely Ginny, shouted, "Leave me the fuck alone! Help!"

The man spun her around, put a hand over her mouth, and pulled her to his left, off the sidewalk and through the open entrance to the construction site. Painted wooden walls nine feet high shielded the remainder of the work zone from the sidewalk.

Jason sprinted forward, reaching for his service weapon. Mike hurried to follow, knowing that his much taller and fitter partner would outpace him by several seconds. When Jason reached the entrance, a high-pitched air horn blasted through the Manhattan street noise. A bay-colored horse pulling a carriage full of tourists stopped, neighing in confusion. Pedestrians stopped walking, turning toward the noise, which continued for five full seconds.

Jason paused, then continued forward to the corner of the entrance, holding his gun to his chest with both hands. Mike panted up behind his partner, nodding for Jason to make his move. When Jason leapt into the entrance, his gun extended, the scene drew his eyes in six directions at once. Mike curled around the edge of the opening a moment later, his own gun drawn, still breathing heavily.

The construction area was level dirt on the left side, sinking abruptly into a deep pit on the right. Mike could see the bottom of the pit only at the far end. Steel rebar spikes rose from the ground every few feet. At the lot's rear, scaffolding stood four stories high against the brick wall of the building abutting the site. Crews of workers in yellow hard hats with wheelbarrows and pallets of building material populated every level of the rear platform. The worker blowing the air horn stood beneath the scaffolding. He ceased his alarm and dropped the horn when he saw two men in suit jackets pointing guns at him.

Mike saw a flash of black hoodie in the back left corner of the work zone. The man was running toward an open door the size of a standard garage.

"NYPD! Where's the girl?" Jason shouted to the nearest worker.

He pointed to the pit. Mike dashed to the edge and saw Ginny lying in a grotesquely unnatural position on the muddy earth. Her head was pressed against a rebar spike like a well-tossed horseshoe.

"Go!" Mike shouted, knowing that Jason had the best shot of catching the suspect. Mike pulled out his phone and dialed central police dispatch. "This is Stoneman, detective, badge number 3641. I'm at a construction site on 48th between Broadway and Eighth. I have an assault suspect on the run toward 47th. Put out an alert for all units in Times Square. Suspect is male, six feet, wearing a black hoodie and a black ball cap and sunglasses. I need an ambulance and a patrol unit at this construction site immediately."

The exit door was half open when Jason burst through into a four-foot-wide passage between two brick buildings. At the far end, a stream of pedestrians spilled down the sidewalk. He saw the black hoodie pause at the mouth of the urban tunnel, then dash left, out of sight.

Jason holstered his weapon and sprinted down the shadowed corridor, emerging into the afternoon sunlight on 47th Street. Cars, delivery trucks, another horse-drawn tourist carriage, and a heavy flow of people clogged his vision. He turned toward the west, scanning for any sign of the hoodie or the black hat. The man was gone.

* * *

BACK AT THE CONSTRUCTION SITE, Jason reported his failure. "I think it could have been Taylor. Are we going to get any information out of Ginny?"

"Not likely." Mike stared at the activity around the pit. "Two construction workers who said they were safety wardens went down into the hole. They shouted up that Ginny was unconscious and not responsive."

A half-hour later, Mike and Jason were directing the uniformed officers and crime scene personnel at the location of Ginny's murder. Two teams of officers were canvasing the area along 47th Street and pulling security video from every camera on the block. Unfortunately, their target was wearing a ball cap and dark glasses, making an identification from the cameras a longshot.

"Union rules don't allow security cameras in a work area," Jason advised Mike after speaking to the site foreman while Mike was interviewing hard-hats. The crew members had been concentrating on their work and saw nothing until Ginny screamed and fell into the pit. Nobody could say what happened before then. They were no help in identifying the man. None of the workers could describe him any better than Mike and Jason.

Mike leaned back, stretching his spine and looking at the sky as the shadows lengthened from west to east. His cell buzzed. He nudged Jason's elbow as soon as he saw their precinct's number on the display. "Stoneman," he answered, pressing the speaker icon.

"Dispatch says you're at a crime scene on a homicide and that you called it in. What the fuck, Stoneman?"

"We happened to be in the right place at the wrong time, Cap."

"Is this related to your internet influencer case?"

"No, it's not." Mike chose not to elaborate.

"OK. Just tell me it has nothing to do with the stupid Ballet Murder case you shouldn't even be looking at."

Mike and Jason exchanged shrugs. Jason said, "I'm afraid it is, Sully. And it's probably significant. We were here for a follow-up interview with one of the actors from *Godfather*. Before we could talk to her, she was abducted off the street and dumped into a construction pit. Mike and I saw it happen, but we missed the assailant."

The silence on the line was more ominous than anything Sully could have said. After ten seconds, their captain's voice was controlled rage. "You start re-investigating this closed case and now somebody tries to dust one of your witnesses? Are you shitting me?!"

"Cap, this means somebody who was involved in the original murder is getting nervous because we've been poking around."

"You think this girl was maybe involved?" Sully was suddenly more interested than angry.

"She was a witness. We spoke to her once already. We were circling back to confront her about lying to us the first time. We were hoping she could help us put a particular bit of evidence in the hands of a possible suspect. We don't think she was involved, but you never know. Should we assume this is now our stiff?"

"Apparently," Sully fumed. "If it's connected to the other thing, that will take care of itself. Work it." Sully hung up without further discussion.

When Mike and Jason returned to the pit's edge, the lead officer who had been down with the EMTs summited a metal ladder onto the level ground. "Done?" Mike asked.

"Yeah," Officer Eddy Cooper responded, handing Jason a cell phone in a yellow plastic case, streaked with mud. "Her phone was on the ground. Before the EMTs carted her off, I used her fingerprint to unlock it."

"Nice trick," Jason said.

"Pretty standard," Mike observed, looking at Jason.

Jason, who had donned blue latex gloves, scrolled through items on the phone, swiping left and right while Mike waited impatiently. "This is significant." Jason stared at the screen. "We talked to her on Monday morning. She lied to us about not knowing the password to the director's laptop. Monday at two o'clock, there's a call to Brock Taylor."

* * *

NOBODY IN THE CAST OR CREW of *Hadestown* had any idea who might have wanted to kill Ginny. She had no conflicts with anyone and no known jealous lovers or drug dealers. One castmate said Ginny often went to a noodle place on Ninth Avenue between shows and that the timing of her return toward the theater was normal. Nobody else had any helpful information.

On the street outside the theater, Jason said, "It could have been an incredibly coincidental act of random street crime. Maybe the assailant did not try to rob her and pulled her into a well-populated construction site instead of a deserted alley because he's very bad at crime."

"Or it was Brock Taylor and his objective was to silence Ginny," Mike replied. "It's not a bad plan, grabbing her on her way back to the theater, along a predictable path. Make it look like an assault or attempted robbery and toss her into that pit with all the rebar spikes. If it was him, he has prevented her from talking to us again."

"Let's say it was him." Jason pulled Mike's sleeve and walked toward the subway entrance. "He's taking a big risk. Why? Why does he think it's so important to ice Ginny?"

"And why did Ginny call him? Was she warning him that we were snooping around and asked about him? She said he was an asshole and she had dumped him. Was she lying?"

Jason scratched his head. "Seems that way. It's possible both Healey and Taylor were involved. She could have helped him access the laptop, knowing what he was doing. Maybe they were still secretly lovers and she didn't want to admit it. Or maybe she didn't know what he was planning, but figured it out afterward."

"Or, maybe she didn't know his plans, but he knows she can finger him as having access to the laptop." Mike paused, allowing a woman in a wheelchair to exit from a restaurant onto the sidewalk.

"For whatever reason, she felt compelled to give him a head's up that we talked to her on Monday."

"She called him after saying she hadn't seen him in months. Either she was scared for herself or she was warning him. Or both."

When they arrived on the platform for the uptown #1 train, Mike tapped out a text to Michelle, letting her know that he would be heading north soon. "She warned him *because* she was scared. Whether she knew what he was doing or not, she must have helped him. She was worried she could be arrested as an accomplice. She probably wanted to know if we had talked to him and how scared she should be. It turned out she should have been very afraid — of him. He decided that having her as a witness connecting him to the laptop was a loose end he couldn't afford."

"You think he came here today intending to kill her?" Jason sounded skeptical.

"Maybe not. Maybe just to scare her, or remind her that if she gave him up, he would take her down with him. It doesn't matter. The guy seems desperate."

"Based on what we now know, Taylor had a perfect opportunity to get into the office, run the searches, then delete them. Between that and setting up a fake alibi, and now maybe killing Ginny, you think the DA will officially re-open the case?"

"No," Mike said. "It's still only a theory, with no hard evidence. We can't say for sure it was Taylor today. She called him, but they are former lovers and fellow actors. We can't say for sure that Ginny gave him the password or that Taylor actually accessed the laptop or planted the searches. We can't definitely put him at the gala spiking the drink. And even if he was there, it's still possible he and Matthews were working together. It's too thin. It might have helped the defense at the trial, but it's not enough to get Matthews released. Not yet. But maybe we can convince the DA to give us a warrant to search Taylor's apartment. What's pretty certain is that we're on the right track."

Chapter 34
Some Things Last Forever

OFFICER ROBYN KONOPKA WAS WAITING for Jason when he arrived at his desk in the bullpen Thursday morning. Mike wasn't there yet, but Jason didn't wait. "What's got you here so early this morning, Konopka?"

"We've been watching the YouTube videos by The Pharmacist. We didn't find any recommendations for taking fentanyl, but we did find ones where he talked about the Montezuma's Delight. There's also an older one where he suggested using digoxin as part of a cocktail he called a Mount Rushmore. I'm still not sure why this is relevant to The Influencer case."

"Thanks, Konopka. Good work. Can you send me the videos?"

"Sure, Detective. I already did." When Jason had no further questions, Konopka left, passing by Mike on his way in.

"What was that about?" Mike asked.

"Konopka found a video where The Pharmacist recommended a cocktail involving digoxin. She sent me the file, but I haven't looked at it yet. I had to blow her off when she asked me how this related to Kayleigh."

"I understand. Don't worry about keeping her in the dark on that. It's what Sully would want."

"Do you think The Pharmacist was intentionally lying about not remembering it?"

Mike remained standing next to Jason's desk. "Hard to say. He talks about a lot of drugs, so he might not remember. He also might be squeamish about telling a homicide detective that he recommended something that could potentially kill somebody. It's not a crime to be forgetful."

"You want to go see if we can jog his memory?"

* * *

BEFORE ELEVEN O'CLOCK, Mike and Jason occupied two of the three chairs around the tiny dining table in the West Village apartment of Craig Goldstein, a.k.a. The Pharmacist. When they arrived unannounced, the aging hippy's attitude was resigned acceptance, inviting the detectives in without any argument.

"Do you know why we're here?" Mike asked.

"I have an idea." The man's gray ponytail was not pulled back as tightly, and was oilier than during their prior interview. Bags under his half-opened eyes suggested someone who had not slept much the night before.

"It's about the video where you recommend a drug cocktail involving digoxin. It was from September of 2021. You called it a Mount Rushmore. Do you need us to play it for you, or do you remember it?"

"I know what you're talkin' about." Goldstien kept his head up, making eye contact with Mike. "After we talked last time, I looked it up."

"We told you to call us if you thought of anything," Jason scolded.

"Yeah. I know. But that was a request, not a requirement. I figured you would try to connect it to the case they just convicted that Broadway director for. I figured, since he was guilty, it didn't really matter."

Mike didn't believe the response, but let it go. "Did you prescribe the digoxin for somebody around April or May of 2022?"

"Yeah. I did. The thing is, like I said in my video, the drug has the same chemical characteristics as homeopathic oleander. When people ask for it, I tell 'em they can get it cheaper by ordering commercially available oleander or getting it at a GNC store. Most people say thank you and go that route rather than bothering with a prescription. This person contacted me and not only wanted the digoxin, but he wanted it in a large dosage, more concentrated than what's normally prescribed. I told him it wasn't necessary to get the dosage that high, but he was very, well, insistent."

"Were you worried about the effects of a high dosage?" Mike asked.

"Not really. People can take as much as they want. It's not going to kill you, unless you're also taking a beta blocker. I tell that to everyone when they ask me for it, and I mentioned it in my video. Anyway, pharmacies don't stock it in a high dosage, so it was a special order. I couldn't just write a normal prescription. He offered to pay me if I would fill the prescription for him and let him meet me to pick it up."

"That sounds unusual and suspicious," Jason observed.

The Pharmacist scowled at Jason. "I don't ask questions or make assumptions. I don't interrogate customers about how they plan to use the ingredients. He was willing to pay.

He didn't want me to call in a prescription with his name on it. I get that. People don't want to be identified and leave a paper trail. It's not a controlled substance, but people get squirrely about these things. It's not unusual. So, I did it for him."

"How much did he pay you?" Mike asked.

"Nine hundred dollars. Cash."

"I take it you delivered the order, as requested?"

"Sure I did."

Jason pulled out his phone and maneuvered to his case file. He handed the phone to their host. "Do you recognize this man?"

"I thought you already convicted the guy," he said.

"We think the man who got the drug from you was an accomplice," Jason explained.

The Pharmacist scrutinized the picture. "No. I can't say that this was him. In fact, the man I met with definitely didn't look like this."

Jason clicked off the image of Brock Taylor's headshot. "Can you describe him, compared to that photo?"

"You have to understand, I wasn't trying to identify the dude. Most people don't want me to know who they are. I meet with people from time to time to deliver certain things that they don't want to get for themselves. Even with a prescription, people aren't always comfortable walking into a pharmacy where there are security cameras and picking up something that could be embarrassing. And pharmacies don't like giving out drugs to somebody other than the person for whom they're prescribed. So, I sometimes do personal deliveries. New York is a big city, with lots of sophisticated drug users. When I do a meeting, it tends to be in a very public space. It is often loud and dark. The client comes in, we make the exchange, and then they leave. I'm not taking selfies with them or taking notes about what they look like. This guy was older. He walked with a limp, I remember, and he had a gray moustache. He was wearing a hat, so I didn't see his hair. That's all I can tell you."

"What about height?" Jason pressed. "Was he particularly tall or short?"

"Not sure. Like I said, he walked with a limp, which probably made him seem shorter than he actually was. He was not particularly tall, no more than six feet, I'd say."

"Where did the meeting happen?" Mike asked.

"It was a little bar on 4th street. Don't bother going there to ask about security cameras. They don't have any. That's why I used the place."

Jason stepped in close. "This was eighteen months ago. You have a pretty specific memory about it. Why?"

Goldstein held Jason's gaze, then dropped his chin. "It wasn't long afterward that Alex Bishop was poisoned. I put two and two together and figured the person who wanted the heavy dose of digoxin might have been involved. I thought about it. A lot. I even thought about going to the cops about it. But then you arrested him. So, I figured it wasn't my problem. And I didn't want to be connected to it, so I never said anything. It's not like I could have picked the man out of lineup anyway. But I still thought about it."

"OK, Mr. Goldstein. I'm not happy that you held out on us, but thank you for being honest this time. I'm taking your word for the fact that you don't have any additional information you're not telling us. If we find out you do, you'd be guilty of obstructing justice and we'd throw your ass in jail. At that point, the medical certification board might become interested in the status of your license to write prescriptions."

"I get it," the man said with resignation. "I told you everything I know."

"And we'll need you to cooperate with our investigation. I need to tell you that another witness in this case was murdered yesterday. It's not impossible that the guy whose picture we showed you, or somebody else, might come gunning for you if they think you're a loose end. If you hear from the man who ordered the digoxin again, you tell us immediately. Understand?"

"Sure. But how will I know whether it's the same person over the phone?"

"You don't happen to have a phone number for him, from the last time?" Jason asked.

"No. I trashed my phone about a year ago and lost all my call history. But even if I had it, when folks call me for buys like that, they don't use their own phones." The Pharmacist sat placidly in his chair, as if discussing the prior night's Mets score.

"How about this," Jason leaned in, "if you get any unusual calls at all, you call us and tell us about them."

"And don't leave town in the next few weeks," Mike admonished as he stood to leave.

"There's nowhere else in the world with more fucked up people. Why would I ever leave?"

Chapter 35
Substitution

THAT EVENING, the informal Ballet Murder task force ate slices of mushroom pizza in Mike's apartment and talked about their information. JJ was home with his grandmother, leaving Topsy without a playmate, although she found a home on Star's lap.

Rachel, Star, and Jackie had divided the internet in a quest to find other drag performers doing renditions of "I Am What I Am." They hoped to identify the imposter who performed in place of Brock Taylor at the Stress Factory. Jackie looked at websites for drag queens, while Rachel focused on other actors. Star trolled for general instances of performance videos, including on Instagram and YouTube.

It was Star who found paydirt. She sent the video to Michelle by email, so she could use her laptop to play it on the television. It was unanimous that the attributes of the song's performance were a fundamental match for the video captured at the club in New Jersey. Star beamed when Jason and Mike congratulated her on spotting what could be a significant lead. The performer's drag name was Lilith Juteuse. Lilith's real name was Lawrence Teel.

"Whoa," Mike exclaimed when Star said the name. "Jason, that's the guy Sterling got into the fight with. He's the guy that Taylor was meeting with last week. Maybe that's what they were arguing about, that Teel was Taylor's alibi. You think they were in it together?"

"Could be." Jason made eye contact with Rachel, who was clearly excited about the connection. "Maybe Teel didn't know. Maybe he did Taylor a favor and found out later that he was an accessory to the murder. Maybe he was shaking Taylor down over it. Who knows for sure? What's certain is that we need to talk to him."

"Wait a minute." Mike rose slowly from the sofa, tapping his index finger against his drink glass. "Jason, that name — Lawrence Teel — wasn't it on the list?"

Jason's eyes widened as he realized where Mike was going. "The waiter list?"

"Yeah. Do you have it?"

"It's still in my email." Jason snatched his phone and navigated to the email with the list attachment. He sent it to Michelle, who pulled it up on her laptop. A quick word search found Lawrence Teel on the list of paid waiters at the Broadway Cares gala.

"He certainly wasn't there if he was performing at the Stress Factory," Rachel said.

"Of course," Mike walked to the window and looked out over 68th street. "Teel's name was on the list at the ballet and Taylor's name was on the performer list at the Stress Factory. They swapped places. Taylor signed in at the gala as Teel. He knew Teel wouldn't be there."

"You think Teel was in on the whole scheme?" Jason asked.

"Maybe. Or maybe not," Mike replied. "If Taylor asked Teel to impersonate him in Jersey, he could have registered as Teel for the gala without Teel knowing."

"Taylor would have to know Teel's password to log into the catering company's assignment system," Rachel pointed out.

"And Teel got paid," Jason said.

"Yeah, That's right . . ." Mike's voice trailed off. "That would explain how Teel may have connected the dots and figured out what Taylor did, which resulted in their argument."

"Regardless," Jason slapped his hand on the table, startling Topsy, who leapt to the floor and scurried to her favorite pillow on the sofa, "Teel is a key piece now. We need to squeeze him and see if he'll give up Taylor."

Jason said he would run the name through the NYPD's database in the morning to get Teel's address, although the way actors tended to move around, it was unlikely that it would be current. "We could contact him by email and set up a meeting."

"We need to catch him off guard," Mike stated the obvious. "Does his website indicate where he's currently performing?"

"I'm on that," Jackie said, munching on a pizza crust. "He's got nothing tonight, but tomorrow night he's performing at a club on 8th Street, according to his Instagram."

"OK. We'll try to catch him before his performance tomorrow," Mike said. "Jason, let's get Sterling to come along. He might be helpful."

Chapter 36
Home Turf

FRIDAY MORNING, at the district attorney's office in Foley Square, Mike and Jason walked into a meeting with Keith Harris. He was still basking in the glow of his successful prosecution of Nathan Matthews. They did not look forward to the discussion.

"Good morning, Mike." Keith stretched out his hand to shake with his favorite witness.

"Thanks for seeing us, Keith. You see Mauricio's home run last night? Man, the kid's got some power."

Jason sat quietly while Mike and Keith spent several minutes commiserating over the failures of the New York Mets season, followed by hopeful speculation about the young players on the team. When the baseball discussion waned, Keith asked, "So, guys, I got your request for the search warrant for Brock Taylor. I'm confused. Nathan Matthews is on his way to Sing Sing as soon as the judge sentences him next week. Why are you interested in a minor witness in a closed case?"

"We think Taylor may be an accomplice to the murder," Mike said. It wasn't entirely a lie. If Taylor was the actual murderer, then he was, in a sense, an accomplice. And it still wasn't out of the question that Taylor and Matthews could have been working together, at least until Taylor fingered Matthews as someone with a motive to kill Alex Bishop.

Keith asked the obvious question. "What makes you think Matthews had help?"

Mike and Jason walked the ADA through the evidence they uncovered. "It's something that came to light recently. It turns out Taylor faked his alibi for the night of the murder. We also think he had a grudge against Bishop because he came in as the big name lead and stole away Taylor's chance to be the star. And we think he might have worked as a waiter during the Broadway Cares gala when Bishop got poisoned, under the name of the guy who was faking his performance in Jersey to establish the alibi."

Keith sat back in his chair and crossed his arms. "Did this information come to light through Matthews' attorney — who claims his client was framed?"

Mike sighed. He and Jason had discussed this. "It's true, Keith, that the original tip came from the private investigator working with the defense attorney. But we chased it down independently. The facts are solid. We'd like you to allow us to investigate what happened. We're looking for the truth, whatever it happens to be. Right?"

"Mike. Jason. You're letting the defense team use you to do their work for them. They want to have the basis for an appeal. We nailed Matthews. It's a win. How is this other actor supposed to have helped Matthews?"

"If he was the one who spiked the drink at the gala, then he's the actual murderer and Matthews was the mastermind. They may both be guilty. I'm sure you don't want to let one guy get off just because you caught the other one."

"Look, I'll admit that if this information had been available before the trial, it might have made a difference, but now it's mere speculation. I agree it seems suspicious, but there are plenty of reasons why Taylor might have wanted to slip away and it just happened to be the same night as the murder. Do you have evidence that he was at the gala?"

"Only the circumstantial evidence that somebody registered to work under the name of Lawrence Teel, while Teel was performing in Jersey pretending to be Taylor," Mike admitted.

"And your conclusion that Teel was impersonating Taylor is based on the discrepancies in the performance?" Keith was obviously skeptical.

"That's right," Jason said. "I know that, from your perspective, it seems like a lot of circumstantial connections. That's why we want to search Taylor's apartment. And we're going to talk to Teel. We'll see if he admits that he doubled for Taylor at the Jersey show."

"That will prove he wasn't at the gala. It won't prove that Taylor was there in his place," Keith observed.

"That's why we want a warrant to search his apartment and examine his phone and internet records." Jason put his palms on the table and half-stood to emphasize the point.

"What? You think he might have a bottle of digoxin in his medicine cabinet? C'mon, Jason. That's not much to go on. I'm not going to give the press and the defense attorney a platform to re-open the case after the trial. The press on that will be ridiculous. No. We got the guy. We're done. Let it go."

"We also think Taylor may have murdered Ginny Healey two days ago," Mike said. "What about a warrant for that? We need a DNA sample from him."

"Do you have a witness who has identified him as the assailant?"

"No," Mike admitted. "Jason and I were nearby and saw him, but we didn't get a good enough look to say for sure it was him."

"So, you want me to ask for a warrant based on a 'maybe' identification? Mike, c'mon. You know that can't happen."

Mike and Jason exchanged a glance. "OK, Keith. We won't push it, at least for now. We also wanted to talk with you about the Kayleigh Bronson case. We're still not sure it was a homicide, but we want to have you give us some cover before we move. We want to arrest Logan Summers."

"Wow," Keith exclaimed. "That will generate some media coverage. How sure are you?"

"There's a lot of smoke. I think there's enough." Mike and Jason then recounted the investigation.

While Jason was describing their interview with Summers' wife, Mike's phone buzzed. He checked the text message quickly and saw that it was from Sully, who never sent texts. Before Jason finished his summary, Mike cut in.

"This discussion just became moot. They found Logan Summers dead in Kayleigh's apartment. We won't be needing that arrest warrant."

* * *

BACK AT THE PARK TOWERS, Jason and Mike spoke to the building manager and interviewed the doormen. They learned that Summers had moved into the apartment he owned two days earlier. He had been mostly keeping to himself. No wild parties, although a lady had come to visit him the night before. The building security kept a lookout for his wife's PI and snuck the girl in through the breezeway.

That afternoon, the housekeeper arrived to clean the place and found Summers naked on the bathroom floor. There was nobody else there; the doormen and security said that his guest left around midnight. The first arriving officers assessed the scene quickly and backed away, sealing off the apartment until the detectives could arrive. They knew this same apartment had been a crime scene less than two weeks earlier and knew better than to risk spoiling any evidence. The assistant medical examiner, Natalie, was already in the hallway, waiting for clearance to enter.

Mike and Jason went in first. The apartment looked significantly different from the night after the Labor Day party. There were only two discarded glasses. The marble bar contained only one half-empty bottle of Grey Goose, an ice bucket with a puddle of water at the bottom, and a tray of half-eaten sushi on the coffee table. They carefully traversed the area, working their way to the bedroom suite. The bed was rumpled, the main blanket lying half-off the left side. In the bathroom, they observed the plump, naked body lying on the tile floor, one arm splayed out above his head. On the marble counter, a razor blade lay flat next to a dim line of white powder residue. A hundred dollar bill, mostly rolled into a tube, lay in the sink.

They left the body untouched. Natalie would conduct the examination. The forensics team would bag the razor blade, sweep up the powder residue, and dust for fingerprints. There was not much more for the detectives in the bathroom.

Back in the bedroom, they found Summers' phone. The battery was dead, so they left that to the forensics team. A small quantity of clothing and a single pair of dress shoes in the closet indicated that the tycoon had not fully moved in. They exited, giving the green light for Natalie to enter.

"I don't suppose there's any chance we'll be able to find the hooker he was here with last night, is there?" Mike asked.

"You never know," Jason replied. "Maybe he's stupid and arrogant enough to have booked her on his cell phone through an escort service."

"It's never that easy," Mike said, then caught himself. "Well, almost never."

"Regardless," Jason said, "whatever case there might have been against this asshole is over. Where does that leave us?"

"If he killed Kayleigh, regardless of the reason, then it leaves us with a closed case file. If Kayleigh's death was an accidental overdose, it's still a closed file."

Jason scanned the bedroom, recalling where Kayleigh's body had been splayed out on the same seafoam green comforter. "What if Taylor had something to do with it? We haven't found a motive for him yet, but he's still in play."

"Yeah." Mike took two steps toward the door, then stopped. "He's still in play, but more for the Ballet Murder, and the murder of Ginny Healey. If we take him down for either of those, maybe it's two for the price of one."

Chapter 37
Circling Back

AT THE LENA HORNE THEATER, the former home of *Godfather: The Musical*, the cast was trickling in before the eight o'clock show of *Sharknado: The Musical*, which had opened a month earlier. The stage manager for the show, Rich Cohen, had carried over from *Godfather*. He was directing traffic from the same backstage office as when the detectives had interviewed him sixteen months earlier after Alex Bishop's murder. Five hours before the curtain went up, Cohen was reasonably relaxed when they entered his office.

"I was surprised to hear from you again, Detectives." He greeted them with a firm handshake. "You said you would tell me what this is about when you arrived. So?"

"We're investigating whether there was another person involved in the Alex Bishop murder," Mike said. "We've uncovered new evidence and need you to confirm some information from last May."

"I'll do my best." The stage manager leaned back in his chair, seemingly unconcerned.

Jason took over the questioning. "Did you know the password for Nathan Matthews' laptop computer?"

Cohen furrowed his brow. "You mean his show computer? The one he kept in his office? Sure. I knew it. I needed to access information about the cast and show sometimes when Nathan was busy or not around. Sure."

"Did you ever tell anyone else the password?"

Cohen's eyes lifted to the ceiling. "I don't think so. I'm pretty sure our choreographer also had it. Nathan's personal secretary, obviously. Maybe a few others. It wasn't a state secret. But I don't think anybody ever asked me for it. They would have asked Nathan."

"We understood from several witnesses we spoke to last year that Matthews was very protective of his privacy and always kept his office locked up. Is that true?"

"Yes, for the most part." Cohen scratched his neck with the back of his left hand. "He didn't like people in his space. But that didn't apply to me. I had a key. I have access to the whole house, but that's normal. It's my house."

"Did anybody else have a key?"

"Only me and the chief of security, besides Nathan, of course. And Julie, his secretary."

Jason paused, scrutinizing the stage manager. "Do you know whether Ginny Healey had a key, when she was sleeping with Matthews?"

Cohen's face fell. "I heard about Ginny. Is that why you're really here? She was murdered, right?"

"We can't say," Mike interjected. "What's the answer to Detective Dickson's question?"

"About Ginny having a key? I don't think she had one, although I suppose it's possible. But she wouldn't have needed one." Mike's puzzled look prompted Cohen to volunteer the answer to the unasked follow-up question. "The door to that office has a bad latch. It locks, so if you try to turn the knob when it's locked it won't turn. But if you lift up on the handle and pull hard enough, the latch will pop out and you can pull it open without unlocking it."

"And you didn't fix it?" Jason was skeptical.

"No. It was actually kinda perfect because it meant that if somebody really needed to get in or if Nathan forgot his key, we knew how to get the door open. It was only the same people who had keys who knew about it. But I'm guessing Ginny probably knew also."

Jason leaned forward in the small chair in which he was sitting. "If one of the actors wanted to get into the office and look at information on the director's laptop, was there anything stopping them from doing that without being seen?"

"You think somebody from the crew helped Nathan kill Alex?"

"Just answer the question," Mike prodded.

"Well, I'd have to say yes. If somebody wanted to get in there and they knew how to jimmy open the door, they could do it. There isn't any other security and the office is kind of out of the way. Doing it without being seen wouldn't be that hard, especially if it was at a time when there weren't a lot of people around backstage. If the person knew the password, they could get into the laptop. I followed Nathan's trial. You think somebody besides Nathan ran those internet searches to identify the drug that killed Alex?"

"We can't talk about our investigation," Mike replied. "You've been very helpful. It would also be helpful for us if you would not tell anyone about our questions today. We don't want anybody to get the wrong idea, and we wouldn't want anyone to think you identified a potential suspect. That might put you in danger."

Cohen's eyes widened like a camera lens. "Whoa. Are you saying Ginny's murder is connected to this? That somebody might want to kill me if they thought I knew something that could get them convicted?"

Mike exchanged a glance with Jason. "You're jumping to conclusions, Mr. Cohen. We can't confirm or deny anything like that. You can imagine how the press might react. But no matter what the reason, You should keep this conversation to yourself. Do you understand?"

"Absolutely," Cohen responded quickly. "I won't say shit to anyone."

Outside the theater, Jason said, "He's telling the truth."

"Yeah. Agreed," Mike walked toward Broadway. "I don't think he's involved, but I would not put it past him to tell other people that we came around asking questions. I hope he doesn't tell anyone who might kill him over it."

Chapter 38
The Blue Room

FRIDAY NIGHT, three detectives met outside the Blue Room on West 8th Street in Greenwich Village. The scheduled show was advertised as a humorous parody of Broadway classics and was supposed to start at eight o'clock. It was a quarter past six when Mike flashed his NYPD badge and ID at an usher wearing a statue of liberty costume. Jason and Sterling Wright followed behind him without contest. After brief conversations with two other staff members at the dinner theater venue, they were directed to a cramped backstage area.

There, they were confronted by a large woman holding a clipboard. "Can I help you, gentlemen?" She was clearly in charge and certainly not a performer, wearing a blue track suit with her hair covered by a red, white, and blue scarf.

"NYPD," Mike said, not bothering to introduce himself while flashing his badge. "You have a performer here named Lawrence Teel."

The woman consulted her clipboard. "Yeah. He's here. What kinda trouble is he in?"

"Probably none, ma'am. We need to talk to him. Where can we find him?"

She tilted her head to the left. "They're all in the green room. First door on the right."

When Jason opened the door to the green room, the buzz of conversation ceased, leaving the cluttered space nearly silent except for the beat of hip-hop music coming from an unseen stereo. Seven people, all holding paper plates piled with sandwiches and other catered food from a scruffy buffet, focused on the appearance of the tall, unfamiliar man. Mike barreled through behind Jason. Sterling waited in the hallway in case Teel recognized him.

The two well-dressed detectives immediately made all the performers nervous. They could have been producers or agents, but looked more like government officials of some kind. "Which one of you is Lawrence Teel?" Jason called out.

All the cast members looked around at each other. A man wearing a blue sequined jumpsuit slowly raised his hand. "I'm Lawrence."

"NYPD," Jason said, flashing his badge. "We have a matter that we need to talk to you about. Can you step outside, please?"

Teel looked like a boy caught by his teacher with a dirty magazine hidden in his textbook. He placed his plate on a folding chair and moved toward the door while his fellow cast members watched in silence. Jason gestured down the narrow corridor, where a metal door blocked further movement. When he turned around, there were three men staring at him in the glow of the EXIT sign.

By pre-arrangement, Sterling asked the questions. "Mr. Teel, you're not in any trouble, yet. We need you to verify some information for us in an ongoing murder investigation."

"Hey, man, I haven't murdered anybody," Teel protested. In the sparkling blue jumpsuit, it would have been easy to overlook the man's athletic physique. His eyes darted between the three cops and the exit door. In the dimly lit space, Teel didn't seem to recognize Sterling from their brief altercation in the alley next to the Club Cabana.

Mike waved off Jason's hand signal to frisk their detainee, figuring that concealing a weapon under the sequins was unlikely. Mike blocked the door, while Jason loomed over Teel's left shoulder to ensure he didn't try to bolt.

"We know you didn't kill anybody," Sterling said. "You were an accessory to a murder, but we think you didn't do it intentionally. However, if you aren't straight with us, we'll arrest you. You'll miss this gig and probably a bunch more. You understand?" Teel nodded his head rapidly.

"OK, then. I want you to think back to the night of Monday, May twenty-third of 2022. I know that's a long time ago, but I'll help you remember. A friend of yours, Brock Taylor, was supposed to perform in a drag revue at the Stress Factory in Jersey. He asked you to fill in for him. You did 'I Am What I Am' and killed it. You remember that?"

"Um, I'm — I'm not sure," Teel stammered.

"Let me help you be sure," Sterling continued. "You didn't tell anyone at the venue that you were subbing. You pretended to be Taylor. You dressed in his costume and mimicked his makeup. He got paid for the gig, although he probably paid you back later."

Teel had an awful poker face. His eyes shifted between Sterling and Mike. He furrowed his brow and beads of sweat formed on his forehead.

"You may have noticed that you got paid for a different gig the same night, working as a waiter for Donald J. Stevens catering at the Broadway Cares / Equity Fights Aids benefit at Lincoln Center," Sterling continued. "Does that ring a bell?"

Teel teetered on his heels, adjusting his balance as if having trouble standing upright. "Man, I get paid for a lot of gigs. Plenty of times the money comes in weeks or months later, so I'm never sure which gig is which."

"OK. That's fair. So, maybe you'll be interested to know that your buddy, Brock, registered for that gig under your name and worked it pretending to be you. It turns out he killed somebody and you are his alibi. You may have heard about it, the Alex Bishop murder. So, you're in a load of trouble, Lawrence. We're ready to arrest you right now, unless you want to come clean and cooperate, because it looks to us like you were in on the whole scheme. That's called being an accessory to murder."

Teel's face drained of color. He opened and closed his mouth like a fish on the beach. "I-I — fuck. Really? I mean. Oh, fuck. You already seem to know what happened. I didn't do anything wrong. He asked me to cover for him. He said Vinnie, the owner, would cut off his balls if he didn't show up and he made me promise to pretend to be him and not tell anybody. He paid me after. It was no big deal. I didn't know he was doing anything criminal. He's a — a friend. I owed him a favor. I swear, I didn't know."

"I think you did know," Sterling pressed. "I saw you last week at the Club Cabana. You got into an argument with Taylor. Were you shaking him down? Squeezing him because you're the only person who can finger him as the killer?"

"What? Are you — Was that you? No! I'm not blackmailing him. I — wait, I thought Nathan Matthews killed Alex Bishop, right? You tellin' me Brock was involved? Man, I don't know nothin' about that. I didn't do anything. I'm not going to jail for him."

Sterling looked around the group, then put a hand on Teel's arm. "Calm down, man. It's OK. We can believe you might only have been doing a favor for a friend. I suppose it's possible you didn't know what was really happening. But it looks pretty bad for you now. I'm inclined to believe you, but we'll need you to come in and sign an affidavit swearing to what you just said."

"Anything, man," Teel blurted. "Whatever. I'm telling the truth. I swear."

Jason attached a firm grip to Teel's shoulder. "Did Taylor tell you where he was going to be when you were covering for him?"

"Yeah. He said he had a date with a married woman that he had an arrangement with. He said it was a huge secret because her husband was rich and jealous and had a private eye, so he had to be careful or the old man would have him killed. He never told me the lady's name."

Jason pulled out a business card and handed it to Teel. "You give me a call on Monday and come to the address on that card. If you're not there by ten o'clock, I'll put out an all-points bulletin for your arrest. Understand?" Teel nodded vigorously, without speaking. "Good boy. If you tell anyone what we talked about, you will absolutely be charged as an accomplice to a murder. Now, you go back and do your show. Break a leg."

The actor scurried away toward the green room, not looking back.

The three detectives exited to the sidewalk. Mike said, "We already knew he subbed in for Taylor. He confirmed it, but we didn't learn anything new."

"Yeah, but now it's not based on our analysis of the videos," Jason said. "Now we have a witness who will confirm that Taylor faked his alibi, and we have a record of somebody showing up at the gala using Teel's name. Who else could it have been?"

"It's good," Mike said. "It's not enough yet, but it's good. Maybe we can figure out who the woman was that he was supposedly with, which now will become his new alibi. Of course, she wouldn't confirm it, even if we could find her. Assuming she even really exists."

"So, it's a pretty damned good cover story," Sterling observed.

"Let's regroup tomorrow." Mike waved to his companions on his way to the Broadway subway.

* * *

WHEN JASON HAD READ JJ *Goodnight Moon* and tucked him in, he joined Rachel in their living room. Rachel's mother was watching CSI Las Vegas. Rachel snuggled against Jason's left side and softly asked, "How did it go?"

He put his mouth near Rachel's ear. "We confirmed that Lawrence Teel impersonated Brock Taylor, like we figured. He says he didn't know what Taylor was up to and we think he's telling the truth. The dude was terrified. That doesn't mean he wasn't shaking Taylor down over it, but that's small potatoes. So, we know what we already knew. What we really need is a way to put the digoxin in Taylor's hand. The Pharmacist won't be able to identify him. So, we still don't have any actual evidence linking the guy to the murder."

Rachel looked into Jason's eyes. "What if we could get Taylor to go back for another meeting with The Pharmacist and you could catch him there?"

"That would be ideal. But how could we get him to do that?"

Rachel smiled. "Star, Jackie, and I were talking about it, and we have an idea."

Chapter 39
Workshopping the Problem

SATURDAY WOULD NOT NORMALLY BE a working day for Mike and Jason unless they had a particularly active case that justified paying the detectives overtime. In the off-the-books Ballet Murder re-investigation, however, it figured to be a busy and critical day. Mike wished they had a search warrant allowing them to bust into Brock Taylor's apartment at dawn. But without the support of the DA, not to mention only provisional permission from Sully, they had to come up with an alternate way to corner him somewhere.

Mike bought into Rachel's plan right away. Jason, on the other hand, had reservations. They would need to recruit some help and their gambit's success depended on several pieces coming together. In the end, Jason relented, partly because Rachel was so excited about it.

The conversation with Sully happened by phone on Saturday morning. Jason would have preferred a video call so he could gauge how mad Sully was based on the prominence of his neck veins, but Mike wanted to keep it short. They were honest and explained the whole plan to their captain.

"You two morons should be kicked off the force for even thinking about such nonsense!" Sully had responded. Mike spent three minutes explaining that nobody would ever know and that he would take full responsibility if the shit ever hit the fan. Both detectives pledged to swear that Sully had no knowledge, if Internal Affairs ever asked.

"Then why are you telling me?"

"Because we don't want to go behind your back, Sully," Mike said. "We remember the Alexander Hamilton hotel fiasco and we promised that would never happen again."

"Yeah? Well this sounds like exactly the same kind of shit-show waiting to happen!"

Jason shrugged at Mike, knowing that Sully could not see. "Cap, we're going to take every precaution to keep this under control. But no matter what, it won't be the same, because this time we're telling you in advance."

"But I'm not going to admit that, and you're not going to tell anyone, so it'll be just as bad for you!"

After another five minutes, Sully seemed to get tired of yelling at them and relented, in his own way. "It's Saturday. You two are not working. I'm giving you a direct order to drop this piece of shit investigation. You are not authorized to apprehend anyone or question anyone. Are you both crystal clear about how much trouble you'll be in if you disregard my explicit instructions?"

"We understand, Sir," Mike said into the speaker.

"Good. I expect to see you Monday morning wrapping up the paperwork on The Influencer murder. If you call me again during my weekend, I will cut your balls off. You got that?"

"Got it, Chief," Jason said right before Mike pushed the END button.

"You think he was recording that last part?" Mike asked.

"You can bet on it. If this goes bad, we're completely screwed."

"Yeah." Mike stuffed his phone into his pocket. "Let's make sure it doesn't go bad."

* * *

FINDING BROCK TAYLOR'S WHEREABOUTS on a Saturday afternoon proved to be challenging. Taylor's social media accounts all contained promos for his scheduled eight o'clock performance at a supper club in lower Manhattan. They needed to get to him earlier in the day. The question was where to find him.

Mike's instinct was to stake out Taylor's apartment and follow him when he left home. Jason pointed out the two potential problems with that plan. First, they were not certain that the address they had for him was current. Second, their target might not be spending the night in his own apartment, even if he did live there. Since their plan required them to find him that day, missing him wasn't an option.

Star's review of his online activity over the past month showed that Taylor habitually checked in at virtually every public location he visited. It was a good bet he would self-identify his location if they were patient. He apparently wanted everyone to know where he was and what he was doing all the time. Since he didn't know a team of detectives was looking for him, he would likely follow his normal pattern.

Mike went to the 94th Street precinct to make preparations, including phone calls to several of his police colleagues. Over his many years, Mike had accumulated a deep trove of favors. It was time to call in some of them. Sterling stationed himself in a Times Square café. He wasn't an active cop anymore, but he knew the drill. Star, Rachel, and Jackie monitored Taylor's social media accounts and watched those of his online friends, in case one of them tagged their prey in a post.

Star won the watch party lottery at 1:15 p.m. when Taylor checked in at the Galaxy Diner on Ninth Avenue and 47th Street. It was a popular brunch location. Sterling was closest and first on the scene. He walked in and identified Taylor at a table with three other people, two men and one woman. He walked out and waited for Mike and Jason on a nearby corner. Jason arrived next, narrowly beating Mike to the meet-up. Sterling reported that the group had only recently been served their food and that all were drinking freely.

"Good," Mike said. "I hope he's good and tipsy by the time they come out."

Mike got his wish forty-five minutes later when the group of four stumbled down the step from the restaurant to the sidewalk. The surveillance team watched from next to a food cart selling pretzels. Two of Taylor's three companions walked away to the north, while their mark and the woman walked past Mike's left shoulder and continued down Ninth Avenue. The plan was to wait for Taylor to be alone before confronting him. They could grab him with the woman present and hope she would not make any trouble or start filming, but they preferred not to have any witness.

Luck was on their side when the woman went into a shop between 44th and 43rd. Taylor remained outside and pulled out a vaping pipe. Mike quickly called in their position. Jason walked past Taylor, then turned around, blocking a southbound escape.

Mike approached and stood directly in front of the man, while Sterling established a position to his north. "Brock Taylor?" Mike said, hoping his tone mimicked a fan who might want an autograph or a selfie.

"Yes?" He removed the pipe and smiled.

Mike pulled out his badge and ID wallet. "NYPD. You're under arrest for the murder of Alex Bishop."

Taylor jerked to his right and took half a step before Jason firmly grabbed his arm above the elbow. Sterling repeated the motion on his left arm. A black-and-white NYPD cruiser pulled up, its lights flashing, but without a siren. Jason pulled Taylor's arm behind his back and attached a handcuff, while Sterling twisted the other arm and snapped on the companion. They jointly pushed Taylor forward toward the cruiser, while Mike held open the rear door. He helped the man in without hitting his head, then got into the back seat next to their detainee. Taylor did not struggle. Jason hurried to the front passenger seat. Officer Robyn Konopka then pulled away, leaving Sterling on the sidewalk.

The cops maintained silence during the ride north to the 94th Street precinct building. Konopka had killed the flashing lights by the time she pulled up in front, allowing the men to exit. Mike and Jason pushed Taylor up the stairs into the lobby, where an elderly woman sat on the public bench, likely waiting for a relative to be released. Mike waved at the officer behind the intake window, who buzzed them through a metal security door. They hustled their prisoner down one flight of stairs to the lower level, then into an interrogation room which the cops called "the box." They planted Taylor in a metal chair in front of a metal table. Jason unlocked one handcuff and attached it to a U-bolt on the top of the table. The detectives then left the room in silence, having not spoken to Taylor since the arrest.

In the hallway, Mike placed a phone call. Jason went into the observation cubby next to the interrogation room and confirmed that the recording equipment and camera were turned off. When he emerged, Mike said, "We're ready."

Jason went first into the room, walking deliberately to the table and sitting opposite the restrained prisoner. Mike remained standing, at the back of the cramped space. "You almost got away with it." Jason left the statement hanging in the room, saying nothing further.

After a silence of more than a minute, Taylor said, "I don't know what you're talking about."

"Oh, come on, Brock. You thought you set up an air-tight alibi. Getting Lawrence Teel to cover your gig in Jersey was smart. You knew he could handle your song. He's about your height and build. You had him wear your costume and booked a gig out of town where the audience wouldn't notice that it wasn't you. It was well thought-out. Teel did a terrific job. Although, I must say that his rendition was a little too derivative of the George Hearn version. Yours, on the other hand, had much more originality. It was lucky for us that they still had the video so we could watch."

Mike watched silently, looking for Taylor's reactions. The actor did not give any outward sign of being worried.

After a long pause, Jason said, "You should know that Teel gave you up pretty quickly when we interrogated him. I guess he doesn't fear you enough. See, that's how the mob guys do it. They make sure the patsy knows that if they rat out their bosses, their life is worthless. That's why they do time rather than talk. Teel didn't feel that way. We have his affidavit. So, your carefully constructed alibi is shot."

Jason stared at Taylor, taking his time. He had not yet asked a question. "We have the security video from the American Ballet Theater. Your disguise was impressive, but facial recognition software can see through that. I must say you were not obvious when you spiked the drinks with the digoxin. You worked it out pretty well. Framing your director was, frankly, brilliant. You two had the best motives to kill Bishop. Putting that evidence on Matthews' laptop sealed his fate. We also talked to your girlfriend, Ginny. She told us she gave you the password for the laptop, before you tossed her into that construction pit."

Mike and Jason watched Taylor's reaction to this statement. The actor's mouth twitched, but he otherwise maintained a stony countenance. Then Mike took over the questioning. "So, you waited for Matthews to be gone, but not so gone that he'd have a great alibi like yours. Then you went into his office and planted the evidence. Did Ginny give you the office key, or did she just tell you how to jimmy the latch?"

"I don't have to talk to you." Taylor sat back in his chair, but was held back by his handcuff. Jason leaned forward and unlocked the cuff, allowing the witness some freedom of movement. Taylor rubbed his wrists. "You haven't read me my Miranda rights."

"You have no fucking rights," Jason growled. "We have you. It's over."

"You got shit," Taylor said. Mike and Jason counted on the actor's compulsion to perform. If they waited, they figured he would reward them. "I had a rendezvous with a married lady whose husband is a jealous prick. I needed to be discreet, so I had Larry cover for me. I owed Vinny Brand a favor, so I promised I'd do his crappy show. I told Larry to be me for the night. Lying to the venue owner isn't a crime. And I was never in Nathan's laptop. I don't know what Ginny told you, but it's probably a lie. Your little narrative would make a nice screenplay, but it's fiction. You've got nothing on me. Ha, I always wanted to say that line in cop movie."

Jason scowled. He slapped his palm loudly on the table, causing the witness to flinch. "You're a goddamned killer, Taylor. You're a smug little shit, but we got you. We have the guy who sold you the digoxin. A special, extra strong dose. You had access to the laptop and you had a supply of the exact drug that killed him. You went to a lot of trouble to fabricate an alibi. And we have you working as a waiter at the ballet gala. I'm sure you were following Nathan Matthews' trial. You were probably thrilled when he got convicted. But I tell you what, the evidence we have on you is a whole lot stronger than the evidence you planted. Maybe you two were working together. That should play well with a jury. Don't you think, Mike?"

"It's a great story," Mike agreed.

"Plus we have you for murdering Ginny. Oh, yeah. Your crappy disguise that afternoon wasn't good enough to fool the security cameras. You'll go down for that one, too."

"You got shit." Taylor projected a brave front, but Jason could see the fear in his eyes.

Then, Jason rose from his chair. He moved his intimidating six-foot-three frame around the table, standing over the actor. He reached down and grabbed the back of Taylor's shirt, yanking him backward and pulling the chair off-balance so that Taylor was teetering on the rear legs.

"You think you're a smart little shit. You're scum. You're vermin. You're going to rot in prison." Jason maintained the off-balance position. He reached down with his other hand and slapped the man across the side of the face, then let go. Taylor and the chair tumbled to the floor with a loud clatter.

Mike, who had been leaning against the door, slapped his hand onto the metal surface as he pushed off and rushed toward his partner. "What the hell are you doing?" Mike yelled. "The cameras are on."

"I don't give a shit!" Jason bellowed. He shook off Mike's hand and moved toward Taylor, who was struggling to get up. Jason pulled him up by the back of his jeans, rage in his eyes. He cocked his fist, ready to punch the actor, who cowered.

At that moment, the room's metal door slammed open, banging against the wall. Jason looked up in mid-punch. A man burst in, wearing a blue uniform with a sergeant's epaulette on the shoulder. He yelled, "Dickson! Stoneman! What for the love of Aunt Millie are you doing?"

Mike turned, looking surprised and suddenly nervous. "Captain Sullivan. What are you doing here?"

"I'm here to save the department from a fucking lawsuit!" Sullivan's voice raised an octave as he yelled at the detectives. "Detective Cook told me what you're doing here. Are you having a mental breakdown? We already convicted the killer. It was Nathan freaking Matthews. It's closed. Who gave you permission to re-open a closed case? I got a call from the DA and he's madder than a hornet in a handbag. You've got no probable cause and no jurisdiction. Stand the fuck down!"

"Captain, we've got this bastard cold," Jason yelled back. "Don't shut us down now. The prick is about ready to confess!"

A woman then entered the room. Her dark features were accented by a tailored business suit with a tight skirt. "Captain Sullivan, what's happening here?" she said in a forceful voice. She was obviously used to having men listen to her.

"It's under control, Miss Vega. There's no need for the DA's office to be involved. Why don't we go upstairs?"

"I'm not going anywhere without Mr. Taylor. We closed this case. It's over. You do *not* have the DA's permission to detain this man. I want him released immediately."

The cops all stood frozen, as did Taylor. Sullivan then said, "You heard the ADA, Dickson. Let him go."

"But, Cap!"

"Don't give me any crap, Dickson! You're in enough trouble already. Apologize to the nice man for keeping him from his Saturday afternoon and let him go."

Jason stood straight up, seething. He glared down at Taylor. "I'm not done with you," he said through gritted teeth.

"Dickson!" Sullivan yelled.

Jason snapped his head toward the captain, then back to his detainee. "I'm sorry about interrupting your day, Mr. Taylor. You're free to go."

The cops all watched motionless while Taylor got up, wiped the back of his hand across his mouth where Jason had slapped him, then slowly walked to the door. He nodded at Vega as he exited to the hallway. Taylor retraced his steps to the stairway leading to the lobby. He pushed through the security door when the desk officer buzzed it open, then hustled down the stone steps to 94th Street and turned left, heading toward the Broadway subway station.

Chapter 40
Wrap Party

BACK IN THE BOX, Detective Mariana Vega poked her head through the door, watching Taylor turn the corner to the stairway. "He's gone," she said. "How'd I do?"

Mike gave her a hug. "You did great. You look every bit like an ADA. I don't think I've ever seen you wear this suit."

"I pulled it out of my closet just for this." She ran her hand down the smooth fabric along her left hip. "But I was nothing compared to Dru. I mean, I've heard him do his Sully impression in the car, but that was *amazing!*"

Detective Dru Cook, Mariana's partner, wearing the sergeant's uniform, took a bow, accepting the group's praise. Everyone applauded quietly. "Thank you, thank you. I'll be here all week."

"I've never heard Sully say, 'madder than a hornet in a handbag.' Where did that come from?" Jason said, perching on the metal table with his legs dangling.

"I don't know," Dru said, scratching the back of his head. "It just came out."

They all laughed. "OK, OK," Mike held up his open palms. "We will never speak of this again, no matter how much fun Dru had. It was a good job. That goes for everybody, including

Serpico here," he motioned toward Jason. "You missed Jason's performance as the bad cop. It was frightening."

"Don't cross me, Mike," Jason snarled, then broke into a grin. "Thank you all for helping out. I know how hard it is to break away from life on a Saturday, especially when there's no overtime involved. It's amazing that Mike was able to call in so many favors."

"We're square now, Mike," Dru called out.

"Not even close, Cook," Mike bantered back. "But Vega is good. In fact, I think I may owe *her* one for this."

While they were talking about their successful ruse, Officer Konopka appeared at the door. "Detective Stoneman, I followed Taylor to the 96th Street subway station. He got on a downtown express train. You told me not to follow him after that."

"Nice work, Konopka. Are you still on patrol?"

"Yes, Sir. I'll get back to it. And, like you said, I've been on lunch since I picked you up, right?"

"Right," Mike said. "And thanks."

Konopka beamed at the senior detective, then turned and hurried away.

"You two Shakespeares have a plan for what happens next?" Dru asked. "You never filled us in on what this is really all about."

"Don't worry, Cook. It's better that you don't know. Plausible deniability is a good thing to have."

"OK, Mike. Whatever you say. C'mon, Mariana, we can share a cab. You shouldn't take the subway dressed that well." The two partners walked away laughing.

Mike turned to Jason, the last remaining cop in the room. He was already dialing his phone while Mike closed the door. Jason put the phone on speaker. "Rachel? Michelle?" When both women confirmed that they were connected to the conference call, Jason said, "Everything went about as well as we could have hoped. We dragged him in and staged the interrogation. I told him we had a witness who could put the digoxin in his hand. Dru and Mariana came in as Sully and an ADA. They scolded our asses and told Taylor that he was clear to leave. We'll see if he takes the bait and goes after The Pharmacist."

"You coming home?" Rachel asked.

"No. We have more prep to do. We need to get with Mason and Berkowitz. Goldstein says he's going to cooperate. We'll see if he keeps his end of the deal."

Chapter 41
Intermission

AN HOUR LATER, Mike sat in the side chair next to Jason's desk in the empty bullpen. They were brainstorming what to put into their closure report for The Influencer case. They figured they could not accuse Logan Summers of murdering Kayleigh. They suspected it. Strongly suspected it. But they didn't have any evidence other than that he was at the party, he was likely her source for the Montezuma's Delight mixture, and he was a frequent drug user himself. He had a potential motive to kill her if he thought the relationship was damaging his divorce position, or if he was simply tired of her and wanted her out of the way. Or, she could have been blackmailing him, although that seemed far-fetched. The department had already put out a statement that the death was an accidental overdose. They had no other suspects, although Brock Taylor was still in play. They could simply close it out based on insufficient evidence to continue the investigation.

"We need to wait for the autopsy and tox screen on Summers," Jason said. "Just in case there's something there that alters our conclusions."

"Like what?" Mike asked. Before Jason could answer, Mike's phone buzzed. "Stoneman," he answered. He listened for twenty seconds, then said, "Tonight? What time? . . . OK . . . Yeah, just like we said . . . Thanks."

Jason immediately asked, "Tonight?"

"Yeah. The guy isn't wasting any time. Somebody called The Pharmacist and said he wanted to buy some ecstasy and would pay double the regular price, but he needs it tonight."

"I thought The Pharmacist didn't dispense illegal drugs?"

Mike shrugged. "He says he doesn't. Maybe he's playing along this once for us. Whatever. We can't be one hundred percent sure that this caller is our boy, but it seems to fit, so we're putting act two into effect."

"Are we going to tell Sully?"

Mike swiveled his head around, reconfirming that they were alone. "We told Sully. He said he didn't want to know the details and told us not to call him again. I think we should honor those instructions."

"What time is the meeting?"

"Midnight. That's also consistent with it being Taylor. He would want to do his gig first. His absence would be conspicuous." Mike scrolled through the addresses in his phone. "The Pharmacist did what we told him and set it up for the bar where Star works, on 3rd Street. We need to get organized in a hurry." He pushed a button on the phone and held it to his ear. "George? We're on for tonight. Call Steve and tell him to meet at my apartment at six o'clock. . . . Sure, I'll buy dinner."

Chapter 42
Second Act

THE SCENE IN MIKE'S APARTMENT at seven o'clock was unlike any other night. Brushes, cotton balls and swabs, pods of foundation, and other assorted makeup supplies spilled over one end of the dining table. Partially consumed Chinese food littered the other half. The nine people trying to communicate created a cacophony akin to a Super Bowl party, but without any television. Topsy batted a fallen cotton ball around the room and avoided all the extra feet.

Detective George Mason sat in a straight-backed chair, a white cloth draped over his shoulders and tucked inside his white undershirt. A laptop computer sat open in front of him. White earphone cords snaked up his torso. George had been the most reluctant member of their little theater company, which was understandable. His role was by far the most perilous. He also required the most makeup, in order to resemble The Pharmacist. Molly Charlston, a professional theatrical makeup artist on loan from the Broadway production of *Wicked,* stood behind George, transforming his appearance.

Meanwhile, George watched YouTube videos of The Pharmacist, working on mimicking the man's vocal cadences. George had been an actor in high school, unbeknownst to

Mike and Jason. On one level, he relished the opportunity. After only an hour of study, he was able to do a fair impression of their drug guru. A gray-haired wig, complete with a long pony tail, and aging makeup gave George a passable resemblance to The Pharmacist. He was about the right height and build to begin with, which was why he drew the starring role. With a hat and a leather jacket, he would be sufficiently believable, at least inside a dark bar.

Rachel, Star, and Jackie helped with the makeup for Mike, Jason, and Sterling. Michelle was an interested bystander, but avoided getting her hands and her black dress dirty. She and her chief assistant, Natalie, had tickets to see *Swan Lake* at the New York City Ballet that night at Lincoln Center. The plans had been set for months. So, despite the impending break in the Ballet Murder re-investigation that night, Michelle was previously committed.

While he and Jason were held hostage in their makeup chairs, Mike insisted on reviewing the plan with Sterling, George, and George's partner, Steve Berkowitz.

"The whole point of this afternoon's little charade," Mike said, "was to induce Brock Taylor to think that The Pharmacist has ratted him out. Taylor is scared. He knows we're close and thinks he caught a break today when the ADA cut him loose. He still has an alternate alibi, but he never counted on us being able to connect him to the digoxin. He already knocked off Ginny Healey because she could have testified that she gave Brock the laptop code and access to Matthews' office. If he thinks The Pharmacist is the key witness who can put him away for murder, he may try to take him out."

"You think that's a great strategy?" Michelle's anxious face projected more worry than Mike wanted.

"It was Rachel's idea." Mike turned his head to where Rachel was attaching fake sideburns to Jason's face.

"Hold still!" Star scolded, using her hand to turn Mike's face back to the front.

"Sorry." While keeping his head stationary, Mike looked Michelle in the eyes. "It's a solid plan. The interrogation part worked out like we hoped. Now, Taylor thinks there's a small window of time for him to do something. He thinks The Pharmacist is the last remaining witness who can put him away. If I were him, I'd try to at least threaten the Rock 'n' Roll Doctor."

"You have to give up that whole Rock 'n' Roll Doctor thing," Jason mumbled as Rachel stroked facial glue down his jawbone.

"It's still the best description I have," Mike replied.

"I remember that record!" Molly exclaimed, laughing to herself.

"*Et tu*, Molly? *Et tu*?" Jason shook his head slightly. Rachel squealed in disapproval as her glue brush slipped down her husband's neck.

"Regardless," Michelle seized the floor, "if you're wrong about the call to The Pharmacist tonight, then all this pre-show preparation is for nothing. If you're right, then you are all walking into a dangerous situation, with George playing the part of the victim!"

"He may not try to kill me," George said, now with only one earbud in place as he listened to the discussion.

"George will be wearing a Kevlar vest," Steve said, chewing a steamed pork dumpling. "He'll be fine. And we'll be right there to give him back-up. All he needs to do is keep the guy talking so we can get him on the recording. George is good at talking."

"Screw you," George responded with a grin. "You wanna put on this damned make-up and be the Rock 'n' Roll Doctor, instead?"

"Nah. You're already doing a great job." Steve then gestured toward Jackie and said to Rachel, "Is your brother going to be on the clandestine team tonight?"

Jackie immediately answered, "I'm on hair and makeup, honey. I'm a consultant, not a soldier. You all can go charging into harm's way without me." Jackie's honest assessment drew a hearty round of laughter from the tense group.

"Hey, George," Steve called, "say something in the guy's voice, like for practice."

"You're an idiot," George said in a pretty good simulation of The Pharmacist.

"That was great!" Star gushed.

"I still think it's dangerous!" Michelle threw up her hands. "And what if Star gets in trouble? She just started working at that place. What if they find out she suggested it as the stage for your little drama?"

"Don't worry, Aunt Michelle. They needed someplace near where The Pharmacist lives, and someplace where they have plenty of people and they know the layout. I mean, I've only worked two shifts, but I know how it's laid out and where to sit for the meeting. I'll make sure George gets the table in the back next to the bathrooms. It's perfect."

"Taylor isn't going to do any shooting in the middle of a crowded bar," Mike assured Michelle for the fifth time. "If he's there to threaten The Pharmacist, we'll get a recording of it on George's phone and we'll bust him when he leaves. If he's there to do some harm, he'll need to leave the bar first. We'll get him on the recording forcing George outside and then we'll grab him. Killing The Pharmacist in front of twenty witnesses is no way to save yourself from a murder rap. When he leaves, whether it's with George or alone, we'll be right behind him and Sterling will be outside waiting. Star will stay behind working her shift. She'll be totally out of the picture."

"You should be safe in your dorm room." Michelle gave Star's shoulder a squeeze. "I need to go meet Natalie. I'd skip out on her, but I have the tickets."

"Besides, the whole evening might be one big false alarm. We're not sure that the guy who called The Pharmacist with this big rush buy is really Taylor," Mike helpfully noted.

"Oh, you be careful!" Michelle planted a soft kiss on Mike's lips, which were not engaged in any make-up activities.

After Michelle left and all the makeup was finished, Mike placed a call to their uniformed officer back-up team. He then huddled his drama troupe around Rachel's laptop. It displayed a Google Earth image of 3rd Street around *The Scampering Squirrel*, a bar frequented by NYU students and youthful West Village residents. "OK, let's go over all the possible scenarios again."

Chapter 43
The Scampering Squirrel

THE MUSIC OF BRUNO MARS blared from the bass-overloaded sound system inside *The Scampering Squirrel*. A quarter to midnight on a Saturday was as busy as the place ever got. A tiny dance floor next to a row of booths was packed with enthusiastic couples. The crowd at the bar was two deep watching the fourth quarter of a west coast college football game on the wall-mounted televisions. The excitement coming from one corner suggested that there were wagers riding on the outcome. Mike thought it amazing that New Yorkers would put money on a seemingly meaningless early-season college game involving teams they could not possibly have any other interest in.

He sat on a wooden bench on the far side of the joint in front of a tiny table, wearing a baseball cap, a pair of bushy grey eyebrows, and glasses with thick, black frames. He sipped on a tall Blue Moon and kept his eyes on the door. Mike had arrived five minutes earlier as the first team member. He watched without seeming to notice when Jason took a seat at the corner of the bar farthest from the door, under the television screen. He wore a Fedora, a high-collared maroon sport jacket, and long fake sideburns with a matching goatee and moustache. Mike thought he looked like Samuel L.

Jackson's character from *Pulp Fiction*. Amidst the crowd around the bar, Jason was effectively invisible, but his height allowed him to see over the heads of other patrons.

Steve came in next, without any disguise since Taylor had never seen him, accompanied by Sterling. They claimed another small table, still cluttered with empty glasses as a couple rose to leave. Sterling's disguise included a full afro, but he sat with his back to the door, just in case. From his vantage Sterling could see the rear of the pub, including an empty table against the back wall where a stumpy scotch tumbler sat next to a water glass. A puddle of condensation encircled the taller container, indicating a long period of solitude. No patron sat on the table's bench or chair. The plan called for Sterling to slip out the front door after their mark arrived, to cover his escape route and be in place to follow after he left.

Mike noticed Star across the room, serving drinks, taking orders, and generally hustling for her tips. The cops all knew to ignore her, and she knew to let other servers cover their tables. Her main job was to save the table in the back for George, which she had accomplished.

All four team members occasionally stole glances at the empty table. From Jason's position, he could see the narrow corridor leading to the restrooms. The team was in place well ahead of the scheduled midnight meet-up. The guest of honor was still missing. Mike had admonished the team that Taylor might already be inside the bar when they arrived and he could be in disguise. They needed to play their roles from the beginning and not reveal their true identities, no matter what.

Mike scanned toward the entrance when his attention fully fixed on George, walking through the front door. He slowly traversed the length of the bar and took a seat in front of the orphaned scotch glass. He wore a leather jacket against the slightly chilly evening, although the heavy air inside the bar was warm and tinged with vape smoke, sweat, and spilled beer.

George remained motionless, with his head down. Every few minutes he mumbled "albatross" into his chest, where his iPhone was both recording and transmitting to the four team members listening to the conference call on Bluetooth earbuds. This wasn't an official police operation, so they had to get by with commercial communications tech. It got the job done. George glanced to the side and saw Mike rotate his beer glass. It was the signal that Mike could hear the call. They didn't want George to check the phone, in case someone was watching.

The football game went to commercial, prompting the man sitting next to Jason to dart toward the restroom. As Jason watched the man walk away, he caught Mike's face, which was fixed on the area around the front door. In his peripheral vision, Jason saw a man shamble across the floor. He sported a mop-top of black hair hanging down over his ears and black-rimmed glasses. A bulky NYU hoodie camouflaged his upper body. But his uneven gait and the timing of his entrance had caught Mike's attention.

The man moved down the bar toward the back of the saloon, pausing near the far television set and panning his head side to side. When his eyes stopped scanning, he moved to the little table in the rear. He plopped into the chair opposite George, without seeming to ask for permission. George continued to look down at his scotch glass.

Mike moved his beer glass to the front edge of his table, the signal to the others that the operation was on. Three detectives and one PI focused on the voices in their ears as they surreptitiously watched what was happening at the tiny table in the back. Sterling quietly left the bar and assumed a position a few yards to the east.

The dark-haired man put one hand on the table and said, "I'm here for a pick-up. I'm looking forward to a very enjoyable night." His raspy voice barely cut through the general din of the bar.

"I was hopin' it was you, Taylor," George said in a mumbling approximation of The Pharmacist. He kept his head down. The makeup job was good, but his eyes were the most likely chink in the disguise.

"Who's Taylor?" His companion remained frozen with his hand resting perilously near the puddle of condensation from George's untouched water glass.

"Cut the shit." George was conscious of keeping his words and sentences short. "The cops came sniffing around, asking about you."

"I'm sure I don't know—"

"Save it!" George spat. "You're putting me at risk. I don't need that. I told 'em nothing but we need to get our stories straight."

"I'm sorry," the man said, "but I have no idea what you're talking about. I'm here to pick up a . . . a prescription. I'm a big fan. Who is this Taylor person?"

"Do you know a detective named Stoneman?" George raised his eyes just enough to look at his adversary, still keeping his face in the shadow of his Mets cap. The man's eyes opened wider, but he did not speak. "I told the asshole I don't remember shit. I don't remember if you wanted Adderall or digoxin or Xanax. What do I know? You need to keep these cops off my—"

"Shut up!" the man hissed, his voice clearer and lower than before. "Stop talking, you crazy old coot."

"You listen to me, you little—"

"Zip it!" Now Taylor abandoned all semblance of maintaining a disguised voice. "Not here. We need to talk, but not here." Taylor stood. "Come with me."

George watched Taylor's hoodie disappear around the corner toward the restrooms. Jason saw the backs of his black sneakers disappear into the dim hallway. All three watchers tensed.

George tilted his head toward the departing Taylor, making eye contact with Mike. Mike nodded. A private conversation in the bathroom hallway would be fine for them if Taylor would be more likely to incriminate himself in private. A moment later, George followed Taylor, his gray ponytail sticking out the back of his cap and swinging slightly as he walked.

Mike held up an open palm toward Jason, who remained seated. So did Steve. They did not want to spook Taylor by following him *en masse* into the narrow corridor, but they were all on the edges of their seats, ready to move.

At the end of the dimly lit hallway, Taylor turned and waited for The Pharmacist. George kept to the far wall, stopping a few feet away. Two ladies exited the women's restroom, paying no attention to the odd couple loitering outside the door. Jason, who had moved to a better vantage, could see George's back. Taylor was mostly obscured from Jason's view. In his ear, Jason heard George and Taylor resume their conversation.

"You got my stuff?" Taylor's normal voice said.

"Sure. I've got your stuff, if ya wan' it." George's Pharmacist imitation was getting progressively more twangy. "But I reckon that's not why yer really here."

"Stop talking and start moving."

"What are you gonna do, kid? Shoot me right here in the hallway with the security cameras spinnin'?"

"Gun out!" Mike said into his phone. "Shoot" was an emergency word George was supposed to say if Taylor pulled a gun on him.

Jason then saw the heavy emergency door at the end of the hallway open, a sliver of light breaching the darkness. Taylor held the half-opened door until George, his head down, squeezed past him. "They went out the back door!"

"Shit!" Mike said. "They're in the alley behind the bar. Sterling, circle around. Steve, Jason, meet me at the rear door!"

* * *

STAR HAD BEEN PAYING ATTENTION to where Mike and Jason were sitting. She peeked at them whenever she had a half-second during her serving duties. She also kept an eye on George once he arrived at his little table. She knew not to approach him. She had noticed when the man in the NYU hoodie sat down opposite George, but she immediately got distracted by a table of eight soccer players who were celebrating a big win.

When Star emerged from the kitchen carrying two platters of ultra-hot wings and one pitcher of Coors Light, she glanced at George's table. It was empty. After delivering the food and beer, she looked for Mike, Jason, and Steve. They were all gone. The plan was for the cops to follow Taylor outside if he left the bar.

She suppressed a pout of disappointment at having missed the action. It was likely that there was no real action. Taylor had arrived in a disguise; now he was gone, along with the cops. She would have to wait until after her shift to find out what happened. She gathered up seventeen dollars in cash from a table she had been serving and stuffed the tip in her apron pocket, then retreated to the kitchen.

"Albertson!" her crew chief shouted at Star as soon as she pushed through the swinging doors. "Come here a minute."

Chapter 44
Expect the Unexpected

WHEN THE EXIT DOOR CLANGED SHUT, a pair of rats scurried for cover. George and the disguised Taylor stood in the dim puddle cast by a floodlight mounted on the wall of the brick building, covered with accumulated urban grime. A hulking steel dumpster with two hinged lids dominated the background. The stench of simmering garbage leaked over the asphalt.

George walked quickly to his right, away from the dumpsters, to put some distance between himself and Taylor, who was now openly holding a small snub-nose pistol. George had his own weapon in a shoulder holster under the leather jacket. He didn't have time to reach for it without Taylor firing first. Even wearing a Kevlar vest under his shirt, George preferred not to absorb a close-range bullet. He knew Mike and the rest of the team would be hurrying to his aid. If he was going to get Taylor to say something incriminating, it had to be fast.

"Do you know the police are lookin' for you?"

"Yeah. I know. You shouldn't talk to the police."

"Well, Son, when they come calling it's hard to turn them away. Maybe you ought to talk to 'em yourself."

"I'm not talking to anyone. And neither are you!"

George tensed, his left hand inching toward the half-zipped opening in his jacket. At the same moment, a door behind him swung open. A thin figure wearing an apron and carrying two black plastic garbage bags pushed backward through the door. Taylor swung his gun hand toward the new arrival.

Star spun toward the dumpsters, then stopped short, seeing George. "Oh!" she exclaimed.

"Aw, shit!" George said as Star dropped the garbage bags. In his surprise, George reverted to his normal Brooklyn accent.

At the same moment, the exit door through which George had entered the alley slammed open with a clang like a gong.

An explosion from the muzzle of Taylor's pistol overwhelmed the narrow alley, echoing off the dumpster and the brick walls. The bullet tore through George's leather jacket, sending the Mets cap flying from the ponytail wig as he fell backward, groaning.

Star screamed.

Jason stormed through the open door, with Mike and Steve behind him. The cops dropped to their knees when Taylor's gun fired, their service weapons already drawn. In the dim light, they searched for their target.

The reverberation of the shot had not settled before Taylor leapt toward Star. She was frozen in between the two garbage bags on the alley asphalt. Taylor moved with amazing quickness, grabbing Star's elbow and spinning her around until he was standing behind her. He held a still-smoking pistol against her neck. Star screamed again, both in alarm and pain at the burn inflicted by the gun's muzzle. Taylor's arm encircled Star's shoulder, pinning her against his body, using his hostage as a shield.

Steve scurried toward his partner, lying face up on the grimy asphalt. Mike and Jason crouched in the open space, their guns now aimed at Taylor but not daring to fire with Star in harm's way.

Star screamed again.

Taylor shouted into her ear, "Shut up, bitch." He had no free hand with which to cover her mouth. His right hand still held the gun to her neck, its surface slowly cooling.

Mike stood up, lowering his Glock 17. "It's over, Taylor. You can't win and you can't get away. There's no reason for anyone else to die."

"Who's Taylor?" He was back in character, the raspy voice returned. The professional actor had more stage presence than George.

Mike's pulse raced. *How did Star end up in the middle of their operation? She wasn't supposed to get involved.* His first thought was to protect Michelle's niece. "OK. OK. Fine. Whoever you are, let's all stay calm. We're going to put down our weapons."

"Throw them into the dumpster!" Taylor yelled back. He pressed his gun deeper into Star's neck, prompting a squeal.

Mike motioned to Steve and Jason. Steve tossed his gun on the pavement, where it clattered to a stop near the dumpster. George lay motionless on the ground. Mike and Jason tossed their guns in the direction of the dumpster. Neither made it over the lip, instead loudly banging against the metal wall and dropping to the pavement.

Star whimpered in terror and pain. A red blotch formed on her neck where the muzzle of Taylor's pistol still pressed into her skin.

"I'm leaving this way." Taylor's still-raspy voice was steady as he pulled Star backward, away from the kitchen door and toward the end of the alley. "You stay right there."

Mike and Jason held their ground as Taylor dragged Star, keeping her body between himself and the cops. "It's going to be alright," Mike called out to Star in as calm a voice as he could manage. "Do what he says. He has no reason to hurt you."

Taylor moved awkwardly away, maneuvering his hostage along with him. Then Mike saw a dark figure silhouetted against the lights at the end of the alley, moving stealthily along the building walls. Sterling had rushed around the block and entered the alley from the west, intending to cut off Taylor's escape route. They had not anticipated a hostage situation, but Sterling was still listening in, which gave him a good idea of what was happening.

Mike figured he would make things absolutely clear. "You don't need a hostage," he yelled to the retreating Taylor, louder than necessary. "Let her go. She's got no part in this. We'll stay here while you leave. Just let her go."

Taylor ignored Mike, continuing to back down the alley. All the while he kept his eyes on Mike and Jason. Star could feel Taylor's staccato breaths in her ear. She frantically considered her options. Taylor had to watch the cops and formulate an escape plan. His left arm still clenched her against his chest. She dragged her sneakers across the pavement, forcing him to carry her full weight and hoping it would slow him down.

Mike and Jason both edged toward their service weapons.

Sterling advanced toward Taylor. The sound of a basketball pounding on pavement echoed in the tight space, accompanied by excited shouts from the court bleachers on 3rd Street.

As Sterling approached, music from another bar to his right got louder. The ambient noise masked the sounds of his rubber-soled shoes as he crept into position behind an air conditioning unit, mounted on a concrete platform behind the club. As Taylor backed toward his position, Sterling gripped the end of a three-foot length of wood he had torn from a discarded pallet farther down the alley. He had a gun, but he didn't dare use it with Star in the line of fire.

When Taylor's leg stepped back, Sterling swung his make-shift club left-handed with all the force he could generate into the back of Taylor's right knee. Taylor yelped in pain, momentarily loosening his grip on Star.

"Run!" Sterling yelled. He leapt from behind the air conditioner, gun in his right hand. He swung the wooden slat again toward Taylor's other leg, making contact on his left hamstring.

As soon as they heard Sterling yell, Mike and Jason grabbed their guns and sprinted down the alley. Jason, naturally, pulled in front.

Star felt Taylor's grip loosen. She ducked her head and slithered downward. Then she rolled to her right, diving in the direction of a nearby telephone pole.

Taylor swung his gun hand in an arc, searching for the source of the attack on his legs. The pain in both of them threw off his aim. Taylor's gun fired.

Sterling's gun fired.

When the two shots rang out, reverberating from building to building, Mike and Jason dropped into a ready crouch again, guns extended. They saw Star dive sideways. Taylor lay on the ground. Sterling stood over him, his gun pointed at their suspect. As the detectives rushed forward, blue and red flashing lights from an NYPD cruiser illuminated the alley. Their back-up team rushed in.

"Suspect down!" Jason shouted. Two uniformed officers hurried toward the prone figure of Brock Taylor, each carrying high-powered flashlights. They secured the shooter with handcuffs and called in a request for an ambulance.

"Make it two," Mike suggested, then remembered that someone was unaccounted for. "Star!"

"I'm here, Uncle Mike." Star's voice cut through the surrounding noise like a beacon from the shadows. Mike stumbled onto his knees, ripping a hole in his trousers. Star lurched forward from behind the pole, latching her arms around Mike's neck like a pair of bolas. "I'm sorry. I'm sorry," she sobbed into Mike's shoulder. After a minute of hugging and crying, Star loosened her death grip and pulled her head back, wiping away the salty streaks from her face. She was trembling. "I was so scared, Uncle Mike. I didn't mean to get in the way. I really didn't. I'm so sorry."

"Shhhhhh. Deep breaths, Star. Shhhhhh. It's alright now. It's all fine. It's over." Mike waved a hand toward Sterling, who was standing nearby. "Star, Sweetheart, I have a few things I need to handle. I'm going to tell your boss back at the bar that you were injured during an altercation with this criminal. When the ambulance crews get here, let someone look at that burn, and then Jason will walk you back to your dorm room. You can get anything you left behind tomorrow. You understand? Can you do that?"

Star looked at Mike with eyes like a deer staring at an oncoming semi-truck. She nodded her head without speaking.

"Good girl. You're a tough little cookie. I'm proud of you for handling this so well. You go home and try to calm down. We don't need to tell your Aunt Michelle about this. Right?"

"U-uh-huh." Star nodded again.

Mike patted her on the cheek and told Sterling to stay with Star until Jason came to get her.

Mike jogged back to the back entrance of *The Scampering Squirrel*. George was lying on the ground, moaning and rocking from side to side. Mike put his hand on George's shoulder. "George? You OK?"

"Christ!" came George's groaning voice. Mike and Steve grabbed an arm each and hauled George to a sitting position. George shouted, "You owe me bigtime for this, Stoneman!"

"I think the Kevlar vest did the job," Steve said.

"That and his natural padding," Mike quipped back, looking at the pained face of his fellow detective. At the range from which the shot was fired, a Kevlar vest would prevent penetration of the average bullet, but it still felt like getting hit in the chest with a sledge hammer. Fortunately for George, the shooter aimed for center mass and didn't hit him in the arm or the face. "You pull yourself together and start working on your statements for the uniforms. None of us fired our service weapons, so there should be no inquiries from Internal Affairs."

"You gonna need a paramedic?" Steve asked.

"Nah," George said, holding up his arms so that Mike and Steve could pull him to his feet. "Damn thing knocked the wind outta me, and it's gonna hurt like hell in the morning, I'm sure. But nothing a few ibuprofen tabs won't take care of." George then looked at Mike. "You're covering for me the next ten times I ask you."

Mike chuckled. "Got it, Buddy. Thanks for being part of our little drama troupe tonight. Tell your wife I appreciate her giving you up on a Saturday night."

"Are you out of your mind?" George coughed twice, each one making him wince. "I am never telling my wife about this shit show. And neither are you."

"Fair enough," Mike agreed. "None of us shall ever speak of this. I'm sure our officer friends will give an entirely accurate account of how they received a call about a gunshot, burst into a confrontation here in this alley, and how Sterling took down this shooter. Am I right, Officers?"

"Exactly right, Sir," chirped Officer Frank Prince, currently kneeling on their suspect's back.

"And there's no need to mention the bystander who briefly breached the crime scene, but walked away entirely unharmed. We have plenty of other witnesses without dragging her into it. Agreed?"

Prince smiled. "What bystander was that, Sir?"

As Mike walked back toward Star, a siren wailed in the distance. He shouted to the nearest officer, "Call in your situation. Tell the other units not to come barging back here with guns drawn thinking there's an active shooter. This operation was not on the dispatcher's radar, so he'll need to tell those street units to stand down."

Mike then returned to where Taylor was lying on the ground. His curly brown hair protruded from under the black wig, now askew and hanging down the side of the actor's face. He was breathing in shallow gasps and groaning.

"Nice shooting." Mike patted Sterling's back. "The DA will appreciate that we kept him alive. He'll want to interrogate this scumbag."

Jason then sidled up to Mike while they waited for the ambulance. "A cop got shot tonight, Mike. Not killed, but shot. When we take the vest back, we'll have to report that. Sully's going to find out."

"Yeah. I know," Mike sighed. "It's unfortunate that we didn't take him down before he got off the shot. At least we got our man. Sully's gotta give us credit for that, right?"

"As long as he never finds out about Dru impersonating him in the perp room."

"I won't tell," Mike laughed. "Listen, you need to go get Star out of here after the paramedics treat that burn on her neck. Walk her back to her dorm, then get the hell home. I'll take care of things here."

"How did Star get into the middle of that?"

Mike threw his head back, stretching his neck and looking at the glow of the Manhattan night. Few stars could penetrate the ambient light. "I don't know. Somehow, she was in the wrong place at the wrong time. As far as I'm concerned, everything went according to plan. Taylor shot George, Sterling shot Taylor. Star stumbled outside and heard the shots, but that's it. You took her home and she's fine. Sound plausible?"

"I like it. Rachel and Michelle will like it, too." Jason went to get Star.

Mike turned to Officer Janice Harris, who was standing nearby, making sure their suspect remained under control. "Looks like this asshole will be spending some time in the hospital. Make sure he's kept under guard when he gets there. One of you ride along with the EMT. Make sure to frisk him. Let's not have another ambulance escape incident, OK?"

"Absolutely, Sir," she replied.

Mike went back through the metal exit door. The football game was over, which had cleared out some of the bar area. The rest of the place was still crowded and hopping. The loud music had apparently muted the gunfire in the back alley. Or, perhaps these New Yorkers were not distracted by a few shots in the dark.

* * *

ALTHOUGH IT WAS NEARLY three o'clock in the morning by the time Mike arrived back at the apartment, Michelle was wide awake. She rushed to her husband, wrapping him in a tight hug. He had sent a text message ahead, but the sense of relief in the room was intense. A few minutes later, Mike sat in a straight-backed dining chair while Michelle removed his makeup. Mike gave her a summary of the events, leaving out the part where Star was taken hostage and put within a hair's breadth of dying.

"Taylor incriminated himself enough that the DA should be willing to indict him for Bishop's murder." Mike wiped the remnants of cold cream off his neck. "They will also have Taylor for attempted murder for shooting at George, even if we can't get him for Ginny Healey's murder. The fact that he took the bait and went after The Pharmacist should be enough to convince Keith to let Matthews go, unless he seriously thinks Matthews was working with Taylor the whole time. It will mean Keith will have to prep for a new trial, but that's what he gets paid for, right?"

"But this time the defense will be able to point to another suspect, someone who was previously convicted of the same crime. Won't that be a problem?"

"It will if Taylor can come up with a good explanation for why he called The Pharmacist today, insisted on an immediate meeting, and then tried to kill him. If he can do that, then he's a true escape artist."

Chapter 45
Facing the Music

"SHUT THE DOOR, DICKSON." Sully took a seat behind his oversized desk, flanked by photographs of himself with various politicians and other luminaries. Mike and Jason occupied the two chairs facing their superior officer. Sully's voice was uncharacteristically quiet and calm. "I understand you arrested Brock Taylor on Saturday afternoon and brought him in for interrogation."

"That's right, Cap. Just like we told you."

"But there's no booking report. No fingerprints. No mugshot. And no interrogation report. I assume that was all part of your little scheme?"

"Yes," Mike answered, keeping his voice as even as Sully's and maintaining his poker face.

"Then, later on Saturday night, two uniforms arrested the same Brock Taylor in an alley behind a dive bar in the Village. He was charged with attempted murder. The guy he attempted to murder was none other than homicide detective George Mason. You may know him. He turned in a Kevlar vest with a slug in it this morning, but had no case file number to link it to. It seems he checked it out on Saturday, also without a file number, but nobody knows who gave it to him. Must have been an oversight, huh?"

Mike and Jason exchanged a glance before Mike said, "Yeah. I guess that's probably what happened."

"The arrest report says a private investigator took down Taylor with a wooden club, then shot him in self-defense after Taylor fired his weapon. I don't suppose you two want to explain to me how this ex-cop—" Sully consulted a sheet of paper on his desk, "—Sterling Wright, happened to be involved in this little incident?"

"No, Cap. I don't think either of us want to do that." Mike nodded, maintaining his serious expression.

"I didn't think so." Sully glared at his two detectives. "You two didn't put in any overtime this weekend, did you?"

"No, Cap," Mike and Jason responded simultaneously.

"You recall my explicit instructions that you were not to chase your crazy theories about the Ballet Murder, which is a closed case, right?"

"Sure, Sully." Mike held up a hand toward Jason. "Jason opened a new file on our investigation of Brock Taylor as a possible accomplice in the Ballet Murder case. But we didn't think you would necessarily want an official record. So, off the record, we were successful in getting Taylor to admit that he had lured The Pharmacist — that's a guy named Craig Goldstein — to that bar for the purpose of killing him. Goldstein was a potential witness against him in the Ballet Murder. Sterling Wright, the PI, was there and took down Taylor in an alley. There, he was arrested by two on-duty uniforms who responded to a report of gunfire."

"Whose guns?" Sully asked.

"The only guns that were fired belonged to Taylor and Wright. No police officers fired their weapons." Mike looked hopefully at his captain, expecting a nod of acknowledgement that the operation had gone as well as they could have expected.

Sully grunted, "Hmmff. So, is this guy Taylor also arrested for the murder of Virginia Healey?"

"Not yet, Cap, but we're expecting to add that charge shortly. Taylor is still in St. Mary's, under guard. We've notified the DA's office. So far, there have been no press reports. We're thinking that, with so many charges, Taylor may be smart enough to take a plea and keep the whole thing under the radar."

"Fine!" Sully shouted. Mike presumed that his boss wanted people out in the bullpen who were paying attention to hear him yell, at least a little. "Now, get the hell out of here before I change my mind and have you cited for insubordination!"

Mike and Jason slipped out, leaving the door open.

Chapter 46
Deja Vu

THE BLOOD SAMPLES from Logan Summers had been sent to the lab on Friday and came back late in the day on Monday. Michelle called Mike's mobile phone as soon as the results were in.

"What's the verdict?" Mike said into the speaker. "I'm here with Jason."

Michelle gave her report as if testifying in court. "The cause of death was heart failure, likely caused by a drug overdose. The body showed signs of recent and frequent drug use. There were traces of cocaine inside his nose. The toxicology report showed high blood alcohol and both cocaine and fentanyl."

"Fentanyl?" Mike mumbled. "No carbamazepine or other anti-seizure med, like Kayleigh?"

"Nope." Michelle sounded disappointed. "It wasn't another Montezuma's Delight. Just the cocaine and the fentanyl."

"Is there a way to tell whether the fentanyl was from the same source as the stuff that killed Kayleigh?"

"I can't say for sure that it was the same supply. The lab results on the powder samples from the apartment may be able to tell us whether the specific granules and concentration levels are similar, but there's no way of knowing for sure. Regardless, it seems to be a drug overdose triggering heart failure. Time of death was between midnight and two a.m."

Mike turned to Jason, lifting both eyebrows as Michelle continued. "The forensics team pulled a baggie of powder out of Summers' toiletry bag. It also came back as a mixture of cocaine and fentanyl."

"That apartment is a hotbed of fentanyl use," Jason observed.

Mike didn't respond. His brain was whirring, trying to make sense of another fentanyl overdose. When they hung up the phone, Mike motioned for Jason to join him in the small conference room.

"Does this make any sense to you?" Mike asked as soon as Jason had closed the door.

"Not yet." Jason took three paces, bringing him to the far wall. Then he turned and repeated his steps back toward Mike. "He couldn't have known that the fentanyl was in his cocaine, unless he was intentionally trying to use it — or if he was trying to kill himself."

"I don't buy suicide." Mike gave a dismissive wave of his hand. "He was too much of a hedonist to be so broken up over Kayleigh's death that he wouldn't want to live. That doesn't wash. And I also don't believe he would have been experimenting with a fentanyl high right after Kayleigh died from it, whether he killed her with it or she took it accidentally. He's too smart for that."

"What does that leave us, then, Sherlock?"

Mike rubbed the stubble on his chin. "It leaves somebody spiking the guy's cocaine, the same way that Kayleigh's was tainted. We didn't find the source of the coke that was mixed in with the other ingredient in the Montezuma's Revenge—"

"Delight," Jason corrected.

"Right. Montezuma's Delight." Mike stared out the window toward the bullpen, bustling with normal Monday activity. "The Pharmacist's cocktail recipe had three ingredients, including the mezcal. So, somebody had to mix the dry stuff together into one powder for her to snort. The residue on the bathroom counter had both cocaine and carbamazepine, along with the fentanyl. We never found a baggie of cocaine, so we figured somebody else brought it and removed it. We figured Summers. It could have been somebody else. You think somebody else gave a hit of the tainted Montezuma's Delight to both Kayleigh and Summers, and Summers waited until Friday to take it?"

"That doesn't figure," Jason said. "Michelle just said that the tox repot did not include any carbamazepine or any other anti-seizure medication. He only had the coke, alcohol, and fentanyl. Summers had his own coke supply, so he would not likely be taking somebody else's."

Mike sat on the conference table's corner. "Or Summers' coke supply could have been tainted from the start, and he used it to mix the cocktail for Kayleigh. And then, without realizing that he had been the source of the fentanyl, he used it himself, thinking that it was just pure coke."

"So, he hadn't taken a hit since Kayleigh's death? That doesn't sound like him."

"No," Mike admitted, but then he looked at Jason and raised a finger. "Unless that baggie of coke was hidden somewhere in the apartment. We didn't tear the place apart searching. We had the residue from the bathroom counter, and we weren't looking for a killer that first day. He could have had it stashed there and not used it until he moved into the

Park Towers apartment. When he invited a hooker over, he used his coke. I guess he didn't share."

"OK, if that's true, then Logan got a tainted supply by accident, or . . ."

Mike finished the thought. "Or whoever spiked that coke was gunning for Logan, not Kayleigh."

Chapter 47
Home, Sweet Home

ON TUESDAY, MIKE AND JASON arrived again at the impressive Central Park South apartment now belonging free-and-clear to Mrs. Evalyn Summers. She had withdrawn her divorce action to focus on handling her late husband's estate settlement. Logan had not amended his will, which provided that his wife would inherit the apartment along with all his other real estate holdings and fifty percent of his total assets. The remainder was split between Logan's two children from his prior marriage.

The detectives had not given her any advance warning of their visit, but she greeted them in an impeccable green flowered dress, with the same perfect hair and tasteful but obviously expensive jewelry as their last visit. She led the detectives to the same sofa and perched herself on the edge of the same chair. This time, however, she summoned her housekeeper and asked her to bring tea. She didn't ask Mike or Jason if they wanted any.

"I would say that I'm sorry for your loss," Mike began, "but based on our last conversation I assume that you're not shedding any tears."

"Don't presume anything, Detective," she said primly, her hands in her lap. "We were married for twelve years. Some of them were good years. I was divorcing him, but that doesn't mean I wanted to see him dead. I'm planning his funeral now, so I hope this visit will not take too long."

"My mistake." Mike made eye contact with Jason, handing off an invisible baton.

"Mrs.—"

"Evalyn. Remember?"

"Sorry, Evalyn." Jason composed himself. The woman was intimidating in her own way, like a strict schoolteacher wielding a long ruler. "We got the toxicology report on your husband. The cause of death was a drug overdose."

"Well, I'm not surprised. I told you that Logan was a heavy drug user. He took far too many and far too recklessly. It's amazing it didn't happen sooner."

Jason was poised to ask the next question when they were interrupted by the arrival of their tea. Evalyn watched patiently as her housekeeper poured her cup and handed it to her on a China saucer. Mike and Jason declined tea and the woman retreated. "You may be surprised to know that the drug that triggered his death was not cocaine, but fentanyl."

Mike watched the woman's face as Jason delivered the news. She held Jason's eye contact without changing her expression. The teacup, balanced on her lap, never wobbled.

"I can't say that shocks me, Detectives."

"It was mixed with cocaine. We found a bag of it in his shaving kit. Do you know of anyone who might have wanted to slip some fentanyl into his coke?"

"Wait. Now I recall. Wasn't that the same drug his little girl toy died from?"

"Yes, it was," Mike replied.

"Well, then I guess we know where he got it from. It's a bit ironic, though. He kept her in that apartment so they could have sex and take drugs and host wild parties. Ultimately, it killed them both."

"You didn't answer my question," Jason said.

"Whether I knew anyone who would want Logan dead? Heavens, it would be such a long list. Business rivals, disgruntled ex-employees, former lovers, God knows who else. Maybe he didn't pay his drug dealer enough. My husband was a man with many enemies."

"When we were here before, you said you knew where your husband kept his stash of drugs. It might be important for us to scrutinize that supply. It might help us determine the origins of the drugs and also give us a clue about whether the death was murder or an accidental overdose."

"I suppose. You're the experts in such things," Evalyn said, looking around her immaculate apartment. She appeared to be contemplating the effect that a police search might have on her decorating, artwork, and rugs. "You said there was a bag of cocaine with him uptown. I assume you already searched there or you would not be asking me. Is that right?"

"That's right," Mike said. "Is the stash you know about here in this apartment?"

Evalyn placed her empty teacup on a marble-topped coffee table with hardly a sound, then stood. "Follow me." She turned and strode off toward the entrance to a hallway. The detectives scrambled to their feet and obeyed.

Evalyn opened a heavy wooden door, disappearing inside. Mike hurried into the room to ensure they saw her movements. As he rounded the threshold, it occurred to him that if Evalyn had wanted to tamper with her ex-husband's drug stash, she had plenty of time to do it before they arrived.

Evalyn stopped in front of a massive desk constructed of dark wood and inlaid leather. She gestured toward the remnant of her husband's presence in the apartment as if exposing the grand prize on a television game show. "Bottom left drawer."

"Not locked?" Mike raised an eyebrow.

"Of course it's locked. The key is in the top right drawer, inside a brown envelope marked 'office.'"

Mike snapped on his crime scene gloves. Three minutes later, he and Jason were taking photographs and cataloguing the drugs they extracted from the desk drawer. It was a long list.

"You wouldn't happen to have a box? Or a shopping bag?"

"Of course, Detective. Amelia!" She called out. When they heard the housekeeper's shoes clacking down the hardwood hallway, Evalyn said, "Please bring the detectives a shopping bag for Logan's drugs."

After the housekeeper melted away to fetch the bag, Mike said, "Evalyn, why don't you save us some time and tell us whether the lab analysis on the bag of cocaine is going to test positive for fentanyl?"

Evalyn did not laugh at Mike's comment. "Detective, I'm sure I would not know. I suppose somebody who wanted to kill Logan could have obtained some of that and mixed it with his cocaine, hoping he would die when he used it. It would have been a shame, of course, if anyone else had used the tainted supply and died as a result. I suppose if someone else had to die, I'm not all that sorry it was his vapid social media whore. If you ever find out who did it, please let me know, so I can send a thank-you gift."

Mike scrutinized the woman. Her face, hands, and body language gave no hint of nerves or obfuscation. "It certainly could have happened like that. Do you have any specific suggestions about who we might look at as a possible killer?"

"No. I'm sorry, Detective. I can't help you. I suppose that's your department, so I will leave you to it."

* * *

IN THE ELEVATOR a few minutes later, Jason gave voice to what Mike was also thinking. "If we get a warrant and search that apartment, there's no chance we find any fentanyl, right? And even if we did, it could have been Summers' own stash, which he voluntarily mixed with his coke, or which he planned to give to Kayleigh. Maybe the guy was careless enough to use the lethal mixture himself by mistake? There's no way we tie that to the wife, is there?"

"Not a chance," Mike replied. "She's got ice in her veins. She wasn't surprised when we mentioned the fentanyl. She had no reaction at all. If she was lying to us, she's a much better criminal than her husband ever was."

"Are we going to chase down the possibility that it was Logan's wife the whole time?"

"I'm not sure how," Mike replied glumly. "I hate the idea of her getting away with it. If she wanted to kill her husband by spiking his coke, it would be pretty easy. Getting some fentanyl can't be that hard. It's out there on the street. All you need is someone who can ask around and make a buy. Someone you trust."

"Like your maid? Or your driver. Plenty of options."

"That's the problem," Mike agreed. "Once she has it, all she needs is some of his coke supply. She blends it in and leaves it for him to snort and die from. She told us he gets deliveries periodically. Just spy on him when the new bag comes in, scope out his hiding place, and bingo. Proving that she did it would require us to put the fentanyl in her hand. We'd have to pinpoint her source, then get them to rat her out. Not too likely."

"The big question is whether she intended for him to give the mixture to Kayleigh." Jason stepped forward into the opulent lobby.

"I don't see how she could have anticipated that. No matter how open he was about his affairs, I don't see him announcing to his wife that he's planning to bring some of his new cocaine supply to mix into a Montezuma's Delight he planned to share with his girlfriend. Can you?"

"No. No way. Like the lady said, you can't always account for collateral damage." Jason led the way out the main door to the sidewalk. "So, how do we close this one out?"

Mike stopped under the building's canvas canopy and faced his partner. "I'm thinking that we list Mrs. Evalyn Summers as a suspect and keep the investigation open."

"You really want to chase this?"

"No. We're not chasing it unless we stumble upon something that looks like a legitimate lead. We're going to let it sit open on our case report for a few years."

"Sully won't like that."

Mike smiled. "He might not mind when we explain that by naming her as a suspect, and maybe allowing that fact to leak to the media, we prevent her from recovering on her dead husband's life insurance policies, and maybe delay the settlement of his estate. She may get away with it, but she's not going to make out like a bandit."

Jason frowned. "You think Sully will go for it?"

"I do. But if I'm wrong, then we'll close it out. We say that the prime suspect in Kayleigh's murder, if it was a murder, was Logan Summers. Before we could prove that he did it, he died from his own drug overdose, either intentionally or accidentally. Maybe he figured we were going to pin the murder on him and he decided to check out early. That could be our conclusion. It's bullshit, sure, but it makes some sense. We'll let Sully choose."

Chapter 48
Curtain Call

THE DISTRICT ATTORNEY ANNOUNCED on Friday afternoon that Nathan Matthews was being released from Rikers Island and that the charges against him were being dropped. That announcement came on the heels of a guilty plea entered by Brock Taylor, who was confined in the medical ward of the Elk Grove minimum security state prison. Facing trial for two murders and one attempted murder, Taylor's lawyer cut him a sweet plea deal. The DA wanted to avoid another trial in the same murder and was willing to sacrifice some years to keep the situation under the media radar. Part of the deal included Taylor admitting that he planted the evidence on Matthews' laptop and that he and the director were not acting together. By the time Taylor would qualify for parole, he'd be past his leading man days.

The NYPD and the district attorney's office took flack for Nathan Matthews' wrongful conviction, but also received praise for quickly discovering their mistake and correcting it. The DA's public relations office pointed out that the evidence against Matthews had been compelling enough for a jury to convict him and that it had been stealthily planted by Taylor. The police and the prosecutors were duped by an actor who was a master at creating fabricated stories. The official statement from the prosecutor mentioned how Taylor had faked his alibi by tricking Lawrence Teel into appearing in his place on the night of the murder. Teel submitted a witness statement throwing Taylor under the bus. The break in the case, the DA's office explained, came as the result of the dogged efforts of a former NYPD detective and now private investigator named Sterling Wright. The press ate up the story.

Sterling spun out the elaborate story of how he tracked Taylor, found a chink in his alibi, then lured the actor to a meeting with a man he thought was a key witness against him. Taylor pulled a gun and tried to kill the witness. He was apprehended by two alert NYPD officers. A literary agent approached Sterling about representing him if he wanted to sell the rights to the story, which would certainly make a dynamite Netflix movie. None of the press reports mentioned Mike, Jason, or any other homicide detectives, which was fine with them and fine with Sully.

Matthews, for his part, remained silent and refused to grant any interviews. He claimed that he only wanted to put the unfortunate incident behind him and move ahead with his career. He did say that he was inconsolably sad that Ginny Healey, a fine actress and close friend, had been murdered by Brock Taylor during the investigation. He said he would gladly have stayed in prison if it would have kept Ginny alive.

The City of New York Corporation Counsel reached a quick settlement with Matthews for what might have been a spectacular wrongful prosecution lawsuit. Matthews agreed to a monetary settlement dont and a total confidentiality agreement. He insisted that Sterling and his lawyer, Kevin O'Beaney, get paid for their services. The city agreed.

Matthews wanted to get back to his Broadway career while his name was in the media with a positive spin. Sterling received a check that paid off all his outstanding bills and then some. The publicity he received from getting his famous client released from jail after being convicted of a high-profile murder generated so much new business that he hired a full-time receptionist to handle the calls and organize his new case files.

* * *

IN MID-OCTOBER, Jason and Rachel met Sterling for a drink at Flannagan's Steakhouse in midtown. Sterling was busier than he had ever been since leaving the force, but made the time.

"You see how successful you can be in private practice?" Sterling said, raising a glass.

"Sure, if you catch the biggest break in the history of policing." Jason clinked his scotch against Sterling's Cuba Libre. "I recall a few months ago you were about to go bankrupt and were scrounging for clients."

"Amazing how things change," Sterling laughed.

Rachel snuggled against Jason's shoulder in the little booth. "When Jason finishes his Master of Public Administration, he'll have a lot of options. Kinda like you."

"Except that I'm so much better looking," Sterling said without humility, "so I'm more likely to star in my own life story." He held a straight face for ten seconds before breaking into a grin.

"You are pretty." Jason took a sip of his Macallan 18, which Sterling was paying for. "You better be careful or some jealous boyfriend will mess you up. I won't have to worry about that when I get appointed police commissioner."

"Is that your plan?"

"I don't know." Jason set down his glass. "It's fun to speculate, but I'm not sure what I really want. It was pretty fun bailing out your ass and getting Nathan Matthews out of prison. I liked that part. Not sure I'll have many chances to do that as a PI or a city administrator."

"But you will have time to play with your children and spend time with me." Rachel held out her Diet Coke toward Sterling for a clink.

"We'll see," was all Jason would say.

"Well, I'm glad I gave you and Mike the chance to be heroes, even if the press never reported it."

Jason dropped his head. "We're no heroes. Because we didn't do our job the first time around, Ginny Healey is dead. Nathan Matthews lost a year and a half of his career and almost spent the rest of his life in prison. We screwed it up. I'm glad that didn't get reported."

Rachel squeezed Jason's arm. Sterling nodded solemnly. There was nothing else to say. They drained their glasses and exchanged hugs and handshakes.

When they got home, Olivia was sitting in the living room, waiting for them. "JJ went down without a fight," she reported. "And I've been thinking; I'm having more and more trouble climbing up those stairs. Do you two think it would be a crazy idea if we converted your father's old study next to the kitchen into a downstairs bedroom for me? It would mean you two could have the master bedroom upstairs."

Jason looked at his wife. She raised both eyebrows, thinking about having a bedroom with more than four inches on each side of the bed, and room for a bassinette when the time came. "I think that's a very practical idea, Olivia. I would be happy to help make that happen."

* * *

MIKE AND MICHELLE HAD A WEEK of days with dinner at home together without Mike being pulled away on any new hot cases. When Mike stood naked on the bathroom scale, he was pleased to be nine pounds down from two months earlier. The chicken, fish, and vegetables were doing their job.

The weekend before Halloween, they had Star over for dinner. She regaled them with stories about the people she was meeting in her theater classes, while petting Topsy. Nathan Matthews had sent her a note asking if she would like to work next year's Broadway Cares gala.

"It was fun pretending to be an actor," Mike said. "Jason and I kinda do that all the time when we interrogate suspects, but this time it was a full-blown production. I understand why you love it."

"It's what I've always wanted to do," Star said, her fork full of cucumber. "But I'm beginning to think that being behind the stage is a better career choice than trying to be an actor out front."

When Star went to the bathroom, she placed Topsy softly in Mike's lap. Mike reached to pet her head, but Topsy hissed and leapt to the floor, hurrying to follow Star.

"That cat just doesn't like me," Mike lamented.

"Oh, Mike. That's silly. Of course she likes you. Topsy loves everyone," Michelle soothed, reaching out a hand toward Mike's.

"As long as she makes you happy," Mike muttered.

Later, when Star was leaving, Mike said, "If Matthews ever introduces you to a guy named Max Bloom, you should be careful. He has a well-deserved reputation for corrupting pretty young girls with stars in their eyes."

"Don't worry, Uncle Mike. I've got Star in my name, but my feet are planted on the ground."

Michelle watched out the dining room window until Star disappeared down Broadway toward the 66th Street subway station. "I hope I can do a good enough job of taking care of her."

"She's lucky to have you," Mike said, slipping his arms around Michelle's waist and kissing her softly on the neck. "And I'm lucky to have you, too. What do you say we go do something that would embarrass the hell out of your niece?"

Michelle craned her neck around to kiss Mike. "Break a leg, darling."

[THE END]

Rock n Roll Doctor video:
https://www.youtube.com/watch?v=vv3rtJwffQI

Thank you for reading *Double Takedown*. I truly enjoy hearing from readers about their reactions to my characters and stories. I welcome critical comments and suggestions that can help me improve my writing and urge every reader to **please leave a review**. Even a few words will go a long way and I will be grateful. Post on Goodreads, Amazon and/or BookBub to let other readers know what you think. I want honest reviews – tell other readers exactly what you really think! And feel free to send me an email directly at <u>www.kevingchapman.com</u> to tell me your thoughts about this book.

And please tell your friends (and book club leaders) about this book. As an independent author, I need all the word-of-mouth plugs I can get. Keep reading books by indie authors; there are a lot of great writers out there just waiting for you.

Kevin G. Chapman
[November, 2024]

About the Author

Kevin G. Chapman is, by profession, an attorney specializing in labor and employment law. He is a past Chair of the Labor & Employment Law Network of the Association of Corporate Counsel, leading a group of 6800 in-house employment lawyers. Kevin is a frequent speaker at Continuing Legal Education seminars and enjoys teaching management training courses.

Kevin's Mike Stoneman Thriller series, six full-length novels (so far), includes *Lethal Voyage*, winner of the 2021 Kindle Book Award, and *Fatal Infraction*, winner of the CLUE Award Blue Ribbon as the #1 police procedural of the year. You can preview the series by reading the award-winning short story, *Fool Me Twice*, available free on most ebook retailer websites or you can get it directly from Kevin's website.

Dead Winner, published in 2022, was the Blue-Ribbon winner of the CLUE Award for the best suspense/thriller of 2022. And *The Other Murder*, another stand-alone mystery, was the Grand Prize winner of the 2023 CLUE Award as the best overall suspense/mystery/thriller in all sub-genres.

Kevin has also written a serious work of literary fiction, *A Legacy of One*, originally published in 2016, which was a finalist for the Chanticleer Book Review's Somerset Award for Literary Fiction.

Find Kevin on Facebook (Kevin G. Chapman Author) and at his website: KevinGChapman.com.

<u>Book Club discussion questions for *Double Takedown*</u>

1. How do you feel about Kayleigh in the end? Did your impressions of her change as you got more information?
2. Were you surprised when Nathan Matthews was found guilty?
3. Did you agree with Mike and Jason's decision to pursue the re-investigation of the ballet murder, or did you think they should have stayed on team prosecution to the end?
4. What is your impression of Mike and Michelle's married life issues? Do you think either of them regrets getting married?
5. What about Rachel and Jason? What do you think Jason's long-term future looks like?
6. Was it too obvious how Michelle's instinct to protect and be a surrogate mother to Star shows her hidden regret about not having kids of her own?
7. Were you surprised by the resolution of the Influencer Case? Was it satisfying enough, or did you feel let down?
8. If you read *Dead Winner* and *The Other Murder*, did you recognize the Easter eggs in this book?
9. What did you think of Topsy? What do you think Topsy symbolizes in the story?

If your book club would like to read *Righteous Assassin*, book #1 in the Mike Stoneman Thriller series, please contact me for information about how your group can get discounted or free copies of the ebook and/or audiobook to get you started. Send me a note via my website at www.kevingchapman.com or by email at Kevin@KevinGChapman.com.

AUTHOR'S NOTE & ACKNOWLEDGEMENTS

As always, I must give credit to my wife, Sharon, for supporting me throughout my writing process, including those times when I wasn't sure where to go with this story.

I also thank my brilliant editor-daughter, Samantha (Samanthachapmanediting.com) whose willingness to tell me when I was being stupid or obvious focused the story and helped me avoid stepping off an unintended cliff . She's the editor that every author wants. And kudos again to my cover designer, Peter from bespokebookcovers.com. Peter did a wonderful job creating this eye-catching cover. Also kudos to Jiawie "Peter" Hsu from Fotolux in Princeton Junction, NJ for making me beautiful prints for my publicity posters.

My beta readers provided me with invaluable perspectives and ideas as the book was in development. Thanks so much to, Roxx, Gayle Wilson, Jerilyn Schad, Sue Martin, Davis Shellabarger, Robert Williscroft, and Carly for scrutinizing the early draft and guiding me toward the numerous revisions that made the book what it came to be. Everyone contributed something to the final product that would not have been there otherwise.

I also thank my intrepid band of Typokillers, who combed over the finished manuscript and rooted out the last few errors, large and small, to make the final text as clean as it can be. (But, if you find a flaw, please let me know so I can fix it.) All authors should use the typokillers. Thanks to Jerilyn Schad and Roxx (who did both a Beta and a typokiller read) along with Tad Richards, Wayne Burnop, and Nancy Lee.

I also must acknowledge a great debt of gratitude to my high school friend and pharmacology professor, Terri O'Sullivan, who provided essential consulting about drug interactions and how to kill off a character using readily available prescription medication. Terri usually worries about how to prevent fatal interactions, but humored me by describing the potential interaction of digoxin and metoprolol. And she saved me from having the research history on my laptop.

I also thank all my newsletter subscribers who volunteered their names for use as characters in the book. Coming up with real-sounding names is more difficult than you might think. Using actual names (or parts of them) from my readers spares me some of the angst of fabricating names. (You know who you are.)

Other novels and stories by Kevin G. Chapman

<u>The Mike Stoneman Thriller Series</u>

Righteous Assassin (Mike Stoneman #1)
Deadly Enterprise (Mike Stoneman #2)
Lethal Voyage (Mike Stoneman #3)
Fatal Infraction (Mike Stoneman #4)
Perilous Gambit (Mike Stoneman #5)
Fool Me Twice (A Mike Stoneman Short Story)

<u>Stand-alone Novels</u>

Dead Winner
The Other Murder
A Legacy of One
Identity Crisis: A Rick LaBlonde Mystery

<u>Short Stories & Novellas</u>

The Car, the Dog & the Girl
Ghost Creek (a romantic mystery novella)

Visit me at www.KevinGChapman.com